MW01116181

Copyright © 2024 by Amanda M. Lee

All rights reserved.

No part of this book may be reproduced in any form or by any electronic or mechanical means, including information storage and retrieval systems, without written permission from the author, except for the use of brief quotations in a book review.

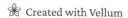 Created with Vellum

TWO BIRDS, ONE CRONE

A SPELLS ANGELS COZY MYSTERY BOOK TWELVE

AMANDA M. LEE

WINCHESTERSHAW PUBLICATIONS

1

ONE

S now was a funny thing I mused as I stared up a rather steep hill and wondered if I would be able to climb it thanks to the crusty snow standing between me and what I was certain was a nest of ghouls.

I, Scout Randall, was in a quandary. The snow on the hill had melted and refrozen so many times it had created a hard layer of ice. If I wanted to climb that hill, it was going to be a slippery affair.

"What are you thinking?" The voice at my left momentarily jolted me out of my reverie, and when I turned, I found my mother watching me. Andrea. Or was it Mother? Or Mom? I was struggling with what to call her. She wasn't the only one either. My father was in town with her. They were both part of the official team. I had cousins, aunts, uncles, and grandparents taking over my life too. The entire thing was a mess.

"I'm thinking that I want to get up that hill," I replied, turning my attention back to the sheet of ice in front of me.

"Because you think there are ghouls up there," Andrea supplied.

"You can't feel them?" I was honestly curious. My powers were in flux. It was hard for me to know from day to day what other people were capable of in comparison to what I was doing because my powers had grown in recent weeks ... and they were showing no signs of slowing down.

Andrea's gaze was clear when it met mine, and she shook her head. "No. I don't feel anything. I mean ... that hill is weird to me. That house on top of the hill is weird to me. That's it, though."

"Huh." I went back to staring at the slope.

"What do you feel, Scout?" Andrea asked pointedly. She was making an effort to get me to open up. That had been obvious since we'd left the Rusty Cauldron with our assignment in hand. Apparently, she and the others—the family who had taken over Hawthorne Hollow and were trying to reclaim the lives they'd had to flee when I was a child—were sick of waiting around for me to come to them.

I should've realized that was coming.

"There's definitely something up there." I cocked my head and turned to look at the third member of our party.

Marissa Martin stood a good twenty feet behind us, arms crossed, and glared at me with open defiance. She was still mad about being sent with us when she requested to be paired with my boyfriend Gunner Stratton instead. Our boss Rooster Tremaine denied that request and sent her with me.

I knew why.

Worse, Marissa knew why.

The same thing that always happened was going to happen again. It didn't bother me as much as it would bother Marissa. In fact, I was kind of looking forward to it.

Everybody was going to pay for Rooster's decision. I could feel it.

"Take one of the snowmobiles," I instructed. We were getting close to when we would be able to trade in the snowmobiles for our bikes. Mine had been in storage for months now, and I desperately missed it. "Ride up there and position yourself in the trees."

Marissa, ever suspicious, narrowed her eyes. "And why would I want to do that?"

"Because we need to approach them from both sides," I replied. "If we go up this way, the ghouls will retreat toward the trees. Whichever ones we don't get, you can easily pick off."

"Oh, right," Marissa scoffed. "Like I'm going to fall for that." She rolled her eyes. "You want to put the ghouls between you and me so you can blow them up. Then all the blood and guts will land on me. I know how your mind works."

"Believe it or not, Marissa, I don't spend all my time thinking about you," I replied in my most reasonable tone. "In fact, I almost never think about you. I figured you would want to take the long way and drive up there because you're useless in a fight. You do you, though."

I turned back to the slope and tested the sole of my boot against the slippery snow. It immediately slid down.

Andrea's gaze was already on me when I looked at her.

"Maybe you should drive up there," I suggested.

"I'm not leaving you, Scout," Andrea insisted. "Whatever is up there, we're going to fight it together."

In truth, I didn't need Andrea to take on a bunch of ghouls. They were lower-level nuisances. Well, at least as far as I was concerned. I could see why other people—normal people—would feel otherwise. They did rob graves and eat body parts. They did steal from the dead. On top of that, when really hungry, they went after the living. That's what everybody was worried about this nest doing.

"Fine." I didn't have it in me to fight with her. I had too much going on. Sure, trying to get to know the mother and father who had abandoned me for my own good when I was a kid should've been high on my list. It really wasn't, though. I didn't know how I was supposed to feel about them. Worse, I didn't know how I wanted to feel about them. Basically, that resulted in me trying to ignore the problem.

It was working for me so far. Well, kind of.

"We're going up," I announced. I didn't wait for them to respond. I merely grabbed one of the rocks on the slope above me to use as an anchor and pulled myself up. It wasn't a ninety-degree climb or anything. In warm weather, it wouldn't even have been that difficult of a climb. The ice was going to make it difficult, though. They would have to figure out their own way to grapple with it.

I was hardly an athlete. I didn't look graceful when throwing a ball or skiing down a hill. I was strong, though, and I was capable. Also, I was determined. Nothing was going to stop me when I set my mind to it. That's what I kept thinking over and over again as I maneuvered up the hill.

I could've opened a plane door and let myself up the hill that way, but I was still coming to grips with that new ability. My friend Poet Parker had recently discovered she could teleport. That was a different ability than I possessed, and yet the outcome was the same. We'd laughed about starting in the same place—a home for unwanted juveniles in Detroit—and ending up with a very similar ability when we found ourselves interacting again as adults. Actually, I'd been doing a lot of laughing with her recently, and I was a happier witch for it.

That didn't mean everything in my life was perfect, of course. Rick and Andrea were desperate to get to know me. The rest of my family watched from afar, but I could tell they had questions. I was the great pink hope of the family. I was the former pixie witch everybody wanted to get their hands on. Now I'd been transformed into the pixie apex, and I had a huge fight in front of me. I wasn't looking forward to that even a little bit.

"What are you thinking?" Andrea asked from my right. Somehow, she was managing to keep up with me even though I had stronger magic and youth on my side. I had to give her credit. She was determined.

"Honestly? I was thinking about Poet. I haven't heard from her in a few days. I want to get an update from her on the lamia situation in Arizona."

Genuine surprise registered on Andrea's features. "That's what you were thinking?"

I nodded. "Yup."

"Huh. And here I thought you were trying to figure out a way to ruin Marissa's day."

My lips quirked. We were on a serious mission and yet Andrea was actually being funny. Since most of my adventures had been with Rick rather than her so far, it was a nice change of pace. "I don't actually have to plan out a way to ruin Marissa's day," I said. "It just magically happens on its own."

"Ah." Andrea's forehead creased with concentration as she pulled herself higher. Thankfully, there were rocks embedded into the slope to help our ascent. "How is Poet? I'm really looking forward to meeting her. You still think that's going to happen, right?"

"I do think that's going to happen." My mind briefly drifted to the prophecy I'd seen. The one where I stood with our group on the field of battle and Poet had been with me. "I actually expect her to teleport in for a chat sooner rather than later. They had a big fight in Phoenix and are on their way to San Diego. Once they're settled there, though, I expect a visit."

"But you saw her in person, right?" Andrea pressed. She seemed intent on the topic. "You got to touch her ... and hug her."

"It almost sounds as if you're going to take that to a dirty place," I said as I gripped another rock. We were close to the top. Two more grabs and we would be on an even level with the house. Then another problem would be facing us down.

"I didn't mean it like that." Andrea gave me a perturbed look as I reached the top and extended my hand to help her the rest of the way up. "You have an absolutely filthy mind," she said, her hands landing on her knees as she leaned over to catch her breath. "You get that from your father."

"See, I'm not sure I want to hear that," I admitted. "It makes me think some very terrible thoughts. We're talking *Flowers in the Attic* thoughts."

"Geez." Andrea burst out laughing. "How do you even know what *Flowers in the Attic* is? That book was way before your time."

She wasn't wrong. "Maybe so, but they had these movies on Lifetime. I think they were made like a decade ago or so. I'm not really sure. I didn't watch them when they first came out. When I was in Detroit, though, there was a blizzard one night and I was locked in my apartment with nothing but a bottle of whiskey and Evan. We watched a whole bunch of those movies."

"You and Evan, huh?" Andrea's lips twitched.

I shrugged. Evan was my best friend. I'd lost him in Detroit, assumed that he was dead, and had only recently gotten him back. He'd been turned into a vampire but somehow—and I was still marveling at how I'd managed this—I'd been able to repair his fragmented soul and put it back where it belonged. Now he could wander around in the day and still boasted his paranormal gifts. He could drink blood or eat food, and both seemed to sustain him. He was my miracle. Actually, he was one of my miracles. Gunner felt like something of a miracle, too. My problem was, my family should've felt like a miracle, but whenever I was in their general vicinity, all I saw was a burden.

"It was a very boring blizzard," I replied. "I know what *Flowers in the Attic* is though. It sparked a lot of 'don't make me send you up to the attic with your brother' jokes when Evan and I were fighting with others in the city."

"I can see that." Andrea and I turned in tandem to watch Marissa make the final ascent. "Are you okay?" she asked the other witch. Her voice was pleasant enough but there was a hint of irritation flitting through her eyes. It was obvious she disliked Marissa. That was hardly earth-shattering news, though. Everybody disliked Marissa.

"I'm fine." Marissa's agitation needed its own ZIP code it was so large. "What's the plan here, Scout?" Her eyes found and held mine.

I shrugged. "I thought we would just scare the ghouls out of the house and then kill them."

"Is that the grand plan of the new pixie apex?" Marissa's tone was clipped, telling me her nose was out of joint about more than just the climb.

"Pretty much," I replied. I studied the house. It had seen better days. Both the roof and the front porch were sagging. It was clear nobody was living inside. Well, other than the ghouls. That meant it was going to be rough ... and likely gross.

"How do you want to handle this?" Andrea asked. She was all business.

"I thought I would just spook them out of the house and kill them."

Andrea blinked. Then she blinked again. "Okay," she said finally. It was clear my response had thrown her. "Let's do this."

I smirked at her obvious discomfort. "I've got this," I assured her. "As Marissa said, I'm the new pixie apex. I might not know what I'm doing all of the time, but somehow my magic keeps responding, so that's all that matters."

"You have faith in yourself." Andrea bobbed her head. "I love that you have faith in yourself. That's such a good trait to have."

I shrugged. "It is what it is." I took a step forward and blew out a sigh. "I think I'm just going to..." I let my magic do the talking after that and threw a wave of purple fire at the house. It, of course, caught on fire—it was ancient and the wood was weathered and dried out—and the inhabitants escaped through the back door fast.

I was like Michael Myers as I followed. Methodical. Plodding. I didn't have a big knife and a mask, but that didn't stop me from imagining I did as I started throwing magic at the scattering ghouls.

I knocked two down right away, causing them to pitch forward. I left them for Andrea and Marissa to finish off and kept going forward. There had to be at least ten ghouls total, and I was curious where they'd come from. With that in mind, I tripped another fleeing ghoul—this one seemingly younger than the rest—and grabbed it by the hair and turned it over so I could demand answers.

"Where did you come from?" I barked.

The girl—even though she looked like a girl, I mentally chastised myself for making assumptions—looked at me with wide-eyed wonder. Then she spit in my face.

"I don't bow to witches," the ghoul screeched.

"Well, then I guess it's good for you that I'm the pixie apex." I smiled when I said it, but the expression didn't last. "You know, apex is a badass word," I said to Andrea, who was busy shoving a knife in the back of the head of one of the ghouls I'd dropped. "Pixie is not a badass word, though. You would think they could've come up with a better word."

Andrea stopped moving long enough to pin me with an incredulous look. "Is that really the sort of thing you spend your time obsessing about?"

"I don't obsess," I replied automatically.

Andrea raised a dubious eyebrow.

"I don't," I insisted. "I don't obsess. I just ... um ... okay, I obsess a little. I wasn't obsessing about this, though."

Andrea didn't respond. She just waited.

"It was an observation," I said. "I'm allowed to observe things." Because I didn't like the way she kept looking at me—*is that how all mothers look at their children?*—I went back to staring at the wiggling ghoul. "You smell like gym socks that haven't been washed in six months," I complained. "I know you guys eat dead bodies and stuff, but how hard is it to take a shower? Or brush your teeth? Or—" Whatever I was going to say died on my lips—it wasn't important, just more ranting—when the ghoul pulled hard against the grip I had on her hair ... and detached her scalp from the rest of her body.

I was grossed out to the extreme as hair and skin came off in my hand and I didn't think. I just flung it to my right. When the hair and viscera smacked Marissa directly on her stupid pouty face, I cringed. Then she started screaming.

"Crap," I muttered.

"I've got it." Andrea hurried toward Marissa. "Don't even worry about it a little."

I turned back to the ghoul, who was aiming for my wrist with her teeth. I fell backwards and scrambled to escape. It wasn't that I was afraid of her. She was gross with all that visible skull space on top of her head, though. I didn't want to touch her.

"I think I'm going to puke," I complained to nobody in particular.

"You're fine," Andrea said as she tried to catch Marissa, who was running around in a circle like a chicken without a head. She was also screaming through the hair and skin that I'd accidentally thrown at her. "Stop moving, Marissa. I can't take that off you if you keep moving. Also, stop making that noise. It's just annoying."

I would've laughed under different circumstances. I didn't have time for that, though. I was too busy trying to escape from the rabid ghoul that was suddenly chasing me. I managed to get to my feet and put a bit of space between us, but the kid—and without hair, she really did look like a kid—was practically foaming at the mouth as she gripped her hands into fists at her sides. Her chest heaved. Her eyes flashed. Then she let loose an unearthly scream and started running toward me.

At a certain point, I would look back and wonder why I did what I did. It was instinct, though, and being turned into the pixie apex had forced me to follow my instincts more often than not. That's why, when the plane door opened directly behind me, I stepped through it.

I didn't give any thought to what I might find on the other side. I didn't wonder if I would be leaving my mother and co-worker to fight the ghouls without me. I just stepped ... and found myself in an entirely different world.

2
TWO

I hadn't meant to run out on Andrea and Marissa. It just sort of happened. The fact that I found myself in a cave was disturbing ... to say the least. It wasn't a normal cave either. There were torches affixed to the walls, casting off an eerie and yet somehow homey glow. There was a couch in the middle of the room and a television to boot. That's not what held my attention, though. No, that honor went to the table at the back corner of the space. There, the horned god Cernunnos sat with several people I didn't recognize—all dark-skinned with painted skull masks covering their faces—and they looked to be deep in conversation.

"One battle is behind us," Cernunnos said. "It went exactly how we thought it would."

"Yes, Charlie did better than I expected," one of the dark-skinned individuals replied. "She did most of it on her own, too, although it was good the mage was with her. If only to bolster her belief in herself."

"Yes, Zoe Lake is a better cheerleader than I envisioned," Cernunnos agreed.

I frowned. I recognized that name. I'd met Zoe Lake-Winters

months before. She was a powerful mage with a mouth that could make even the burliest man fall to his knees and weep. Why were they talking about Zoe? More importantly, why was I here? Did I bring myself here, or did the horned god somehow call me to him and I didn't realize it?

Before I could think too hard on the subject, one of the men at the table shifted his gaze until it landed on me. When he smiled, his teeth were bright white against the dark pallor of his skin. "We have a guest," was all he said.

I straightened—it was instinctive—and then internally cringed when the other individuals at the table turned to look at me.

"Ah, Scout," Cernunnos said when he registered my presence. "You're early. I didn't expect you for another few minutes."

I had no idea what to make of that. "Did you call me here?" I took a step forward, then faltered. What the hell was this? It felt like a meeting I shouldn't be privy to and yet here I was.

"Sit." Cernunnos gestured toward the only open chair at the table. "We have a few things to discuss. Then I'll get to you."

I didn't like his tone. His imperious nature grated. "I thought you left," I challenged, remaining rooted to my spot. The god had been hanging out in Hawthorne Hollow several weeks before. One of his sisters, Skadi, had been wreaking havoc, and he decided it was his job to take her out. She was gone now. He'd done his job. We were still digging out of the mess she'd left, but there was no reason for the god to be present for that. "What are you doing here?"

"This is my home," Cernunnos replied. "I think the more appropriate question is what are you doing here?"

Was he joking? "You called me." Even as I said it, I couldn't decide if that was true. Had he called me here, or had I traveled to him on my own?

"I most certainly didn't call you." Cernunnos shook his head. "I simply unlocked the door from this end. You're the one who found it, opened it, and walked through it."

I chewed on my bottom lip as I debated what he'd said. "Okay, well, then I guess I'll just walk right back out of it." When I turned, I found there was no door to exit. Just a cave wall with a very weird pictograph painted on it. Even though it was in my best interests to flee —I could feel that to my very marrow—I took a moment to commit the pictograph to memory. There were a lot of different people on it— women, men, vampires, shifters—and they all seemed to be working outward from different areas and aiming themselves toward a bright orange circle in the middle. There, a figure that looked suspiciously like Cernunnos stood with other figures. Some of whom I recognized from this very cave. They appeared to be waiting for something.

"You're here now," Cernunnos countered, drawing my attention away from the pictograph. "I think we should talk. Besides, I want you to meet my friends."

I would've preferred leaving. That was my normal response to uncomfortable interactions. I fled. Sure, I was always up for a fight and could trash talk with the best of them, but when it came to heavy conversations—and this one felt like it was going to be a doozy—I preferred running. Unfortunately for me, there was no door to flee through, and I didn't want to risk trying to conjure one in case I failed.

"Fine." I squared my shoulders and turned back. "I really can't stay long. I left two of my co-workers to fight a bunch of ghouls, and it doesn't seem fair that they're cleaning up the mess I made." I trudged toward the table, studying each face in turn before sitting. "I like cleaning up my own messes," I added lamely.

"You like fighting," Cernunnos countered. "It's one of your favorite things to do. That's why you get along so well with Tillie Winchester. She also likes fighting."

I pursed my lips as I regarded the flask he handed me. It was old school, made out of some sort of animal skin, and I waved off the offering. "I'm good, thanks."

"It's just whiskey." Cernunnos took a swig and then handed it to the man on his right. "I believe introductions are in order. Then we have a conversation to finish. Once it's over with, I can discuss a few things with you."

"I can't wait," I lied.

Cernunnos smirked. "First up, my friends are all loas. I believe you've heard that term before."

If I thought I was suspicious before, it was nothing compared to what I was feeling now. "I've heard of loas," I confirmed, my gaze bouncing between faces as I tried to get a handle on what I was dealing with.

"This is Papa Legba," Cernunnos continued. His tone was breezy. "He is the figurehead of the crossroads, essentially standing as an intermediary between higher beings and humans. He also has an entire army of crossroads demons at his disposal."

I scratched my cheek. I knew of one crossroads demon. Harley. I'd met her through the Winchester witches months before. She'd made me laugh—several times—and that wasn't always easy because I had the sense of humor of a ten-year-old boy. "Fun," was all I said.

"This is Baron Samedi." Cernunnos gestured toward the next loa. "I believe he's familiar with your friend Poet."

I rested my elbows on the table as I leaned forward. I'd heard Baron's name multiple times of late. "Weren't you just in Phoenix?" I demanded.

Baron smiled. "Yes. I was with my granddaughter. We were dealing with a lamia situation."

"Poet has mentioned you." I saw no reason to lie about it. Baron knew about my relationship with Poet. Lying would make me look weak, and everything Poet had taught me about the loas suggested that was the wrong way to go.

"My granddaughter has mentioned you as well," Baron said. "She's quite fond of you."

"I'm not sure I can say the same thing about you." I sent him a flat-lipped smile.

"Oh, I'm growing on her." Baron winked at me. "Her fondness for you means that I too am fond of you."

"Yeah, I'm good." I focused on the lone woman at the table. "If he's Baron, does that make you Brigitte?"

Maman Brigitte's eyes twinkled when she nodded. "It does." She cocked her head. "I have to say, you're not what I expected."

"Meaning what?"

"Meaning that I expected someone with more...stature." Brigitte shook her head. "Looks can be deceiving, though."

"If you say so." I found this entire meeting uncomfortable. "You were just talking about Zoe." I turned to Cernunnos. "Is she in trouble?"

"I guess that depends on your definition of the word 'trouble,'" Cernunnos replied. "Right now, she's riding high after a victory. Charlie Rhodes's fight is at an end, and as she moves forward, she will spread joy and light to the world."

That was another name I recognized. Charlie Rhodes was also friends with the Winchesters. "I'll take your word for it. I'm glad she won her fight, though." That was true, if only because I knew that the Winchesters would be crushed if something bad happened to her. "I'm not sure what that has to do with me, though."

"Nothing," Cernunnos replied. "And everything. Charlie is on her own path now. As are several more of your friends, including Poet Parker."

I eyed him with cool resolve. "If you're sitting here plotting about how to make Poet's life harder, I'll kill you all." It was an interesting threat since I was basically sitting around a table with four gods. I meant it, though.

"Oh, you're so cute." Baron's grin was wide enough to swallow his entire face. "I just want to eat you up." He leaned closer and poked my cheek. "How are you so adorable?"

I slapped his hand away. "Did you really just poke me?"

If Baron was bothered by my nasty glare, he didn't show it. "Yes, you're definitely adorable." He turned to Brigitte. "She reminds me of you."

"Because she wants you to die?" Brigitte asked tiredly. "Yes, we are similar in that respect."

Now it was my turn to be confused. "I thought you two were married."

"She's my blushing bride," Baron agreed.

"In name only," Brigitte replied. "The fire went out of our relationship hundreds of years ago."

"And yet it rekindles on a regular basis," Baron insisted. The smile he shot his wife was more of a leer than anything else. "You love me, and you know it."

"If you say so." Brigitte impatiently tapped her fingers on the table. "We need to get moving. I have a pedicure scheduled in the French Quarter, and I don't want to miss it."

"Yes, it's time to cut back the claws," Baron agreed. "It will be flipflop season before you know it."

"God, how do you put up with him?" I complained, not realizing I was going to say the words out loud until they were already out of my mouth. "I would've smothered him in his sleep on the wedding night and called it a day."

Brigitte's eyes twinkled. "Okay, now you really do remind me of me."

"She's perfect," Baron agreed, offering up a chef's kiss.

I turned my impatience to Cernunnos. "What is this?"

"You need to learn temperance, Allegra," the horned god chided.

"I'll smite the crap out of you if you call me Allegra again," I threatened. It might've been my birth name, but I felt so far removed from it that just hearing it chafed. "I mean it."

"Fine." Cernunnos took another swig from his flask. "Your friend Poet enacted a change in Phoenix. It was an important change."

I narrowed my eyes. I was aware of Poet's deeds in Phoenix. How that would be important enough to lure me through a plane door for a ridiculous conversation with four gods, though, was beyond me. Still, I wanted to understand. This felt somehow important.

"You're talking about the lamias," I said finally. "There was some sort of spell making it so the lamias couldn't reproduce. She fixed it."

"And in doing so, she also enacted another curse on the lamias," Cernunnos said. "They can no longer feed on humans."

I waited for him to expand. When he didn't, my eyebrows moved toward my hairline, and I became exasperated. "I don't see how that's a bad thing."

"I didn't say it was a bad thing. Just that it was a change. The lamias, however, see it as a terrible thing. It seems some of them would've preferred being unable to procreate to their new reality."

"Whatever." I couldn't get worked up about a bunch of whining lamias. "What does that have to do with me?"

"Well, since the new lamia apex has marked you as her enemy, it seems to me that having a bunch of disgruntled lamias looking for a new individual to cast enough sun to chase away the shadows haunting them would be a big deal."

It was only then that reality hit me. "You think the Phoenix lamias who are angry about not being able to feed are going to seek out Bonnie in the hope that she can somehow lift the curse," I realized.

"Yes."

I scratched my temple. Bonnie Jenkins had once been a part of our group. I'd considered her a friend. That had been a mistake. Turned out, she'd always been working against us. Then, in a fluke I was still trying to understand, she'd absorbed the lamia apex's power at the same time I'd absorbed the pixie apex's power ... and now we were embroiled in the sort of war that could only end in bloodshed.

"Well, crap," I said finally. "Are they already here?"

"That's what we were just discussing," Cernunnos replied. "It's only been a few days. The disgruntlement in the lamia camp is through the roof, though. The leader there told his people that he was going to fix everything. Instead, he made it worse.

"Sure, they're no longer under the constant threat of mummy attacks and they can birth a child without the female dying, but they really enjoyed their little snacks," he continued. "I fear an uprising is imminent."

My mind drifted back to the battlefield I'd seen in the prophecy again. Shifters were involved in that fight. There had been other creatures I couldn't immediately identify in the brief glimpse I'd received. Were they lamias? It made a strange sort of sense.

"What is it you want me to do?" I asked finally.

"I don't want you to do anything. This is your fight. It's your decision how you will proceed. I figured you would want to know all the facts, though."

I ran my tongue over my teeth. This entire meeting felt strange and odd. "Okay then." I pushed myself to a standing position. "If that's all, I should probably get going."

"Just like that?" Papa Legba asked.

I shrugged. "I'm aware that lamias might show up in the area. You've done your due diligence. The thing is, I haven't seen Bonnie in weeks. For all I know, she might be dead."

"She's not dead," Brigitte countered. "In fact, she's doing better than she was. Absorbing your sister's magic essentially fixed her."

"Fixed her?" My eyes flashed.

"Well, it stopped the weird fluctuations she was dealing with," Brigitte corrected. "From your perspective, it was the exact worst thing that could've happened. The apex was in real danger of running so hot she actually exploded. Now that is no longer a fear."

"Ugh." That was not what I wanted to hear. "Well, lovely." I shook my head. "I guess that means I'm going to have to kill Bonnie."

"Bonnie can't live," Cernunnos agreed. "You can't be the only one there when she dies, though."

"And just why not?"

"Because you're an apex. If you're the only one there, you'll absorb Bonnie's powers on top of your own. At least that's how it's been in the past. You need someone else there to absorb the powers."

That was news to me. "How come nobody mentioned that the other times I fought Bonnie?" I demanded.

"Because there wasn't a fear you would actually kill her then. Now that she's stolen your sister's powers and managed to stop the rot that was threatening to destroy her, she will come after you with new purpose. Now you need to be afraid."

"Unbelievable." I planted my hands on my hips and stared at the ceiling until I was reasonably certain I could speak without losing my mind. "What good are you guys if you just dole out information like this in drips and drabs? It's crap."

"It's like being a loa of four hundred again," Baron mused. "I see so much of your younger self in her, my Brigitte." He mock clutched at his heart. "I almost want to bed her for old times' sake."

"Knock yourself out," Brigitte replied. "As long as you're not trying to bed me, I'm perfectly happy."

I glared at both of them. "Don't push me."

Brigitte chuckled. "You really are a delight. I can see why Poet is so fond of you."

I was over both of them. "Bonnie is a threat," I said when I turned back to Cernunnos. "I can't kill her until I have someone lined up to be the new apex lamia. Am I understanding everything correctly?"

"Pretty much," Cernunnos replied. "There's more, of course—there always is—but those are the salient details."

"Great." I stormed away from the table. "Thanks for all the useful information. I really don't know what I would do without you guys." I paused. "Oh, I know. I would figure it all out myself, like usual."

"I'm in love," Baron murmured.

I ignored him and waved my hand. I was relieved when a plane door opened in front of me. "I'll handle Bonnie," I said to them. "There's no need to worry about me."

"Your ego is healthy," Cernunnos said. "It's going to get you into trouble, though."

"I've got this." I meant it. "Just ... sit back and enjoy the ride." With that, I walked through the door and back into the snow outside the cabin.

It was spotted with blood and bodies. It was also surrounded by familiar faces, and the first one I saw belonged to Gunner.

"What are you doing here?" I asked without thinking.

He stalked toward me, his expression fierce, and when he jerked me into his arms for a hug, I couldn't hide my surprise.

"I wasn't gone that long," I complained.

"You've been gone for hours," Rooster said as he appeared behind Gunner. He looked as relieved as my furious boyfriend. "We were worried."

"Yes, well, you should be worried. I have some stuff to talk with you about." I glanced around. "Are all the ghouls dead?"

"No thanks to you," Marissa screeched from somewhere behind Rooster. I couldn't see her. That wasn't some great loss, though.

"Where did you go?" Gunner asked when he pulled back. The color was coming back to his cheeks. I took that as a good sign.

"It's a long story," I replied. "I think we should discuss it at the Cauldron." I looked back over my shoulder, but the door had been firmly shut in my wake. "We have a new problem."

"Of course we do." Rooster shook his head. "I can't wait to hear about this one."

He was going to regret saying that. We all were.

3
THREE

Whistler was alone behind the bar when we came trudging in. I cast a curious look around the Rusty Cauldron and then asked the obvious question.

"No Tillie?"

Tillie Winchester and Whistler had been spending a lot of time together. Too much time I sometimes thought. I didn't want to know what they were doing with one another either. My mind kept going to a dirty place, something Tillie seemed to realize because she wasn't subtle when she told me all about the *sublime* romance they were embarking on.

It was freaky to think about, so I tried to pretend it wasn't happening. Tillie didn't make it easy.

"I'm going over there tomorrow," Whistler replied. "She's got something brewing in her greenhouse and needs my help."

Well, that wasn't frightening or anything. The only things Tillie brewed in her greenhouse were alcohol and potions.

"I guess it's best she's not here." I tried to picture Tillie's face when she heard about the loas and internally cringed. Pairing her with an entity like Baron Samedi had trouble written all over it. "So, I'm sure you're wondering what happened," I started.

"I'm mad," Gunner countered. He sat on one of the stools and tapped the bar to get Whistler to draw him a beer. "You can't just disappear like that, Scout. You freaked me out."

"You freaked us all out," Rick said. He was with Andrea a couple spots down at the bar. They, too, were drinking.

"You just disappeared," Andrea explained to me. "One second you were there. The next you were gone. I thought you were setting a trap at first or something. When you didn't come back, though..." She trailed off.

"I was actually hoping you wouldn't come back," Marissa offered from the archway that led to the bathrooms. Her face and hair were wet, telling me she'd stuck both under the sink faucet to get the stench of ghoul off her. "Personally, I think we would all be better off without you."

"Nobody asked you, Marissa," Gunner shot back. "I'm pretty sure you don't want to know how many of us think we would be better off without you."

I shot him a quelling look. "To be fair, I did throw a ghoul scalp at her. I didn't mean to, but it still happened."

"I don't care." He shook his head. "She hasn't stopped whining for hours."

"I take it you called them out there," I said to Andrea.

She nodded. "I did. When it became apparent you weren't going to come whistling while walking out of the trees, I panicked. I thought maybe Bonnie somehow kidnapped you and I wanted to make sure we could get you back."

"Well, that was nice. It wasn't Bonnie, though." I leaned on the bar and looked at the beer Whistler slid in front of me. I wasn't in the mood to drink, and yet because it was there, I took a long gulp. "I visited Cernunnos's place," I blurted after I swallowed. "I can't decide if I got myself there or if he pulled me to him, though."

"I thought he was gone," Rooster argued. "I haven't seen him since the whole Skadi thing."

"I haven't either. I don't think his cave is near here."

"Cave." Andrea made a face. "Like ... with snakes?"

"There might've been snakes," I replied. "I didn't see any, though. I just appeared in his domain."

"Did he seem surprised?" Gunner asked.

"No." It was only then that I realized my best friend was missing. "Where is Evan?"

"He was in Hemlock Cove when we got news of you going missing," Rooster replied. "I'm not even sure he realizes we had an incident. Now I'm glad I didn't pull him off the job he was doing. You can handle informing him."

"Well, I guess that's better than him knowing and not coming."

"Yeah, I don't think you ever have to worry about that," Gunner agreed as he brushed my hair away from my face. "Tell us about Cernunnos."

"There's not much to tell." I forced myself to focus on my brief sojourn away from Hawthorne Hollow. "He wasn't alone. He had three loas with him."

"Anyone good?" Whistler asked. "What?" He shrank back when several people pinned him with dark looks. "I happen to like the loas. I've done a lot of reading on them since Scout's friend was just promoted to one of their ranks."

"She's not like them," I countered. "She's just not *not* like them either." For a brief moment, I wished desperately for Poet. Then I forced the thought out of my mind. I was a big girl and could handle this on my own. "It was Papa Legba, Baron Samedi, and Brigitte. They were talking about someone winning a fight. Charlie Rhodes. They seemed happy enough about it."

"What does that have to do with you?" Gunner asked.

"Nothing. The next part revolved around me. Well, Poet and me." I took another swig of my beer. "It seems that Poet's trip to Phoenix turned the lamia population on their ear. I knew part of it—she told me—but I guess I didn't realize what a big deal it was."

"We don't deal with lamias all that often here," Rooster said. "Well, before Bonnie that is. I knew about lamias. I had never really researched them much, though."

"Lamias are weird," I said. "Their origins suggest they were a matriarchy, but at some point, the men took over and turned it into a patriarchy. Poet and I discussed how difficult it would be when the lamias came to grips with their new apex being a woman. It seems she set a few things in motion in Phoenix that might actually force the lamias to embrace Bonnie, though."

"Like what?" Gunner asked.

"Well, for starters, she cast a spell so they can't feed on humans. Or paranormals either. I guess they were making a game out of torturing people. It's not necessary for survival, but they were having fun with it."

"Good for her," Rooster said.

"She also helped get rid of a curse that was stopping the lamias from procreating," I continued. "Apparently the lamias would rather be able to feed on people than reproduce, though."

"Well, that's weird." Rooster rubbed his chin. "What does all of this mean for us?"

"It means that Bonnie could be getting reinforcements, and soon," I replied. "They also told me that the magic Bonnie absorbed from Emma has settled her. She's no longer in danger of killing herself with too much power."

"Well, that's a bummer," Rooster lamented. "I was hoping she would take herself out so we wouldn't have to."

"Me, too, but that doesn't look like it's going to happen." I downed the rest of my beer and shook my head when Whistler hiked an eyebrow to ask if I wanted another. "They told me that I can't kill Bonnie if there's not someone there to become the next lamia apex. I can't handle that much power on top of the power I already have. It will kill me."

"I don't understand." Rooster's forehead creased in concentration. "You've taken on Bonnie before. Why didn't they warn us about this?"

"That was my question," I said. "Basically, their response was that they knew I wouldn't win so it wasn't a concern."

"Well ... maybe it's a good sign that they think you're going to win now," Andrea suggested.

"Or maybe there's more going on than they want to admit," I replied. "Either way, we need to start figuring stuff out."

"Like who can be the new lamia apex," Gunner said.

"Yeah."

He stroked his hand over my hair. "We'll figure it out."

"We can even talk about it tonight," Andrea said.

Now it was my turn to be confused. What was tonight?

Andrea seemed to read my confusion because she immediately started frowning and shaking her head. "You agreed to a family dinner. You can't back out."

"Oh, right." I exhaled heavily. I'd forgotten about family dinner. They were all staying at a cabin outside of town, one that was magically protected and enlarged like something out of a Harry Potter novel. They were all having a grand time being on this plane together, cooking up a storm and making plans for a future they expected me to secure for them.

The whole thing gave me indigestion.

In truth, I would've much preferred grabbing gas station chicken with Gunner on the way home and crawling into bed to eat it. That didn't seem like it was going to be an option, though. Rather than admit I'd forgotten about dinner, I lied.

"I'm looking forward to dinner." I pasted what I hoped was a bright smile on my face. "What are we having?"

"Liver and onions," Rick replied.

I tried—really, I did—to keep my smile in place, but it was impossible. That had Rick breaking out in a wide grin.

"I was just checking to see if you were actually listening," he said.

"It's pasta night. There will be ten different types of pasta and ten different sauces. There will be shrimp, chicken, and meatballs as far as the eye can see. There will also be garlic bread."

"Man, that's going to make romancing you later hard," Gunner complained.

Rick's expression faltered. "Lots and lots of garlic bread," he said.

I had to bite back a smirk. "That actually sounds really good. I'm looking forward to it."

"What are we going to do about the lamia?" Rooster asked. "I mean ... should we be getting prepared for them?"

"How?" I was genuinely curious how he thought we could manage that. "Like ... what are you going to do? Are there snake repellants that will work or something?"

"I don't know what to do." Rooster held his hands palms out. "I was just musing out loud."

"It can't hurt to do some research," I said. "I don't know that there's anything else we can do, though."

Rooster was rueful. "I don't know either. I guess it can't hurt to try."

"Definitely not."

GUNNER DIDN'T PRESS ME DURING THE drive to the cabin. I knew he had questions. He wouldn't ask them until we were alone in our home later that evening, though. His fear had been real. I knew he was constantly worried now that I could walk through plane doors. It wasn't that he thought I would purposely leave him. Some of those doors only opened one way, though. What would happen if I walked through the wrong one?

"I know you're upset about earlier," I started when he parked outside the cabin. "Can we hold off talking about it until later, though?"

"I have no intention of bringing that up here," he assured me.

"I know. I just want you to know that I'm not going to run away from the conversation. I'm willing to have it ... even though I don't know what to say."

"I'm curious about the loas mostly," he admitted. "I know Poet has spent some time with them. She likes them, right?"

"Actually, she's wary of them. She thinks they're up to something. After spending a grand total of ten minutes with them, I can see why she thinks that."

"You realize it was a lot longer for us, right? You were gone for hours."

"Yeah." I cocked my head. "I'm still trying to figure out how that works. Time moves differently on various planes. Since this was what I'm assuming is Cernunnos's private plane, I think he controls it."

"So ... why would he want to keep you away from us for so long?"

"That's a very good question. I can't wait to come up with an answer."

"You and me both." He took my hand for the walk to the cabin. Inside, it was bustling with activity. The scent of pasta sauce hit me like a heavy weight fighter punch, and my mouth instantly started to water when the heavenly aroma wafted by.

"Nice," he said, breaking out into a wide grin.

"Your relationship with food is interesting," I said. My stomach picked that moment to ruthlessly growl.

"Yeah, like I'm the only one who is starving." Gunner ushered me in front of him, placing his hands on my hips as he nudged me to move forward. "Pick a place to sit. I want to start eating."

"I'm shocked. I never would've guessed."

Before he could offer up a snarky response, Andrea waved from across the room. "Scout, over here!" She was a little too enthusiastic for my liking—I was not an upbeat girl—but I nodded. There was no avoiding sitting with them.

"They're just trying to get to know you," Gunner reminded me in a low voice as we walked to the table.

"I know. I like them." That was true. I *did* like them. For the most part. I couldn't just forget the hardships of my past, though. Plus, well, I didn't bond with people all that easily. It took work. This place was bursting at the seams with expectations. I didn't do well under the weight of other people's expectations.

"Sit." Andrea motioned toward the spot across from her and Rick. "Each table has all the sauces to choose from. The same with the meat."

"It looks good." I meant it. Since my sister Emma was at the table, across from me and at the corner, I caught her gaze. "How are things?" I asked. It wasn't the smoothest of openings. Emma had expressed relief when she lost her magic. That response had surprised me, and I expected her to lose her cool after the fact. Now, weeks later, her smile said she was still okay with it.

"I helped with three of the sauces," Emma replied. "If you don't like cream-based sauces, I won't take it personally."

"I like all sauces," I replied.

"Me, too." Gunner already had three types of pasta on his plate— where did he even get the plate?—and was busy eyeing the sauces. "You know, if we both overdose on the garlic tonight, we won't even notice each other's breath."

I could do nothing but shake my head. "I'm going to eat my weight in all things pasta. I don't care about the garlic."

"Yes." He pumped his fist and went to town. I was intrigued as he poured Alfredo sauce on linguini noodles and added shrimp. Then, right next to it, he added tomato sauce and meatballs to mostaccioli. Finally, he threw chicken and some sort of primavera sauce onto regular spaghetti noodles.

He shot me a thumbs-up as he dug in. Rick extended the bread-basket to him so he could grab a hunk of garlic bread with each hand.

"At least he has a healthy appetite," Andrea mused.

I nodded. "He likes food." I opted for regular spaghetti noodles and the tomato sauce. I wasn't much of a fan of meatballs, so I went for the shrimp and threw some vegetables on top for good measure. "I like food too," I explained when Andrea's eyes went wide.

She laughed. "I'm actually glad to see it. When you were little, you were picky and would hardly eat anything. You were actually underweight, and I was worried."

I didn't think before I responded. I should have, but I didn't. "Well, when you spend a lot of time in group homes, you learn fast that nobody cares if you get your fair share. You can't be picky because you really will starve. I think I lost five pounds in the first group home I was at. That didn't happen when I went to the next one." I took a big bite and smiled. "It's good."

When I looked up, I found Rick and Andrea watching me with horrified expressions. "Oh, crap," I muttered around my mouthful of food. When I looked at Gunner for support, I found him studying me with abject anger. "Not you, too," I complained.

"They starved you?" he demanded once he'd swallowed.

"They didn't starve me," I assured him. "Obviously I'm here, and I'm well fed. You just have to learn to stake your claim fast. Plus, you eat what's in front of you. I'm nowhere near as picky as I used to be. I'll eat anything. Well, within reason." I glanced up at Rick. "I don't like liver and onions."

"Nobody does," Rick replied. He looked shaken. "I'm sorry you went hungry."

"Oh, man." I slapped my left hand to my forehead and focused on the food. "I didn't mean to turn this into a thing. It's not a big deal."

"It feels like a big deal to us," Andrea replied. "We can't help feeling as if we failed you."

"Well, you didn't." That was the truth. "As much as we wish we all could've had more choices when I was younger, we didn't. Everybody did what they thought was right. Can you really argue with the outcome?" I gestured toward the room, to the multiple tables, where everybody was excitedly eating and chattering away. "Everybody is together. Maybe we should let go of the guilt, huh?"

"How can we?" Rick countered. "You're still a stranger to us. You work overtime to remain a stranger. We can't be happy with that outcome."

"That's just who I am," I explained. "I don't form attachments easily."

"You're attached to Gunner," Andrea countered. "You're attached to Evan. You're attached to Poet."

"Yes, but all of those relationships took me by surprise. I would've worked against them if I'd realized what was going on. You just need to take a breath. Eventually, you'll wear me down, and all the fight will go out of me."

"Yeah, that doesn't sound like anything we want either," Andrea argued.

"Baby steps." That was all I could offer her. "I'm doing my best here. Just ... take a breath and enjoy dinner."

Andrea clearly recognized the intelligence behind the words because she nodded. "Baby steps."

"Maybe next time you can do eight types of fried chicken," I suggested. "That might be fun, too."

Andrea's lips curved. "If fried chicken is what you want, then that's what you'll get."

Gunner pumped his fist. "Score." He had sauce all over his face. "You need to eat, baby. This food is amazing."

I dug in. "It looks amazing." When I glanced up, I found Emma watching me with amusement. She really did seem like a different person. "I'll get to your sauce eventually," I promised.

"Take your time." Emma waved me off. "We have all night."

For once, that didn't sound like a threat. No, it sounded like a nice evening. "Then bring it on."

4
FOUR

My favorite part of dinner was when Andrea attacked Gunner's face with a wet nap once we were finished eating.

"You're a messy eater," she complained as he tried to pull back. "It must be a boy thing."

Gunner gave me a wide-eyed look, but all I could do was shrug. "She's not wrong," I offered.

Even though he was clearly irritated, he let her clean his face. Then he managed a smile when she leaned back to study her handiwork. "Good?" he asked.

"You're a handsome boy," Andrea said. "You shouldn't ruin those looks of yours with pasta sauce."

"You should see him when he eats chicken in bed," I offered. "The sheets are greasy enough to slide on."

"Oh, right." Gunner shot me a wounded look. "Like I'm the only one who is messy in bed."

A quick glance at Rick showed me he was uncomfortable with the conversational turn, so I decided to take control. "We should get going."

"Wait." Andrea reached out to grab my arm. "We haven't talked about what happened to you yet." She was desperate to keep me from leaving. Unfortunately for her, I was tired and needed to think. I couldn't think when I was with them. I was too busy trying to be on my best behavior.

"We'll talk more about it tomorrow," I assured her. "I'm not sure what to think about it right now."

"I didn't even know horned gods hung out with loas," Emma mused. "It's an interesting turn of events."

That was an understatement. "It feels choreographed," I agreed. "I just don't know what they're up to. If they're watching Zoe, Charlie, Poet, and me ... does that mean something big is brewing?"

"I'm guessing they've been watching powerful beings for a long time," Rick said. "Maybe this is simply normal for them."

That didn't feel right. "They said Charlie had done her part ... with a little assist from Zoe. I know that Cernunnos has been watching Zoe for a long time. The loas feel newer and yet they seem a bit more dangerous too."

"Are you afraid of them?" Rick looked worried.

"Actually, I found Baron Samedi downright annoying. Poet kind of told me what he was like, but I thought she had to be exaggerating. Obviously, she wasn't."

"You could call Poet," Andrea suggested. "She might give you some ideas."

"That's on the agenda," I agreed. "I need some sleep, too. I'll start figuring stuff out tomorrow."

Andrea hesitated, then nodded. "Okay, well, you didn't have dessert. At least let us send dessert home with you."

"I'm already stuffed."

"Hold up," Gunner interjected, holding out his hand. "What sort of dessert are we talking about?"

Andrea's lips twitched. "Chocolate cake."

"I think we could take some with us," Gunner said. "It will make a nice snack for later."

"Yes, you can eat it in bed," Andrea agreed.

"Oh, geez," Rick muttered under his breath.

I was amused despite myself. Weariness continued to wear me down as I waited for Andrea to pack up the cake. When it was time to leave, I waved them off, and inhaled deeply as I stepped outside. The relief I felt about having a bit of space didn't last because I was barely through the door when I registered a brand new problem.

"What in the hell?" I took four steps forward, my eyes going wide as I realized we were surrounded by a magical wall. The cabin had been warded to an nth degree, but this wasn't my magic surrounding it. This was someone else's magic.

"What is that?" Gunner asked as he clutched the container of cake closer to his chest. "Did you do that?"

I shot him a dirty look when his accusatory eyes met mine. "I was with you the entire time."

"I know, but you do weird magical stuff all the time."

"Why would I want to trap myself here?"

His expression told me he hadn't thought that far ahead. "Who did it then?"

Unfortunately, there were a few options. "Well, we know a god is close. There are loas in the mix now. There's a vampire apex not too far away." I was careful when moving closer to the wall. It almost seemed to be undulating, as if it were a living, breathing magical manifestation. "Does that look like a snakeskin to you?"

Gunner sent me a knowing look. "Bonnie." He followed up her name with a series of curses.

"Bonnie," I agreed.

The door opened behind us, and I risked a glance. Andrea, Rick, my grandfather Ezekiel, and Emma were on the front porch of the cabin, and they looked dumbfounded.

"Did you do this?" Rick asked.

I graced him with the same glare I'd lobbed at Gunner. "Why would I do this?"

He shrugged. "You do weird stuff all the time."

"Geez." I flicked my angry glare toward Gunner. "They say you fall in love with someone who is just like your father. I always assumed that was crap."

Gunner managed a smile, but it was wan. "What do we do here?"

That was the question of the evening. "I'm not sure. Hold on." I raised my hands and moved them closer to the wall. The magic rippling beneath the surface was strong. It was like nothing I'd ever seen, though.

"It looks reflexive," Emma announced from a spot closer than I'd last seen her. She was out and staring at the magic. It wasn't fear scrolling across her face when I shifted my gaze to her, though. It was curiosity.

"Meaning what?" I challenged.

"Meaning that if you feed magic into it, then the barrier will just get stronger."

I thought about it—she made a decent amount of sense—and then I extended my hand once again. "What happens if I draw the magic out?"

The question seemed to throw Emma. "I ... don't ... know. Can you do that?"

"I can try." I lifted my chin to warn the others to back off. "Give me a bit of space."

"Wait." Gunner shook his head. He was no longer obsessed with the cake and had turned his attention to me. "What if you get hurt and we're trapped in here?"

It was a fair question. It didn't matter, though. "I don't have a choice, Gunner. We can't do nothing. We can't just sit here. I have to try something."

"Why not try to open a door to get to the other side?" he argued. "At least that way you could warn the others something was going on here."

I wanted to kick myself for not considering that myself. "Oh, right. Duh." The laugh that escaped was thin and weak. "I'll try that first."

Gunner's smile was flat. "Just be careful."

"I'm always careful."

"Yeah. That's the word I think of first when I see your face. Careful."

"Your sarcasm is duly noted." I drew a door with my finger and pushed magic into it. When it opened, I leaned closer to see what was on the other side. Unfortunately, it was too dark to make out my surroundings. "Wait here."

"Hold up." Rick sounded like a nervous wreck behind me. "Maybe one of us should test out the door to make sure it works. You're too important to lose."

"That's sweet." I cast him a tight smile. "I appreciate it. You can't go through that door, though."

"Why not?"

"Because what if it shuts?"

"Better that it happens to me and not to you."

"Okay, but I can open another door. You can't."

"I..." Rick exhaled heavily, defeat dragging down his shoulders. "I didn't consider that."

"That's okay. I'm comfortable being the brains of the operation." I winked at him before glancing at Gunner. "You need to stay here."

I knew he would argue and wasn't disappointed. "No way." He shook his head. "I'm going with you."

"No, you're not." I was firm on this. "You have to stay here."

"And why is that?"

"Because if there's something bad over there, I might have to open up another door fast. I won't leave you over there, so it puts us both at risk. It has to be me."

"Oh, you just made that up," Gunner complained.

I grinned because I couldn't help myself. "I can take care of myself."

"Oh, I know. I just don't like it when you go through creepy doors and I can't follow. We're supposed to be a team."

"Eat your cake," I suggested. "You won't even know that I'm gone."

"I'll know." He held my gaze. "Be careful when you're over there, and kick whatever asses need to be kicked."

I squeezed his hand. "Don't I always?"

I could feel their gazes on me as I walked through the plane door. I made sure to do it with more swagger than was necessary because I wanted them to be okay. Me? I was feeling a bit of trepidation.

I made it three steps over the threshold before the plane door swung shut behind me, blocking out Gunner and my family, and leaving me in a dim cave environment that had me cursing Cernunnos under my breath.

"Again?" I demanded, looking around. "Did you forget something earlier, or are you just trying to irritate me?"

It wasn't Cernunnos who stepped into view. No, it was a woman. Or at least she'd once been a woman. Now her skin had a weird green tint to it and she looked as if she was boasting scales. Her eyes had slitted to look like those of a snake, and she moved differently than when I'd known her. There were no more soft steps but rather a silky —and creepy—glide.

"I think you have the wrong god," Bonnie said in a voice I didn't recognize. She almost looked surprised to see me. "What are you doing here?"

I'd thought for sure she somehow chose my destination when I opened the plane door. Obviously, I'd been wrong. "I thought we could spend some quality time together," I lied. "Don't you miss me?" I spoke with more bravado than I felt. This was a sketchy situation.

"How did you find me?" Bonnie looked more irritated than anything else. "You should've stayed away, Scout." She shook her head. "You could've lived just a little bit longer."

"Oh, I like living my life on the edge," I countered. I could sense other beings close. They weren't close enough that I risked taking my eyes off Bonnie. "So...is this your new place?" I tried to imagine it as if she were throwing a housewarming party. "Show me around."

"Why would I possibly do that?" Bonnie didn't crack a smile. She didn't appear intrigued. She looked tired, as if the weight of the world was dragging her down. Since that's how I often felt, I understood what she was feeling.

At least mostly.

"Well, how am I going to know what to get you as a gift for your new digs if I don't see the space?" I challenged. "I mean...a plant is clearly out. You don't have any windows." I lifted my nose to sniff, committing the scent to memory in case I could use that information at a later date. For what, I had no idea. I was basically buying time at this point. "Do you have indoor or outdoor bathroom facilities?" I asked. "A nice toilet paper basket might work."

Bonnie had been my friend at one point. Okay, maybe she hadn't been my true friend. She was always working undercover, always plotting against us. Everything she did was for her own gain. I'd thought she was my friend, though. I'd genuinely enjoyed talking to her. There was nothing of the woman I used to know reflected back at me from the creature making hissing noises.

"No?" I said when she didn't respond. "It was just a thought."

"I used to hate it when you thought you were funny," Bonnie offered. She slithered—yes, slithered—to her right, making sure to maintain a safe distance from me. "I would have to sit there and laugh, pretend you were one good joke away from making the traveling comedy circuit. All the while I daydreamed about snapping your neck."

"Well, I'm no George Carlin, but I have my moments." I crossed my arms over my chest. I wasn't certain what I was supposed to do here. Clearly Cernunnos and his buddies had brought me here—or somehow arranged it—and I'd followed their plan to a tee. I couldn't worry about that now, though. I had to deal with Bonnie in the present. "It's not nice to talk about the appearance of others, but you don't look so good."

"Do you think appearances are important?" Bonnie challenged. "Wait ... look who I'm talking about." She held up a stilling hand. "You're the most superficial person I know. I mean ... you were in a fight for your life and kept going on and on about Ann Taylor Loft."

"Actually, I found out it's just referred to as Loft now," I offered. "Apparently, they decided to rebrand, and they thought that was trendier."

Bonnie merely stared, her mouth open and a creepy snake tongue zipping out. Well, *that* was gross. I couldn't exactly comment, though, because it would only serve as proof of the superficial claim.

"I'm just saying." I held out my hands. "Personally, I don't think the clothes are terrible if you wear them to an office. They're inappropriate for a witch fight, though."

"Still vapid," Bonnie muttered.

"I'll probably die vapid," I agreed. "Since we're going there, though, what is up with your skin?" I leaned closer so I could see a little better under the muted lights. Bonnie had thrown up a magical net to illuminate her cave. It wasn't doing a very good job, though. "Did the magic split your skin like that?"

"It's my pattern," Bonnie argued. "All lamia have a pattern."

"Just like snakes," I mused. I considered it, then shook my head. "Here's my problem. You have the pattern, but your skin actually split in some places. It looks as if it has been sewn back together. You're kind of like Bride of Frankensnake." I didn't have to consider it long before I started nodding. "That's exactly who you are."

"If you're trying to distract me, it's not going to work," Bonnie rasped. "You came onto my turf. Tell me what you want."

"I would appreciate it if you would die." The words were out before I could internally debate how smart they were to utter. "I mean ... if we're being honest here, my life is going to be a lot better when you're gone."

For the first time since I'd invaded her territory, Bonnie smiled. "I could say the same thing about you."

"Yeah, but I'm the good guy."

"And here I thought you didn't look at the world through a black-and-white lens."

"I don't." She was trying to get under my skin. She was actually good at it because she'd spent so much time with me before I saw her true colors. She knew what I liked. More importantly, she knew what I didn't like. She could torture me better than most ... and I knew that was her ultimate goal.

"You weren't meant for the power you possess," I continued. "You took Emma's power to anchor it, but I'm betting you can't wield it properly."

"Or perhaps that's simply what you wish," Bonnie suggested. "Maybe you're afraid that with Emma's power, I will crush you."

"Okay, Skeletor." I shook my head. "That was just sad."

"You're afraid of me," Bonnie insisted. "I can feel your fear."

"I'm not sure 'fear' is the right word. I am worried about what you're going to do. The influx of new powers has forced the cheese to fall off your cracker. It's a little disconcerting. There's nothing more dangerous than a nut."

"Do you think insulting me is going to make me spare you?"

"I don't expect you to spare me." She had a lot of turmoil bubbling under the surface, and it wasn't of the good variety. She could claim to be in control as much as she wanted—and she was certainly better than she had been last time I'd seen her—but she had too much magic in her, and it was trying to escape. That wasn't a good sign. For her.

"I'm not afraid of you," I continued. "You're nothing to me. Like ... nothing. It helps that you don't look anything like the woman I used to know. That will make it easier."

"It will make what easier?"

"Ending you." The smile I offered up was feral. "We both know that this town isn't big enough for the both of us. That's some Clint Eastwood smack I'm talking right there, but it's true. Only one of us will make it out."

"I won't bow to you," Bonnie argued. "The whispers say you're the new queen, but I will wear the crown."

"What whispers? You know it's a bad sign when you hear whispers, right? Like ... a really bad sign."

She lashed out. I was expecting it. I had a unique ability to torture others to the point of no return. I deflected her magic toward the ceiling, and it was only a split second before it hit that I realized what a mistake that was. We were underground. She'd sent out a killing blow.

"Oh, crap," I said just as her magic made contact with the rocky surface above.

Her eyes went wide. Mine did as well. Then everything above us crashed down, and I lost sight of her as the darkness overwhelmed me. The last thought that entered my mind was a doozy.

I'm going to be buried alive. Well, at least I'm not dressed inappropriately for the occasion.

Then everything that hurt swept away, and I wondered if I would ever feel anything again.

5
FIVE

"Ow!" I jerked into consciousness when a piercing pain convinced me that my shoulder was actually being separated from my body.

I had to blink multiple times to adjust to the bright lights above me. Then I took a breath and tried to absorb my new surroundings.

The cave was gone. It was no more. I wasn't in the cabin, though. I wasn't on the ground in front of it. I wasn't outside of it. I wasn't in my own bed either. No, I was somewhere else, with other people.

Thankfully, it happened to be a place I loved and people I absolutely adored.

"What's up, Pooh," I drawled—or rather slurred—as Winnie Winchester tried to wipe down the open wound on my shoulder. "How the hell did I get here?"

Winnie gave me her patented "don't push things too far" look. "Did you just call me Pooh?" she demanded rather than answer my questions.

"I did." I smiled. "I mean ... Winnie the Pooh. It was right there."

Winnie rolled her eyes. "You're the only person I know who would say something that stupid right after almost dying."

"I have a gift," I agreed. "Ow!" I glared at her again. "Are you trying to kill me?"

"Yes," Winnie deadpanned. "That's my ultimate goal. I'm going to kill you, have Aunt Tillie grind up your body, and then we'll use you as fertilizer for the gardens."

I narrowed my eyes. "You are much darker than anybody gives you credit for."

"And you're a mess," Winnie said. "You're a walking bruise. You have open wounds. Aunt Tillie is mixing some ingredients for poultices. We'll pack you down and when you wake up tomorrow morning, you'll be as good as new."

Since everything hurt—hardcore—I had my doubts. "I'm pretty sore. I guess sleeping in my own bed will fix that. Will the poultices stay on for the drive?" Something occurred to me. "Wait ... how am I going to get home?"

Panic threatened to overtake me. "Gunner. He's trapped at the cabin!" I reared up to a sitting position and had to hold back a scream when the bolts of pain rocketed through me. "Oh, Goddess!"

Winnie nudged me back. "What did I say about pain?"

"Gunner," I whined. "He's out there. He's trapped."

"I don't know about the trap." Winnie was calm. "Lay down."

"I have to get out there." I refused to back down. "There's a wall of magic surrounding the cabin. That's how I ended up ... wherever I ended up." My mind was working fast, but I was still slow from being unconscious. "How did you even find me?"

"We didn't. A friend brought you here. You were a bloody mess. We started working on you. Then we called Gunner."

"And he's okay?" I needed to hear it from her. Even in my weakened state, she wouldn't lie to me.

"Other than being panicked about you, he's fine," Winnie assured me. "He's on his way with Evan."

Well, that was something at least. "What about the wall?"

"You'll have to ask him." Winnie looked toward the door when her sister Twila appeared with a bowl of something that smelled foul even from ten feet away. "Is that the healing mixture?"

Twila nodded. "Aunt Tillie just finished it. She said not to be stingy."

"I'm sure we're going to use all of it." Winnie took the bowl from Twila. "Lay back, Scout."

I glared at her but did as I was told. She took the mixture and rubbed it into my shoulder, causing me to hiss and squeeze my eyes shut. After a few seconds, the pain that I'd been feeling in that area floated away, and it went pleasantly numb.

"There we go." Winnie's voice was soothing. "I have to put this all over you. Your clothes were already ruined, but you can borrow something from Bay to get home."

"Whatever," I muttered. I no longer cared about anything but the blessed peace the medicine was bringing me. "Wake me when Gunner gets here. He'll want to take me home."

"Yes, well, we'll talk about that when he gets here." There was an edge to her voice, but I didn't push further. I was too tired.

I floated for a bit—how long was anybody's guess—but I slowly emerged from the cloud of relaxation at the sound of voices.

"How did she get here?" The voice was familiar. I knew the face it belonged to, but the name escaped me.

"The gentleman down in the dining room brought her," Winnie replied. I remembered her name, but probably because she was the last person I'd talked to.

"We didn't stop in the dining room," another voice said. I knew that voice too. "We came right up here. This is where Marnie directed us."

"Well, we have a guest."

"I want to see Scout," the first voice demanded. Gunner. Now I remembered his name. My brain was starting to work again.

"She's right here. Just...be careful," Winnie warned him. "We have the poultices where we want them. She's going to need to be still all night."

It was Gunner's sharp intake of breath that forced me to open my eyes. He stood at the end of the bed, an anguished look on his face. The way he stared at me suggested that I looked pretty bad. I hadn't even considered my appearance until now.

"I'm fine," I said automatically.

"You don't look fine," Evan countered. He had a better poker face than Gunner, but it was impossible to ignore the concern in his eyes. "Her face isn't going to stay like that, is it?"

That was enough to have me groping for my phone. "What's wrong with my face?" I had every intention of taking a selfie so I could see the damage for myself.

"I have your phone," Winnie assured me. "It was in your pocket when you were brought here. Take a breath."

"I want to see my face," I gritted out.

"No, you don't," Winnie replied. "The swelling will be gone in the morning. Most of the cuts, too. I know you want to go home—"

"I *am* going home," I insisted.

Winnie ignored me. "You're staying here so we can monitor you."

"No." I sounded petulant, but I couldn't seem to stop myself. "I'm going home."

Gunner was the one to take control. "We're staying here." He edged himself onto the bed next to me. "It will be better this way. I won't be as worried. We can sleep, then tomorrow we can get up and have a big breakfast." He turned his puppy dog eyes to Winnie. "Right?"

Winnie chuckled. "I guarantee a big breakfast is on the table."

It wasn't what I wanted. I didn't have the strength to fight them, though. They seemed to know that. "Whatever. Tell me what happened."

"I don't know what happened." Gunner stroked his hand over my hair. "You went through the plane door. It closed right behind you. A few minutes after that—only five or ten at the most—the wall came down. I assumed you did something and that you would reappear. You didn't, though.

"I tried calling you," he continued. "You probably have ten notifications from me. Then I called Evan for help. We were going to start a search—even though we had no idea where to start—and that's when we got the call from Winnie. He'd only been at the cabin a good ten minutes when she called and said you were here."

My brain wasn't as fuzzy as it had been, which made it easier to think. "And how did I get here?"

"A gentleman brought you here," Winnie replied. "We were in the dining room, enjoying some wine, and he just came strolling in with you in his arms. He said he brought you to us because he knew we could help. Then he handed you over to Landon and started drinking the wine."

That made zero sense. Not the part about him handing me over to Landon Michaels, who was married to Winnie's daughter Bay, but the other stuff. "Who is he?"

"I don't know." Winnie held out her hands. "I didn't get a name. I came straight up here to start working on you. Bay and Landon stuck with him. I think they've been drilling him with questions."

I frowned. "I don't understand."

"I don't either," Gunner said. "Where did you go? When you walked through that door, where did you end up?"

That part of my memory was a little fuzzier. "Um ... Bonnie. I saw Bonnie. I think I was in her lair."

"Did you purposely seek out Bonnie when you left?" Gunner looked anxious. "Did you know you were going to see her?"

"No. I was just looking for an escape. Take a breath."

He frowned but did as instructed.

"I'm not sure why I ended up with Bonnie," I admitted. "I was just there. She seemed as surprised as me. That magical wall was definitely erected by her, though."

"What happened with Bonnie?" Evan asked.

"We said snarky things to one another. She got annoyed and threw magic at me. We were in a cave, and I didn't think before I deflected the magic. It went into the ceiling and everything came down on us."

Evan shook his head. "Smooth move."

I shrugged, then cringed when I felt a twinge. "It happened fast. Then everything went dark." I tried to readjust, but it hurt too much. "I don't remember anything after that until waking up here."

"So, I think it's time we figure out who the mystery guest is." Evan started back toward the door but pulled up short when a man appeared in front of him. The dark suit, top hat, and skull makeup might've thrown Evan, but I knew who we were dealing with right away.

"Oh, geez!" I threw up one hand, then made a growling noise. "Did you do this?" I demanded of him.

Baron Samedi, a glass of wine clutched in his hand, sent me a sunny smile. "You're welcome."

"Who is this?" Winnie asked.

"He's a lush," a voice said from behind the loa. It belonged to Tillie Winchester, and she sounded disgruntled. "He drank two whole bottles of my special blend all by himself."

"It's quite good," Baron said. "Normally, I tend to shy away from home blends unless it's someone in New Orleans doing the fermenting, but you're gifted." He lifted his glass and took a big sip. Then he turned back to me. "You've looked better."

I narrowed my eyes to dangerous slits. "Why did you do this to me?" I demanded.

"I didn't do this to you." Baron looked affronted at the charge. "I simply swooped in and saved you when you did this to yourself." His grin was cheeky. "Bet I'm not looking so bad as a paramour as you initially thought now, am I?"

Next to me, Gunner shifted. "Did he just say what I think he said?"

"Ignore him," I growled. "He's just trying to irritate you."

"He's doing a good job of it."

I waved him off, battling back the jolt of pain that swept through my shoulder. "If you didn't do this to me, who did?"

"You did. I just told you that." Baron was blasé as he wandered into the room. "You need more skulls," he said to Winnie. "This place looks like a knitting circle threw up."

"What an odd insult," Winnie muttered.

"As for what happened to you, it's best you don't throw around blame," Baron continued. "You opened the door into the lamia's lair. You literally brought the roof down because you were being lazy with your magic."

It was harder to think than I would've liked. "She put the wall up around the cabin." I was certain of that. The snakeskin undulation of the magic was a dead giveaway.

Baron nodded. "Yes, and you opened a door to solve your problem, and it led you to her. You really should start concentrating more when you do things like this. This whole ordeal could've been avoided."

I shot him the finger, refusing to grimace when I felt another jolt of pain. "What about Bonnie?" I asked after a beat. "If you swooped in and saved me, did someone do the same for her?"

"She was buried under the rubble when I left," Baron replied. "I didn't pay her much heed. She wasn't my primary concern."

"Why didn't you kill her?" Evan demanded. "I mean ... you were right there. She was down. You could've ended it all."

"It's not my place to end her," Baron replied. "This isn't even my fight. The only reason I got involved in the first place is because I was watching her." He gestured toward me. "She reminds me of my Brigitte."

"Who is Brigitte?" Gunner asked.

"His wife," I replied.

Gunner made a face. "Someone married you?"

"Yes, and she's a better woman for it." Baron showed his teeth when he smiled. "As for the lamia, she's not dead. I'm sure she's gone from the cave. I can check, though."

"I'll go with you," Tillie offered. "I mean ... you can teleport, right? I've always wanted to teleport."

"I can." Baron looked her up and down. "I was actually thinking you and I could go on a different adventure, though."

Was he hitting on her? It almost sounded as if he was hitting on her. He was so gross. Not that Tillie wasn't vital or anything, because she was. She had a boyfriend, though. I opened my mouth to say just that, but it was already too late.

"Don't wait up," Tillie instructed Winnie as she grabbed Baron's arm and dragged him to the hallway. "We're going on an adventure."

"Don't get into trouble," Winnie called after her.

Tillie didn't respond. She was already focused on her new friend.

"Does anybody else think they're going to be trouble?" Gunner asked as he stared in their wake.

"I'm on it." Evan leaned over and dropped a quick kiss on the top of my head. "I'll see you in the morning."

"Are you going to watch her?" Winnie asked Evan, who was striding toward the door.

"I'm going to give it my best shot." Evan shrugged. "I can't teleport. We'll see what they're up to, though." With that, he was gone.

"Well, at least someone responsible will be with them," Winnie said.

Evan couldn't always be called responsible when paired with Tillie. She was a bad influence on him. I wasn't worried about her leading him into danger, though. He could take care of himself.

"I'm tired," I admitted. "Everything hurts, and I'm tired."

"You need sleep." Winnie was firm. "You're going to sleep here. In the morning, you're going to feel better." She slid her eyes to Gunner. "No funny business."

Gunner shot her a dirty look. "Yes, because I'm going to molest my bruised and battered girlfriend thanks to my lack of control. That sounds just like me."

"There are cookies in the kitchen if you need a midnight snack," Winnie said, opting not to rise to the bait. "She needs a solid ten hours of sleep. She'll be much better in the morning." She checked my poultices one more time and then slipped out the door, leaving only Gunner and me.

"I'm sorry I freaked you out," I said to him as he stripped out of his shirt and pants.

"It's not as if you did it on purpose."

"No, but you're still upset."

He killed all the lights but the bedside lamp and crawled in beside me. "I am upset," he agreed. "I didn't know where to even start looking for you." He extended an arm and I thought he was going to try to pull me toward him. Then he thought better of it and linked his fingers with mine. "Your new abilities are something we're going to have to get used to."

"Especially since I didn't even realize I was going to be walking into Bonnie's lair," I agreed. "At first, I thought she brought me to her, but she was surprised. I think... I think something inside of me reacted to her magic."

"Well, it's done. If we're lucky, she's hurt even worse than you."

"Yeah." I closed my eyes. "Why do you think Baron was there? I mean ... why would he come for me?"

"He seems to have a thing for you."

I made a face. "That's not why. I think he flirts with everybody."

"Then maybe it's because of Poet. He seems enamored with her."

"He *is* enamored with her," I agreed. "This feels somehow different. They were all in that room talking. It was as if they were moving chess pieces around a board."

His lips brushed my cheek. "You're not a chess piece. You're way more than that."

"To you, but what are we to them?"

"I don't know." He pulled the covers up and snuggled me in. "You need to sleep. I can't look at you when you're in so much pain. I'll be here if you need something during the night."

"You're always here. And ... I'm fine. I'm a little sore, but otherwise fine."

"Yeah, I'll believe that when your face doesn't look like you've been through a war."

Again, I wanted to see my face. Winnie had conveniently taken my phone with her, though. That was on purpose. She wouldn't want me freaking out … or spending my time researching loas when I should be sleeping.

"It will be okay in the morning." Weariness was overtaking me. "We'll figure it out then."

"I'll be here when you wake up."

"Okay."

"I might run down to get some of those cookies that Winnie mentioned, but I won't be gone long."

That elicited a smile. "Eat two for me."

"You can eat your own in ten hours."

"Even better."

6

SIX

I woke to the sound of munching the next morning. My eyes snapped open like rubber bands and I jerked my chin to the side, where I found Gunner reading on his phone with cookie crumbs all over his chest.

"How many of those have you eaten?" I asked. My voice was rusty, and I had to clear my throat. "Did you save any for me?"

Gunner had a smile at the ready as he angled himself to get a better look. "As much as I wanted to eat them all, I did save some for you." He reached out to brush my hair away from my face. "You look better."

"Am I back to my beautiful self?" I was hopeful.

"You're always beautiful to me." He gave me a soft kiss.

As earnest and sweet as he was being, that wasn't enough for me. "Give me your phone." I snagged the device before his reflexes could kick in and hit the camera app. I had to switch the viewer to get a gander at my reflection, and when I did, an involuntary gasp escaped.

If this was better, then I didn't even want to know how I looked the night before.

I had a series of small cuts on my face. They looked as if they'd been healing, which meant they were way worse hours earlier. My coloring was off. Everything looked to have been bruised at some point. The bruising had turned green at the edges, though. A sure sign that the worst of it was behind us. And yet still, it was jarring.

"Oh, crap." I wanted to cry. I wasn't as vain as some people assumed. This was just too much, though.

"Don't, baby," Gunner chided. He slipped his arm around my waist and tugged me to him. "Just ... don't cry. I can't stand it when you cry."

I didn't want to cry. To me, it was a sign of weakness. I hadn't been prepared for my face, though. "Don't." I shoved his face away from mine. "I look like I belong in a horror movie."

"You're healing," he argued. "You're way better than you were last night."

"That doesn't make me feel better." I covered my face. "Don't look at me."

He sounded exasperated when he sighed. Thankfully for both of us, the sound of the bedroom door opening had us looking up.

Winnie, smiling and dressed for the day, stepped inside the room. "You look much better." She placed my cell phone on the nightstand without commenting on it.

"Don't say that." I was starting to get irritated. "I look as if I've gone ten rounds with Jason Voorhees and lost."

"If you'd lost you would be dead," Gunner argued.

"Are those crumbs all over your chest?" Winnie asked him.

Gunner turned sheepish. "I got hungry. I eat when I'm stressed."

"Yes, because you don't eat otherwise." Winnie rolled her eyes until they landed on me. "As for you, stop being a baby. Your face will be back to normal before you know it. I'm actually more concerned about your other injuries."

Before I could respond—or turn into an even bigger baby—she removed the poultice from my shoulder. The open wound had healed, but the skin looked fresh and tight.

"Much better." Winnie's smile was bright. "You're well on your way to recovery. How do you feel?"

That felt like a loaded question. "I look like I got run over by a truck."

"That's not what I asked." Winnie folded her arms across her chest and waited.

"Man, you didn't let Bay get away with anything when she was growing up, did you?" I groused. "Like ... she couldn't even feel sorry for herself for five minutes."

"Bay was actually a bit of a moper when she was a teenager," Winnie countered. "She got away with murder because Aunt Tillie used to tap her for adventures, and as you well know, there's no controlling Aunt Tillie."

That reminded me of the previous evening. "Did she come home?"

"Yes, and she kept her friend close." Winnie's lips curved down. "Even now, he's tucked away in the corner suite one floor up. You can hear him snoring from a full floor away out in the hallway."

"Well, that's good at least. They couldn't have gotten into too much trouble."

"We'll see." Winnie didn't look convinced. "Just because we haven't heard anything yet, that does not mean they didn't get into trouble. We'll worry about that over breakfast, though." She snapped her fingers, causing my eyebrows to fly up my forehead. "You, young lady, need to shower because you smell."

"I think that's the poultice," I argued.

"No, it's you," Gunner replied.

"Then you two need to head down to breakfast. We're going to have a full house this morning."

"Guests?" I asked, suddenly alarmed. I didn't want strangers asking questions about my injuries.

"No. It's too early in the week for guests. You'll see who is there when you get downstairs. You have a half hour. Don't dillydally." With that, she turned on her heel and left.

"I'm not used to so much heavy parenting," I complained to Gunner as I slid out of bed. I wasn't moving as fast as normal, but nothing hurt as badly as it had the previous evening. It was more of an achy feeling, telling me that I was indeed healing.

"I kind of like it," Gunner said as he joined me. "My mother wasn't lovey-dovey. Winnie is the mother I never got to enjoy."

"It's weird."

"You're weird," he fired back.

"Whatever." I cocked my head. "Do you think it's wrong for us to shower together?"

"Since I'm afraid of you getting lightheaded and potentially falling, it's happening," Gunner replied. "If they don't like it, they'll live."

That was good enough for me. "I'm kind of hungry," I admitted.

"I'm starving."

"You just ate your weight in cookies."

"That's not a real breakfast."

"If you say so."

CLOTHES MYSTERIOUSLY APPEARED IN the bedroom when Gunner and I were showering. They were my clothes, and his, and I had to wonder where they'd come from.

"Evan," Gunner said as he pulled on a shirt. "I'm guessing he ran to our place to grab clothes and check on Merlin."

Merlin was our cat, who we treated like a son. I hadn't even thought of him the previous evening. "Man, we are bad cat parents," I complained as I pulled on a pair of jeans. "He was probably starving."

"I'm sure Evan took care of him."

"Yeah." I stared at my hair in the mirror for a beat. "Do you feel up to braiding this for me?" I gestured toward the tangled mess.

"I could possibly be persuaded."

I was instantly suspicious. "What do you need to persuade you?"

"A kiss."

It wasn't the worst request I'd ever heard. "Fine. I can manage a kiss." The kiss lingered longer than I was expecting. Gunner was quick when braiding my hair, though. It didn't look quite as good as if I'd done it myself, but my shoulder wasn't ready for heavy contorting and it wasn't as if my face looked perfect anyway. The braid would hardly be a distraction.

"Let's eat," I said, forcing some brightness.

Gunner studied me for several seconds, then nodded. "Let's eat."

I was slower going down the stairs than I would've liked, but I didn't exactly hobble either. Voices greeted us from the dining room as we pushed open the swinging door. There, at the table, I was greeted by more faces than I was expecting.

"You're okay." Andrea started to stand—who invited her and Rick anyway?—but I held up my hand.

"I'm a little sore," I said. "No hugs."

Andrea automatically nodded. She'd become accustomed to the fact that I wasn't big on public displays of affection.

"I bet Gunner got a hug," Rick said in a low voice.

"Gunner was covered in cookie crumbs this morning, and I woke starving," I countered. "There's a difference."

"I look good with cookie crumbs on my chest," Gunner argued. He pulled out a chair for me. "Sit."

I did as instructed—but only because arguing with him seemed like too much work—and then I took in the other faces watching me. On top of Rick and Andrea, Evan, Baron, Tillie, Bay, Landon, Marnie, Twila, Winnie, Hemlock Cove Police Chief Terry Davenport, and Gunner's father Graham Stratton were all seated at the table. "You weren't kidding about having a full house," I said to Winnie.

She smiled. "I happen to enjoy a big, boisterous breakfast," she said. "I have no doubt that's what's in store for us this morning."

She was right. It was going to be a loud meal. "Just point me toward the food."

Gunner, to my surprise, grabbed my plate and started filling it up. He didn't ask what I wanted—he knew what I did and didn't like at this point—and by the time he was finished I had twice as much food as I would've gathered for myself.

"Eat," he ordered before adding even more food to his own plate. "You need your strength."

I was about to tell him what he could do with his bossy attitude when my stomach let loose a ruthless growl. "I'm eating, but only because I feel it's necessary. I'm not doing it because you think I should." I shot him a dirty look before shoveling a forkful of eggs into my mouth. I immediately felt better, stronger even. Yes, breakfast was definitely necessary.

"As long as you eat, I don't care," Gunner replied around a mouthful of food. His eyes darted across the table, to where his father was sitting next to Marnie. "Did you spend the night here?"

Graham had been silent since we entered the room. His expression didn't change in the face of Gunner's question, but unless I was very much mistaken, his ears were turning pink. "What does that matter?" He didn't meet his son's gaze and reached for his juice.

"I'm just curious."

"You spent the night here," Graham noted.

"Because my girlfriend almost died and that guy brought her here." He jabbed his index finger at Baron.

"He's right," Baron said. "I did bring her here. I knew that this would be the best place for her."

"And how did you know that?" Bay asked. "I mean...it's not that we're not grateful you brought her here—because we are—but I'm still a little fuzzy on why you were there."

"I wasn't there. I was elsewhere." Baron reached for the bacon platter at the same time Landon did. "You're not going to eat it all, are you?" he asked when Landon shot him a dirty look.

"I just might," Landon replied. "Answer my wife's question."

"I don't believe she asked a question. She said she was fuzzy." Baron winked at Bay. "I happen to like a fuzzy woman."

That was weird for anybody to say, but especially him. "Do you always have to take it to a weird place?" I groused.

"Yes," Baron replied.

"Speaking of weird places, I've received no less than three calls today," Terry interjected. "It seems someone—I don't know who but someone—painted a series of erotic images on the outside of the Unicorn Emporium last night."

I jerked my eyes to him. The Unicorn Emporium was just what it sounded like. A store that sold unicorns of every shape and size. Pewter, metal, ceramic, resin, and even brass unicorns. It was owned by Margaret Little, who just so happened to be Tillie's arch nemesis.

"Why are you looking at me?" Tillie demanded. "I can't paint."

"I don't know," Terry replied evenly. "Perhaps it's because half of the naked images had skulls for faces." His gaze moved to Baron. "It's just a hunch, though."

"Well, I don't appreciate being blamed for everything that goes wrong in Margaret's life," Tillie argued. "It's not my fault someone painted her store. Personally, I think a little doggy style delight would do her some good."

Terry looked pained. "How did you know that some of the images depicted doggy style?"

Tillie seemed to realize she was caught because her eyebrows moved up her forehead. She caught herself fast, though, and shrugged. "What other style is there?"

Gunner's hand went into the air, as if he wanted to answer the question. Since his mouth was full, he couldn't speak right away. That allowed me enough time to slap his hand down.

"Don't," I warned.

He looked chagrined.

"I got another call from Bea's Beauty Boutique," Terry said. "It seems someone stripped the mannequin in her window and put a cigar in her hand. There's also something that looks like shaving cream—although it's not shaving cream—over the mannequin's private parts."

Landon choked on his bacon.

"Mannequins don't have private parts," Baron offered helpfully. "They're not anatomically correct."

Terry blinked. "What does that have to do with anything?"

"I'm just pointing out the folly of your statement."

Terry held up a hand to silence the loa. "I thought you guys were on a serious mission last night," he pressed. "That's what Winnie said you were doing."

"We were on a serious mission," Baron replied. "We went to the cave. It's empty, well, other than a few bodies."

Well, now he had my full attention. I straightened and opened my mouth.

"None of those bodies belong to the lamia," Baron continued before I could ask the obvious question. "She's gone."

"Who do the bodies belong to?" Landon asked. "Should we be retrieving these bodies?"

"Not unless you have a portal to another plane, because that's where she got her minions." Baron didn't look all that disturbed about the deaths. "They're not locals."

Bay darted a questioning look toward me but didn't say anything.

"Who are they?" I asked.

"I don't know." Baron shrugged. "I just know they're not from this plane. They don't belong here."

I shoved some hash browns in my mouth to buy time to debate my next move. I didn't speak again until I'd swallowed. "I want you to take me to the cave when we're done here."

"Why?" Baron looked baffled. "I already told you the lamia isn't there. You're not ready to face her anyway."

"I don't care about her. Or, well, not right at this second. That was her lair, though. There might be clues."

"Fine." Baron sounded bored. "I'll take you, but only if you're not a kvetch about it."

I recognized the word. It was one of Tillie's favorites.

"Oh, crap," Bay muttered under her breath. "They've bonded."

"We have," Baron agreed. "I find Tillie to be an absolute delight. If she was fifty years younger, I would be all over her." He winked.

"Hey!" Tillie's annoyance came out to play. "I'm middle aged."

"Maybe at heart," Baron agreed. He was a blunt creature. I had to give him that. "Externally, you look like my grandmother when I disinterred her ten years after her death."

My appetite disappeared in an instant. "Why would you disinter your grandmother?"

"We don't need to know the answer to that question," Landon barked.

"Definitely not," Rick agreed. "Just ... pretend she didn't ask it."

Baron was not one to pretend anything unless it was in his best interests. "My grandmother was a mean old coot. She insisted on being buried with all of her jewelry, including a very rare rune. When I needed the rune, I retrieved the rune."

That was horrifying. "You're kind of a monster, aren't you?" I complained.

"I am a man of many talents," Baron replied. "She didn't miss the rune. Trust me."

All I could do was shake my head.

"I'm middle aged," Tillie insisted to Winnie. "Can you believe he's suggesting I'm old? He's way older than me."

"I'm young at heart," Baron countered.

"So am I." Tillie shot him a death glare. "I'm not old."

"You're quite long-lived for a human," Baron countered. "I'm still in my prime as a loa. There's a difference. Although ... if you're quite set on taking a tumble, I can probably make it happen."

"Don't do that," Graham blurted.

"Please don't do that," Terry intoned.

"You two mind your own business," Tillie warned. "I'm the one who decides who to tumble with, and I'm not ruling it out."

This conversation was spiraling out of control ... and fast. "Let's talk about something else," I said.

"What about Whistler?" Gunner challenged. "I can't just sit back and watch you do my boy wrong."

"We're not exclusive," Tillie replied. "I'm under no obligation to only slap his salami."

"Oh, geez." Terry slammed his hand to his forehead. "Someone make the weird skull guy go away. I cannot tolerate this conversation a second longer."

He wasn't the only one chafing under the heated glances Baron kept gracing Tillie with. "You're taking me to the cave," I ordered. "After that, you're free to go and do ... whatever it is you do."

"Normally, I would take you up on your offer and flee this place as soon as humanly possible," Baron replied. "You don't even have any proper absinthe in this godforsaken place."

"I have absinthe," Tillie countered. "It's hidden in my secret stash."

"And just where is that?" Winnie demanded.

Suddenly, Tillie became fixated on her plate. "This is a really good breakfast." She shoveled eggs into her mouth.

"This place amuses me despite the fact that there's no good music to enjoy when walking around," Baron said. "I think I'm going to stick around for a while."

That was not good news. "Why?"

"Because you're going to need me."

"Why?"

"Because I said so." Baron shot me a pointed look. "You should eat your breakfast. It's going to be a long day."

Just what did he know that I didn't know? I couldn't wrap my head around why he was here. I didn't like it, though.

"We're not done talking about this," I said when I was reasonably certain I could speak without losing my cool. "We're going to save the rest of this conversation so it's not had over breakfast, though. I don't want to ruin everybody else's morning."

"That's quite gracious of you," Baron said. "I'd heard you were a bit of a turd when it came to manners. I'm happy to hear that not all of the stories swirling around you were true."

"You're the turd," I fired back.

"Yes," Baron agreed. "We're a match made in Heaven."

"Next to me," Gunner growled.

Yes, this was definitely going to be a long day.

7
SEVEN

From what I could tell, Baron seemed to rub everybody the wrong way. Even Tillie, who he went out and wreaked havoc with the night before wasn't speaking to him by the time breakfast was over. As for the loa, he didn't seem to care. There was a cunning light glittering in his eyes when he took in all the faces around the table.

He was up to something.

Despite that, deep down, I realized I trusted him. I didn't trust him to do the right thing by me necessarily. I did trust him to do the right thing for the greatest amount of people, though.

"What are you thinking?" Bay asked when she found me in the library staring out the window. She looked genuinely concerned.

"I think that he's not telling us something," I replied. I didn't bother asking what she was referring to. I already knew.

"What does Poet say?"

"I haven't called her yet. Later."

Bay opened her mouth, then shut it. "What's the plan?"

"I want to see the cave where Bonnie was living. After that, I'm not certain."

"Well, I'm going with you." She sounded determined enough that I just nodded. "You should invite your parents too."

I frowned. "I don't even understand what they're doing here," I admitted. "I mean ... who called them?"

"My mother called them, and she means business." Bay was firm. "I know you don't want to deal with certain things right now—your family being one of them—but my mother and aunts have decided they're going to force you to deal with those things whether you want to or not."

"Ugh." I could just picture Winnie opting to take control of things. "She's going to be difficult, isn't she?"

"Oh, really difficult," Bay agreed. She managed a smile despite my dark glare. "She thinks of you as her own now. She wants you happy."

"I've been better," I insisted. "The whole reason I got into trouble last night is because I was out at the cabin having a family dinner."

Bay looked momentarily sympathetic. Then she shook herself out of it. "Why didn't you call your parents last night to at least tell them you were okay?"

"I was out of it." The answer came quick and fast. It didn't feel entirely truthful, though.

"Uh-huh." Bay's smile was flat. "Why didn't Gunner call to tell them that you were okay?"

"He probably didn't think about it."

"He *is* forgetful," Graham agreed as he joined us. He looked concerned as he stroked his hand over my hair and stared into my eyes. "My son doesn't think past his own emotions most of the time. He's a pain."

I scratched my cheek. "I happen to like him."

Graham smirked. "I'm well aware. I'm just suggesting that you're the only thing he thinks about with any regularity. If you would've put a priority on your parents, he would've made sure they knew you were okay. They wouldn't have had to practically invite themselves out here for breakfast."

He had a point. "I'll try to be better," I managed.

"That's all anybody asks." Graham was earnest as he stared into my eyes. "Kid, your face makes me want to cry."

"Well, thanks for that."

He chuckled. "I just mean that I don't like seeing you hurt. Your parents don't like it either. Personally, I think they've been saints where you're concerned. You haven't exactly been welcoming, and they haven't done more than stand tall in the face of that mouth of yours."

I was genuinely fond of Graham, but he was starting to bug me. "They left me. They can't expect me just to instantly warm up to them."

"Maybe not, but you're holding a grudge just to hold a grudge at this point."

I narrowed my eyes. "That is not true."

"It is. I think you have multiple things going on in that head of yours, including the fact that you have an independent streak a mile wide and don't want to take others into consideration. That's not the only reason you're doing this, though."

I folded my arms over my chest and stared him down. He clearly wasn't done.

"You say you understand why they gave you up—and I think part of you does—but you're still angry about it," Graham continued. "That's okay, kid. You have a right to be angry about it. I would be angry, too. It's no different than Gunner being mad at me for all those years because he didn't think I did enough to protect him from his mother."

My heart stuttered. Yolanda Stratton had been a terrible mother. Sure, she'd been mentally ill—which gave her a bit of a pass—but she was evil incarnate. She'd tried to kill Gunner as a child because she was trying to avoid the same prophecy fueling me now. Gunner had been marked by that incident. That didn't mean Graham was to blame.

"See, I really wish you wouldn't compare us," I admitted. "Gunner's anger for you was misdirected."

"Weird." Graham grinned. "I wonder if that means your anger for your parents could possibly be misdirected."

"Unbelievable," I muttered under my breath. "I should've seen that coming."

"You really should have," Graham agreed. He wasn't backing down. "The thing is, you're entitled to your anger. You're dealing with so much right now I can't help but feel that you're being unfairly overwhelmed.

"Despite that, though," he continued, "you can't have everything your way." He leaned close. "Next time, just call your parents to tell them you're okay. It's not too much to ask."

"Fine." I heaved out an annoyed sigh. "I'll do it. Under one condition."

Now Graham was the one who was suspicious. "And what's that?"

"I'll do it if you tell me what's going on with you and Marnie," I pressed. "Are you guys spending every night together now?"

Rather than respond, Graham lightly pushed my face away from him. "You need to learn to mind your own business."

"Um...you just spent five minutes telling me I was a bad daughter," I argued. "How was that your business?"

"No." Graham straightened quickly. "Kid, that's not what I was saying to you. That anger you're carrying around, it's okay. You deserve to hoard that anger like gold if you want to. I just think you can be conscientious of your parents' issues at the same time. You all need to work together on this. You're not a bad daughter, though. I should know. I kind of think of you as my daughter now, and I happen to believe you're great."

"Aw," Bay teased.

Graham glared at her. "Marnie has told me quite a few stories about you and your cousins growing up. You guys were bad daughters."

Rather than be offended by the comment, Bay snickered. "They weren't exactly stellar adults."

"Just ... behave." Graham was stern until his eyes moved back to me. Then his gaze softened. "You're one of my favorite people. I think you're the best thing that ever happened to my son. He was a hapless idiot before you came along."

"I love you too, Dad," Gunner called out as he passed the library and kept going.

I smirked at their interplay. They argued. A lot. They also loved one another, although they would never admit that in front of an audience.

"Just be more cognizant," Graham said. "It doesn't cost you anything to be kind occasionally."

"I said I was sorry. My thoughts were kind of scattered last night."

"So, you get a pass," Graham acknowledged. "Numb-nuts out there doesn't. You need to train him better."

"I have the best father in the world," Gunner yelled out from somewhere in the hallway. "People everywhere are jealous because my dad is so great."

Graham chuckled. "Just be careful," he said to me. "Something big feels as if it's happening here, and I don't think we have a clear view of what that something is. That means we're essentially blind ... and it's not good for us to be blind when we're dealing with gods and apexes."

I was right there with him. "You'll check to see if anything weird has popped up overnight?" I prodded.

He nodded. "I will. You be careful going to your cave. It would be great if you didn't get hurt again in the next few days."

"I'll give it my best shot."

"Yeah, try a little harder than that."

. . .

BARON DIDN'T PUT UP A FIGHT WHEN I said that we were taking a big crew to the cave. Even though I hadn't initially thought about including Andrea and Rick, Graham's insistence that I do better had me inviting them. Bay invited herself. Gunner and Evan weren't going to be left behind. And Tillie, well, Tillie was going to do whatever she wanted. So, she might've been annoyed by Baron, but that didn't mean she was going to be left behind.

"Ugh. It really is a cave," Bay complained when we landed in our destination. The ceiling had caved in, but we could still move around the space. At least some.

"Why would I exaggerate about a cave?" I demanded.

She shrugged. "I don't know. You just tend to exaggerate sometimes."

I turned my incredulous stare toward Evan and Gunner, who were surveying the fallen rocks.

"You do exaggerate," Evan confirmed without looking up. "It's just part of the wonder that is you."

"Oh, stuff it." I was at the end of my rope. "I'm a truth teller."

Rather than agree, Gunner lifted his chin. "I don't feel comfortable hanging around in this cave knowing it's likely the rest of the ceiling could give in any second."

Baron shot him a dubious look. "Geez." He waved his hand and all the rubble started to lift from the ground. More than that, it returned to the ceiling. The loa's magic swirled for a few seconds. When he was finished, everything was back the way it had been before the initial fall.

Well, except for the bodies that were stretched out at the far ends of the cave room.

"Where did they come from?" I frowned as I moved closer to one of the bodies. It was somehow different from what I was expecting. The legs were shorter, the torso thicker. "They're not humans," I realized.

"They're dwarves," Baron replied. He didn't look all that worked up about the bodies. "They're from another plane."

I took a moment to consider that. He'd mentioned it before, but I'd glossed over what it could possibly mean. "Poet has a friend who is a dwarf from another plane," I said finally. "He wears dresses and carries around a big axe."

"Yes, he's one of my favorites," Baron agreed. "He doesn't give me 'the look' when I arrive without an invitation. Poet's harem gives me 'the look' and it drives me crazy."

"Poet's harem?" It took me a moment to understand who he was referring to. "I forgot she said that girl in Texas said she had a reverse harem. That is kind of funny."

"She only has sex with the whiny one," Baron argued. "That's not a true harem."

"She gets emotional fulfillment from all of them," I argued. "I think they're cute...although I'm not looking forward to having to deal with Luke when I finally get to meet him in person."

"Why are you going to have to deal with Luke?" Evan asked.

"He's got his nose out of joint. He thinks I'm trying to steal his best friend."

"He sounds high strung."

"He is, but Poet loves him." I moved to a corner of the cave and studied the stuff that had spilled on the floor. "Does this look like potion ingredients to anybody else?"

Baron shifted so he was closer. "It looks like green dirt and leaves."

"Yes, that would be potion ingredients." He was trying my patience.

"We can try to find something to bag it up," Andrea offered. When I'd included her and Rick in the trip, she looked so happy I thought she was going to try to hug me. I was careful to nip that instinct in the bud. I didn't want a bunch of unnecessary hugs slowing me down.

"Thank you." I smiled at her. "The Winchesters should be able to tell us what we're dealing with. If they can't, Doc can send the samples to the regional office."

"What do you think she was doing here?" Gunner asked as he finished frisking one of the dead dwarves.

"Why are you feeling him up?" Evan asked before I could answer.

"I wasn't feeling him up," Gunner shot back. He and Evan got along like middle school-aged brothers. "I was seeing if he had identification on him."

"Because you want to look him up at the DMV?" Evan gave him a dirty look. "That's not really how it works. He's from another plane."

Gunner threw his hands into the air. "I can't even deal with him right now," he said to me. "How are you friends with this guy?"

For the first time since the ceiling had fallen in on me, I managed a genuine laugh. I was still a bit sore and achy. I didn't want to look at my face too closely. These guys, though, they always knew how to make me feel better.

"Well, that was nice to see." Gunner leaned closer and studied my face. "Are you feeling better?" He looked hopeful.

"I'm fine," I assured him. "By tomorrow, you won't even be able to tell anything happened to me."

"I'll know."

"Yes, well ... I'm fine." I didn't like it when people hovered. "I'm just curious where she got these guys."

"Really, I'm more curious why she felt the need to get them," Evan said. "I mean ... she's the lamia apex. Why does she have to bring in minions from another plane?"

Actually, I could answer that question. "Because she's a woman. The lamia of the present have fashioned themselves as a patriarchy. Poet explained it all to me."

"Well, try to explain it to me."

"The lamia men are basically jerks. The first lamia apex was a woman. The men decided to take over. They made sure that it was always men close to the apex when it was time for a shift in power after that."

"Only they couldn't control this shift in power," Evan surmised. "Bonnie taking over for Zeno wasn't anticipated."

"No," I agreed. "She stole the power. Now she's augmented it with pixie power. I'm not even sure she is a true lamia any longer." I thought back to her appearance the previous evening. "Although ... she looks like a snake. She has weird scars, though. Like ... it almost seems as if the magic was ripping her apart from the inside. She managed to stop that. She looks rough, though."

"She's more than an apex now," Baron confirmed. "She's keeping more magic inside of her than is wise. She won't be able to control all that power."

"Which begs the question, again, of why you didn't kill her when you had the chance," Gunner complained.

"It wasn't my place," Baron replied. "I mean ... where do you think that power goes when she dies?"

Gunner looked confused by the question. "I'm not sure. I guess I've never really thought about it."

"I can't absorb that power." Baron was matter of fact. "It would change me."

"And I can't absorb that power because the same thing that happened to her would happen to me," I said. "So, you're basically saying we need to arrange it so there's another lamia present to become the new apex when it's time."

"I don't know that I would boil it down to that, but essentially, that's true," Baron said. "Do you know a lamia who might be open to taking the job?"

"I don't know a lot of lamias," I replied. Something occurred to me, though. "Poet has a lamia friend. Maybe she can do it."

"Raven." Baron nodded. "I've considered her. The problem is, I'm not certain she would be open to the job. She seems to have her eyes on a different prize right now. He dresses as a clown and wears chaps."

"The clown with the fake accent." I nodded. Poet had given me a rundown of all of her people, and I'd laughed really hard when she was telling me about Percival the clown, who apparently decided that being British somehow made the fact that he performed in heavy makeup and a red wig somehow more palatable.

"I like him," Baron said. "He doesn't care that the others make fun of him behind his back. His love for Raven is obvious. That's a very eclectic crew."

"But you don't think Raven would be up for the job," I surmised.

"I don't think she wants it," Baron replied. "She seems more interested in severing her ties to the lamias and living a peaceful life on Moonstone Bay. Forcing her to become something she doesn't want to be won't make things better."

He was right, of course. I just had one problem. "I don't think we should let a male lamia take over the position again. They've screwed the females in their group enough. If we contact them, they're going to send a man."

"They are," Baron agreed.

"Even if she doesn't want the job, Raven probably knows others who might want it," I said. "I'll text Poet and set up a video call. It can't possibly hurt."

"That's probably smart," Baron agreed. He was curious as he looked around the cave. "I have a question."

I waited for him to ask it.

"Why would she pick a lair that's underground?"

It wasn't the question I was expecting. "Um ... because she's a snake? Lamias are snakes in human form, right? Don't snakes like caves?"

"Some," he replied. "They also like to sun themselves. They prefer warm and arid climates, like Phoenix."

"She came here because she knew I would eventually come here," I said. "That was all part of their plan from the beginning. They wanted to stop me from winning this big battle that they keep freaking out about."

"Okay, but that still doesn't explain why she wouldn't go for a different lair." Baron was insistent. "Something drew her here."

I looked around the cave again, hoping to find something to

pique my interest. The only things that stood out were the ingredients on the floor and the dead dwarves. "I don't know what to tell you," I said finally. "I don't know why she picked this spot."

"Perhaps she doesn't know either," Baron suggested. "She was never meant for these powers. The person you knew is no longer here."

"I'm not sure the person I knew was ever real."

"No, but she would've allowed real bits of her personality to shine through. Otherwise, it's too much work to keep up the charade." He rolled his neck. "It's just something to consider."

"I'll take your word for it."

8
EIGHT

Our next stop was the Rusty Cauldron. Evan handled introductions—Baron seemed more interested in Whistler and the beer tap than the people—and I set up my computer so I could call Poet.

She was fresh-faced and happy when she saw me come on the screen. "Hey." Her smile immediately disappeared. "What happened to you?"

"I got in a fight with a cave ceiling and lost," I replied. "Don't worry about it. I'm fine. How is married life?"

"It's great. I want to talk about your face, though. You look..." She didn't finish it out.

When her computer screen shifted and I found Luke staring back at me, however, he didn't have that problem. "You look like you should be in a Lifetime movie about spousal abuse," he said. "Are you permanently disfigured? I'm betting you are."

I glared at him. "I know that would make you happy, but I'm going to have to disappoint you. I'm fine."

"Okay, *Allegra*." He said my birth name in his grating way, which was designed to irritate me. It worked.

"Luke, can you put Poet back on?" I asked. "I don't have time for your nonsense today."

"Yes, he can," Poet replied. She wrestled the computer away from Luke, giving him a dirty look in the process. "Why do you always have to be so difficult? She's clearly had a bad day."

"Hey, I was just thinking about her," Luke replied. "If she doesn't have her looks to fall back on, she's never going to make it far in life because her personality is lacking."

"That's what people say about you, too." Poet graced him with another glare before turning back to me. "Seriously, what happened to your face?"

I caught her up. It didn't take long. When I explained about the dead dwarves, she looked confused.

"I can ask Nellie about why they would be working with her," Poet said. "He might not know, but it can't hurt to ask."

"The dwarves aren't actually my biggest concern," I admitted. "My biggest concern is that it's been explained to me that I can't kill Bonnie when I'm alone."

"What are you supposed to do?" a male voice asked as another figure came into the frame. I recognized it as belonging to Kade, her husband. He slung an arm around Poet's shoulders and smiled at me in greeting. "I mean ... if it's just the two of you, are you supposed to let her kill you instead of killing her?"

"Apparently, if I kill her it will be the same as killing myself because someone has to absorb her powers."

Realization washed over Poet's face. "I didn't think of that. What are you going to do?"

That was the question I'd been driving myself crazy with over the past hour. "I don't suppose Raven wants to be the apex, does she?" I was hopeful but it felt like a long shot.

"I can ask but that wouldn't be my first inclination," Poet replied. "She's actually looking for an easier life."

"I think the next apex should be a female."

"I agree."

"Maybe ask Raven if she can think of somebody who would be good at the job," I suggested. "I'm not sure when I'm going to see Bonnie next, but this feels like the sort of thing we should have a plan in place for."

"It does," Poet agreed. "I'll talk to her. Now, tell me about Baron." She was serious. "What is he doing there?"

I lifted the computer and angled it so she could catch a glimpse of him at the bar. Doc and Rooster were on either side of him, and they seemed to be grilling him for information. "He appears to be drinking and entertaining anybody who wants to listen to him."

"That sounds like him." Poet made a face. "He's kind of a pain."

"I've noticed." I glanced over one more time to make sure he wasn't listening and lowered my voice. "The meeting with him and the other loas was weird enough. They're obviously up to something."

"I think the loas have figured out a way to keep themselves from disappearing into obscurity. That's why I absorbed the magic of one of their least savory loas, and now it appears Charlie Rhodes has done the same if what you heard is correct."

"I don't see why they would lie about it." I rolled my neck. "You don't think they want to make me one, too, do you?"

Poet hesitated, seemingly taking it all in, and then shook her head. "That doesn't feel right to me. You're something entirely different. I had loa blood to start with, and Charlie was a hodge-podge of a million different things. She could absorb loa powers because she didn't have anything else inside of her fighting the transformation. Or, if she did, there was nothing inside of her powerful enough to override it. You're different."

"Oh, in so many ways," I agreed.

She smirked. "I'm just saying that overriding the magic you already have inside of you is going to be an uphill battle."

"So, why is he here?"

"It's hard to tell with Baron. He seems to go wherever the wind takes him. It's possible he was just intrigued by you after the meeting with Cernunnos ... although it's weird to me that he's having meetings with a horned god."

"I already think the horned god is as weird as they come," I said. "I figured that out when he was fighting Skadi."

"And we know he's been hanging out and doing stuff in Detroit," Poet said. "It wasn't just Charlie that he was helping there. He's involved with the reapers, too."

"So ... what are they doing?" All of the scenarios I'd come up with were bad. "Do you think they're intent on world domination?"

Poet snorted. "I forgot you're a conspiracy theorist."

I glared at her. "I am not. It's a legitimate question."

"They could already have dominated the world if that's what they were after. No, I think they're trying to find some sort of balance. Like ... maybe evil was getting too big of a foothold and they're trying to combat it."

"Oh, it's cute that you still have such shiny thoughts." I rolled my eyes. "I can't figure out what his plan is. He stuck around for a reason."

"The thing with Baron is, eventually, he will tell you what he's doing. You might not like it, but he *will* tell you."

I glanced at the loa in question again. He seemed to be having a grand time with his beer and rapt audience. "He pulled me from that rubble, and I'm grateful because Bonnie would've killed me if she woke up and found me still there."

"You think they knew that was going to happen," Poet surmised.

I shrugged. "I think they know way more than they're telling us. I'm not encouraged by the fact that he seems to have bonded with Tillie Winchester."

Poet's face lit up with amusement. "Well, that sounds like a fun combination."

"Then I'm telling the story wrong, because it's not."

"No, I think it sounds fun." She beamed at me. "I'm almost sorry I'm going to miss it."

"You could pop in," I suggested. "You know ... just for a meal or something. You could eat at the inn and see the Winchesters." I'd seen her in person only once since we'd found each other again. Sure, I'd interrupted her honeymoon when it happened, but it had been one of the best hours of my life. "I sounded a little pathetic when I suggested that, didn't I?" I asked ruefully.

"Yes," Luke answered from somewhere near Poet.

"No," she replied. "We'll see each other again. If you need help, you know where to find me."

"You're going to end up out here eventually."

"I will," she agreed. "I'm looking forward to it."

"I'll keep you updated on what he's doing." I glanced at Baron again. "Something tells me he won't be able to keep his true intentions under wraps for very long."

"Definitely not," Poet agreed. "Just because he tells you something, though, don't assume he's telling you everything."

We said our goodbyes, and when I closed the laptop, I remained in my spot in the booth and watched Baron weave his web of enchantment over my friends. I was so lost in thought, that I almost jumped out of my skin when Rick slid in across from me.

"Penny for your thoughts." He extended his index finger, and there was an actual penny resting on it.

Without thinking, I took the penny and rolled it through my fingers. "Did you pay me pennies for my thoughts when I was a kid?" I asked.

He nodded. "You had a huge bag of pennies at one time. You thought you were rich."

"Did you send the pennies with me when you put me in the system?"

He shook his head. "No. We didn't want anything that could be traced to us. It was hard enough to let you go. We couldn't leave a bunch of trinkets with you in the hope that you would somehow remember us."

If he thought that admission was going to bother me, I had bad news for him. "I don't remember much of anything. There are images in my head. I remember that farm."

"Ezekiel wants to reclaim the farm when this is all over."

"What if it's never over?"

"I don't believe that is a concern we need to be entertaining." Rick was calm, a heavy sadness dragging down his shoulders. "We did what we thought was necessary to protect you. We were being led down a specific route. If I believed that all of this had been for nothing and it would never end, I wouldn't be able to get out of bed."

His words sparked something in the back of my brain. "We were led down a specific route."

"That's what I said. We knew you were destined for great things. That's the only reason we did what we did."

"I'm not giving you grief over it." I meant it. "In fact, maybe we should stop bringing it up. I'm including myself in that. I'll stop bringing it up, and you can stop apologizing."

"I'm not sure I can stop apologizing. It hurts to think that you had such a tough upbringing."

"Okay, but ... it's in the past. My present is pretty good. You can't keep apologizing. I can't keep whining like a little girl."

"You're allowed to feel what you feel."

"I know that. I just don't want to keep dragging people into the past. It's not doing us any good. I want to look at the future."

"Okay. What does that have to do with what I said about the route?"

"Well, I'm curious." I shifted my gaze to Baron again. "It's clear that he and his buddies are up to something. What if they're the reason behind the route?"

Rick's face was blank. "I don't understand."

"I'm not sure I do either. It's just a hunch."

"You think he's behind everything that's happened?" Bafflement ran roughshod over Rick's features as he turned his attention to the loa. "That doesn't feel right to me."

"I think that he's part of a group of entities who are trying to get to a specific outcome," I clarified. "Now, I don't know what that outcome is, but I think we're part of it. Charlie Rhodes was part of it, although she's apparently fulfilled her part. I think Poet is a part of it."

"What about the Winchesters?"

That was a good question. "They don't feel like they're part of it other than however they're going to help me ... and they *will* help me. That's a foregone conclusion."

"What about Stormy?"

Stormy Morgan was another witch from a nearby town. She was a powerful hellcat who had only recently come into her powers. I'd met her through the Winchesters. "I don't think she's part of it either. I mean ... she's going to fight with us, but she's not the central figure."

"You are," Rick guessed.

"I think I am one of the central figures. I think the loas and Cernunnos have a lot of irons in a variety of fires. It's not just me. They're fighting multiple battles."

"So, what do we do?"

That was a very good question. "For now, we just watch him. He's not going to tell us what he doesn't think we're ready to hear. He's in Hawthorne Hollow for a specific reason, though. We have to figure out what that reason is." I looked up when Gunner crossed over to me and sat, trapping me in the booth. "Why do you have that look on your face?"

"I was just thinking about my dad."

That was not the response I was expecting. "Do you want to check on him or something?" I asked. "Do you feel as if he's in trouble?"

"No." Gunner's upper lip curved into a sneer. "It's just ... do you think he and Marnie are serious?"

I burst out laughing before I could regulate my response.

"What?" he demanded. "It's a simple question."

"Would it be so terrible if he and Marnie were serious?" I asked.

"Personally, I believe they're a solid match. Plus, if she moves in with your dad, then we're going to have good breakfasts in our future."

"Oh, trust me, I've considered the food. I would trade my dad for the food alone. It's just ... can you see Marnie moving away from her sisters?"

It was something I hadn't considered. "I don't know. It's not as if Hawthorne Hollow is that far away. She can drive twenty minutes to work every day. It's not the end of the world."

"Yeah, but they do stuff together," Gunner said. "They dance naked on the bluff. The family's magic is tied to that bluff. I think it's far more likely, if they get married or something, that my dad will move in there."

I tried to picture that. "He is tight with Terry. They could be brothers-in-law under the same roof. It's kind of cute."

"It's weird is what it is. Plus, well, he has breakfast with us a lot. He's going to stop doing that if he moves in with Marnie."

And that was what was bothering him, I realized. He and his father had suffered through rough years together. Their relationship wasn't great because of it. In recent months, Graham had taken to bringing breakfast out to our place a couple of times a week. He had grown close with his son because of it.

"It's going to be okay." I patted Gunner's wrist. "We're going to keep having meals with your dad. If some of them happen to be at The Overlook, that's not the end of the world. You like their cooking anyway."

"If I wasn't already in love with you, I would totally marry Twila just for access to the pot roast," he agreed.

I had to press my lips together to keep from laughing. "Good to know."

He kissed my temple. "I know I'm being a baby. It just weirded me out to see him this morning. I wasn't expecting it."

"It's going to be okay. In fact..." I trailed off when I realized Rooster was heading in our direction.

"How goes it with the loa?" Gunner asked.

"He's interesting," Rooster replied. "He's full of himself—and clearly hiding something—but he's interesting all the same."

"Yes, he's a true joy," I agreed. "Is something up?"

"Yeah." Rooster was no longer smiling. "We have a job."

"Don't you think he takes precedence over whatever job has come in?" I asked, gesturing toward Baron, who had Whistler and Doc cackling with laughter.

"Normally, I would say yes, but we are looking for a new lair for Bonnie, correct?"

I nodded. "Why? Did you find one already?" The odds on that felt long, but I was game to go look.

"I don't know." Rooster held out his hands. "We do have a report of unusual activity out at Lakes of the North."

My eyebrows moved toward one another. "Where is Lakes of the North?"

"It's on the north side of town," Rooster replied. "Actually, it's closer to Gaylord than here, but everything melts together. There's a small chain of cabins up there. They're on the lake. They're not open this time of year."

I turned a questioning look toward Gunner. "Why wouldn't they be open? It's snowmobile season, right?"

"It is snowmobile season," Gunner replied. "Those particular cabins aren't insulated, though. They were designed for summer fishing and camping."

"Well, somebody is out there," Rooster said. "The neighbors have seen activity over the past few days."

"Would Bonnie know about those cabins?" I asked.

Rooster bobbed his head. "Yes. We've had jobs out there before. The lake has played host to more than its fair share of monsters. She knows about the cabins."

"And she might think because they don't keep the road up in snow that it's a good place to hide," Gunner said. "It's worth a shot."

"I'm sending the two of you and Evan," Rooster said. "If you do find Bonnie, I don't want you to engage with her. I just want you to report back."

"Okay." I was going to do what I wanted to do, and he couldn't stop me, but there was no reason to embark on that argument just yet. "What if it's just some random squatters?"

"Get rid of them. Same if it's random paranormals. It will just be something to cross off our list."

"We can manage that," I said. "In fact, I could use some fresh air." I looked at Baron one more time. "Try to keep him here."

"We can't control him, but I'll do my best."

"He's sneaky. Watch him closely."

9
NINE

Gunner drove. He knew the area better than me. I sat in the passenger seat and Evan took the back, where he proceeded to read from his phone.

"There's a golf course, what looks to be cabins and cottages, and even a campsite out here," he said. "I had no idea."

"You don't strike me as much of a camper," Gunner noted.

"He's not," I replied. "I'm not either."

"Oh, come on," Gunner complained. "Camping is fun."

"Maybe in your world." I shook my head. "There's no fun to be had from sleeping on the ground."

"Even though I could camp now with minimal discomfort—being a vampire does have its perks—that doesn't mean I would want to." Evan looked horrified at the thought. "Just ... no."

"Everybody says that hanging around next to a campfire is fun," I complained. "I've never found it fun."

"Man, some of the best memories of my childhood are from when my dad took me camping," Gunner insisted. "He would take us fishing and we were allowed to swear as long as nobody else was around."

"Who is 'us'?" I asked.

"Brandon."

Brandon was Gunner's best friend. I hadn't seen much of him since the snow had arrived. Before then, he'd had a rough go of it because a nest of vampires had taken control of him—all sorts of nefarious intentions fueling their efforts. I couldn't help but think we should probably check in on him.

Perhaps reading my mind, Gunner continued. "I talked to him two days ago. He's gearing up for the busy season at the lumberyard. We're close to spring, and that's when people decide they're going to do a lot of projects."

That made sense. "We should probably go to dinner with him. You know, when we're not dealing with loas and dwarves from another plane." I shifted on my seat. "How does that even work? Why would you come to this plane and work for an apex you don't even know?"

"Money," Gunner and Evan replied in tandem.

"But ... how does she even have money?"

"Maybe Zeno did," Gunner replied. "I'm sure, given how long he was alive, that he managed to amass a decent amount of cash."

"And a lamia probably didn't keep it in the bank," I mused.

"Probably not," Gunner agreed. "My guess is, Zeno had a bunch of gold and silver bars—that stuff is valuable on multiple planes from what I've learned throughout the years—and that's how she's paying her new mercenaries."

"Or she just kidnapped them from whatever plane they were on and forced them into slave labor," Evan suggested.

I froze in place. I didn't like that possibility one little bit. "Crap," I muttered. "Now I feel bad the little buggers died. Do you think that's what she did?"

Evan shrugged. "I have no idea. She doesn't strike me as somebody who would care about taking advantage of others."

"Yeah." I stewed in my own juices until Gunner pulled to the side of the road. We were in the middle of nowhere as far as I could tell.

There was a lake a good half a mile away, and I could see some cabins in that direction. What I couldn't see was a way to get to the cabins. "What are we doing?"

Gunner arched an eyebrow. "We're checking out the cabins."

I made a big show of looking around. "Where are they?"

He pointed toward the cabins near the lake.

"Okay, but how are we going to get there?" I asked.

"We're going to hike in. My truck can't drive through two feet of snow."

Was he joking? "I can't hike through two feet of snow either."

"I was wondering." The look on his face didn't change and I was instantly suspicious.

"What's the plan here?" I snapped.

"The plan is we hike in." Gunner shoved open his door.

I was in a hurry and practically tripped getting to the front of the truck to meet him. He calmly pulled on a pair of gloves as he regarded me.

"If you don't think you can do it, Evan and I can scout ahead," Gunner offered.

I murdered him with a single glare. "I can do it." To prove it, I took a huge step into the snow...and sank like a stone. When I tried to take another step, I grunted. They were big steps and a lot of snow. I was instantly cold. When I turned back to him, I was furious. "This isn't funny. I'm going to freeze to death before we get out there."

"You're being a little dramatic."

"Okay, Mr. My Daddy is Dating, and I'm Sad," I hissed. "I guess we make a good couple because we're both dramatic."

"That's a legitimate concern," he fired back.

"Whatever." I girded myself to take another step, but Evan caught me around the waist and hauled me out of the snow before I could.

"Let's not turn this into an elementary school playground show-down, huh?" Evan suggested in his most reasonable tone. That only served to make me angrier. "You're not hiking out there, Scout. Even though I think, with enough determination, you could make it, that's not what you need given the fact that your body is still healing."

"You could've let me mess with her for another two minutes," Gunner complained.

"At the rate you were going, you were going to be sleeping on the couch and she would've hurt herself just to prove a point," Evan replied. "You're not hiking out there, Scout."

"Well, I'm not staying here." I would die before I let them have all the fun ... or glory. I didn't want anybody else to get either. I was the hero ... and they were going to have to get used to it. "I'm going."

"Then start moving." Gunner gestured toward the snow.

I didn't like his attitude. I would indeed freeze to death before I gave up, though. "Fine." My attitude was poor when I started toward the snow again. Evan didn't allow me to make it more than a single step.

"Stop getting her riled up," he ordered Gunner.

"She's fun when she's mad," Gunner argued.

"Well, I'm too tired to listen to her rant and rave today," Evan shot back. "You guys were tucked into bed before ten o'clock last night. I had to chase Tillie and Baron all over Hemlock Cove. Tillie had a list of people she wanted to torture, and when she found out Baron could basically beam her to wherever she wanted to go, she was unstoppable."

When I tried to picture what he was describing, I couldn't hold in my laughter. "Was it even more than Terry mentioned this morning over breakfast?"

"So much more."

"Aw." I was momentarily amused. Then I remembered the snow. "What's your plan? Do you have a sled or something?"

"Actually, I do have a sled," Gunner said. He gestured toward the back of the truck. "I keep it in case I need it when somebody goes off the road. Something tells me you're not going to be comfortable allowing me to pull you to the cabins, though."

I took a moment to consider it. "I might be persuaded." Even saying it, I knew I wouldn't be okay with that option. "Or not."

He smirked. "I'm going to carry you."

How did he think that was better than the sled? "Um ... excuse me? You can't make it through this snow any better than I can."

"Actually, I can. I'm taller than you by a good eight inches."

"Six inches."

"Eight inches," he repeated. "I also have shifter strength. I can easily make it across the snow."

"And if he gets tired, I can take you the rest of the way," Evan said. "I won't even break a sweat, unlike him. He'll be breathing heavily the whole way. I know better than suggesting I be the one to take you at the start, though. I'm just going to swoop in when his back starts screaming at the extra weight."

"I don't weigh that much." I stared out at the cabins. As much as I wanted to make the trek myself, I knew I couldn't. "Fine. I don't want to hear you guys bringing this up, though. If word gets out that I let you carry me, it's going to be the death knell of my badassery."

"I think it's cute that you think there's a chance we're not going to give you a hard time about this later," Gunner teased. He turned so his back was to me. "Hop on."

I stared for a moment, debating, and then took a leap of faith. Literally. Gunner caught me, hooked his hands around my knees, and then we were off.

Gunner and Evan made good time. Evan, true to his word, had zero issues. Gunner made it through the first half of the trip without a problem. He started to labor after that.

"Let me take her," Evan prodded when he got tired of listening to Gunner wheeze. "You might need your strength when we get over there."

"I've got her," Gunner countered. "She's my girlfriend."

"Yes, but she's my friend."

"I said I've got her." Gunner made it five more steps and then groaned. "Fine. You take her. What is wrong with me? I'm out of shape or something."

"The snow is two feet deep, and she's an extra hundred and fifty pounds to grapple with," Evan said as he shifted so I could move to his back.

"A hundred and thirty," I corrected.

Evan angled his head and raised an eyebrow. It was obvious he didn't believe me.

"Eight," I said out of nowhere. "I weigh a hundred and thirty-eight pounds." I thought about it a bit longer. "On days that we don't eat gas station chicken."

"Uh-huh." Evan's feet were light despite my added weight dragging him down as we made the rest of the trip. Once we were near the cabins, he unceremoniously dumped me on the ground and scanned the area. "Do you smell that?" he asked Gunner, who was a full twenty seconds behind us.

"I can't smell anything," Gunner complained. "Wait ... is that burnt toast? Isn't it the sign of a heart attack if you smell burnt toast?"

"Or you're smelling that." Evan pointed toward a spot behind one of the cabins. It was obvious someone had hosted a bonfire party...and recently.

"Suck it up, big guy." I slapped Gunner's back a little harder than was necessary. "You're the one who said you would have no problem making the hike."

"You can plane jump," Gunner argued. "Why can't you just open a door for us to walk through when we go back?"

In truth, the notion hadn't even occurred to me. "Maybe I don't want to flaunt my new powers," I sniffed, refusing to meet his gaze.

"Whatever." Gunner gave my butt a friendly slap to mimic the one I'd already given him. Then he sobered. "What's that other smell?"

"Caught that, did you?" Evan was grim. "There's definitely someone here."

They had my full attention. "Bonnie?"

"It doesn't smell like a snake," Evan replied. "That doesn't mean she hasn't been out here. I don't think she's out here now, though."

"If it doesn't smell like a snake, what is it?"

Evan slowly trained his eyes on me. "Do you remember that time we had to go into the old Packard Plant downtown and we were overrun with those strange creepy-crawly creatures we'd never crossed paths with before?"

I frowned. "Those were Arachnids."

He nodded. "It smells very similar to that ... only more potent because I'm a vampire now."

My stomach bottomed out. I wasn't afraid of much—spicy Thai food notwithstanding—but Arachnids were not a favorite of mine. "How certain are you?"

"Pretty certain."

"What's an Arachnid?" Gunner asked. "I mean...other than a spider. I know you're not talking about a giant spider."

Evan shot him a pitying look.

"Oh, no way." Gunner's face drained of color. "Are you being serious right now? I do not want to fight a giant spider. This is not *It*."

It took me a moment to grasp the reference. "See, I think the giant spiders in Harry Potter are way more terrifying than the Penny-wise spider in *It*."

Gunner shot me an incredulous look. "That spider had a clown face. You can't combine a spider and a clown. That's an assault against nature."

"It's a good thing we're not fighting either of those spiders," Evan interjected. He looked annoyed. "Arachnids are different. They're humans with spider characteristics."

Gunner's mouth fell open. "Is that supposed to be better?"

"I'm just saying that we're not actually going to be fighting a giant spider."

"Can it spin a web, trap me in it, and eat me when I'm still alive like a regular spider?"

Evan blinked twice. "Yes," he said finally.

"Then that's all I need to know." Gunner shot me a death glare. "Let's head back. We told Rooster we would just scout the area and then give him an update. Hop on." He leaned over so I could climb onto his back.

"We said we would not get into a fight if it was Bonnie," I countered. "These are Arachnids."

"Don't finish what you're going to say," Gunner warned.

"We can take Arachnids. They're not great thinkers."

"I told you not to say it," Gunner hissed. "I don't like spiders, Scout."

I didn't like them either. "We don't have to get close to them," I assured him.

"You guys finally have a shared phobia," Evan cooed. "It's adorable."

"I will hurt you," I growled.

"I know what I'm dressing up as next Halloween," he sang out.

I sensed danger before I saw it and threw up a magical wall just as a web shot in our direction. It bounced back, disappearing into the snow, and when I raised my eyes, I found five Arachnids creeping out from behind the nearest cabin.

They were just as bad as I remembered. They scuttled like crabs and raced toward us, intent to wrestle us down—and, yes, trap us in a web so they could eat us over the course of several days—before we could make an escape.

I blasted the first three with pixie fire, internally cringing when they screamed as they were roasted alive. Evan caught the fourth around the neck and the accompanying snap as he twisted the creature's head made me want to throw up. That only left the fifth for Gunner, who did the one thing I wasn't expecting.

As the Arachnid launched itself at him, he ducked, and the creature went sailing over his head and landed in the snow.

I stared at the creature for a beat, dumbfounded, and then I turned my incredulous gaze to Gunner. "Seriously?"

"They are freaky, Scout," he shot back.

"I've got it." Evan was quick as he darted over and caught the Arachnid. The creature had realized all of its buddies were dead and was opting for escape. Evan ripped it apart without a single flinch, and when he turned back to us, he was grinning. "You really shouldn't have given me all this ammunition to use against you."

"Don't look at me." Gunner covered his face.

Me? I pressed my lips together, debated if I should soothe my boyfriend, and instead shifted to look at the first Arachnid Evan had killed. "What are they doing here?"

"Haunting my nightmares," Gunner replied, peeking out from between his fingers. When he caught me looking at him, he covered his eyes again. "Stop looking at me."

I left him to recover from his mental breakdown and poked the dead Arachnid. "I just mean that they're usually not found out in the snow. I wouldn't say they would never end up in Hawthorne Hollow —the summers get hot enough—but there's no conceivable way they would be here of their own volition in the middle of winter."

"They're barely down in Detroit," Evan agreed. "The winters are much milder down there." He kicked at the body of the last Arachnid that he'd dropped. "They didn't come to this place on a fluke."

"What does that mean?" Gunner finally lowered his hands from his face. "Did someone bring them here for a specific reason?"

"It makes more sense than all of our other options," Evan replied. "The thing is ... there's only one person I can think of who would potentially think it's a good idea to bring Arachnids here."

"Bonnie," I said on an exhale.

"Bonnie," Evan agreed. "Arachnids aren't powerful, though. At most, they're a nuisance."

"What if she didn't expect us to find them so fast?" I asked. "What if they're only pieces of a bigger army?"

"It seems weird that she would be building an army now." Evan cocked his head, then lifted his eyes to the cabins. "We have to make sure there are no more of them loitering in there."

"You guys do that," Gunner said. "I'll watch your backs."

I smirked but didn't say anything. I was fine if he wanted to stay behind. There was no reason to torture him when it wasn't necessary. Evan and I could easily take out a nest of Arachnids. Heck, we'd done it before Evan had been turned into a vampire.

"Maybe the Arachnids came from another plane too," Evan suggested after a few seconds. "Maybe the dwarves and Arachnids were both brought from the same plane, and they're supposed to be doing something specific."

"What, though?" That was the part I couldn't wrap my head around. "Arachnids can't be strategic. They take over an area, eat everything in sight, and then move on."

"So, we're back to them being a distraction," Evan mused. After a few seconds, he shook his head. "We can't just sit out here. We'll check for others, get rid of them, and then head back."

"What if there are more of them?" Gunner asked. "Like ... not here. What if she planned on keeping them in the cave but had to send them out to different places?"

"Then we'll figure out where they are soon enough," I replied. "For now, we just have to make sure this area is clear. There's nothing else we can do."

Gunner didn't look thrilled with the news, but he nodded. "I'll stay here. Just call if you need me."

I squeezed his hand. "I think we can manage."

"I'm not scared or anything. I'm just making sure they don't sneak up behind you and kill you."

"You're very wise. That's a solid plan."

Evan shot me a dubious look. I didn't respond, though. We all had our weak spots. Mine had made an appearance more than once in the past few weeks. I wasn't going to give Gunner grief about this.

No, we had other things to worry about. Plus, well, he was kind of cute. Dramatic, but cute all the same. How could I punish him for that?

10

TEN

I opened plane doors when it was time to make our escape. Gunner couldn't get away from the spider people fast enough. Evan, however, said we couldn't leave the bodies out for some random person to find—especially with a thaw right around the corner—so we burned them in the fire pit.

Gunner cringed the whole time.

Once the bodies were gone and the rest of the cabins secured—we didn't find more spider people, which was a relief to all of us—we headed back.

"You're getting good at opening the plane doors," Evan encouraged.

"You could've opened them on the way out," Gunner complained as he hopped behind the wheel of his truck.

"I thought you were in the best shape ever," Evan taunted.

"Don't you start," Gunner complained. "Not all of us have vampire strength to call on."

Evan's smirk told me he was having a good time. I opted not to chastise him. It was good for Gunner to get some pushback occasionally. It kept his ego in check.

The Rusty Cauldron was bustling with activity when we returned. There was no Baron in sight, though.

"Where is he?" I asked Rooster before he could question me about the job.

"He took off about an hour ago," Rooster replied. "He said he had places to be and then just poofed himself away."

"Lovely." I didn't like the idea of a loa running around Hawthorne Hollow with no supervision. If he paired up with Tillie again, they could wreak a lot of havoc. "Did he say anything after we left?"

"Just that things were starting to bubble up. I didn't take that as a good thing, but he seemed excited."

"That sounds about right," I muttered, shaking my head.

"What about you guys?" Rooster's gaze bounced between faces. "What did you find? I'm assuming it wasn't Bonnie."

"No Bonnie, but we did find some Arachnids," Evan replied.

"Arachnids?" Rooster's forehead creased. "Why are there Arachnids in this area?"

"I have no idea," Evan replied. "I can theorize, though."

Rooster didn't need him to theorize. "Bonnie. She's trying to build up some sort of army."

"Well, doesn't that make sense?" Whistler challenged. "Scout saw the prophecy. When the big fight comes, there will be a whole army working against us. Shifters. Ghouls. Vampires. Why wouldn't Bonnie increase her forces?"

"I don't want to put too much focus on that prophecy," I argued. "We'll make mistakes if we do that. Mama Moon told me that little things in prophecies change all the time. If we focus on too many little details, we might miss some big details ... and then we're going to be in trouble."

"Scout is right," Rooster said. "I think we need to ignore the prophecy entirely and strategize as if we don't know anything ... including the fact that she's going to bring in her friend Poet eventually. We can't count on that. What if something shifts and Poet can't make it to us in time?"

Given the fact that Poet could now teleport, that seemed unlikely. She would drop everything—unless she was in the middle of a battle of her own—to get to me. "Let's not worry about that," I said. "Let's worry about Bonnie. I very much doubt she's going back to the other lair because we know where it's located now."

"I can't see how she would think that was smart," Rooster agreed.

"So, she has to be setting up shop somewhere new." I thanked Whistler with a nod when he pushed an iced tea in front of me.

"How would you do it if it was you?" Evan asked.

"I would put my lair in a town outside Hawthorne Hollow. Close, but not too close."

Evan nodded. "Well, I can do some reconnaissance in Hemlock Cove. We can tell Stormy to be on the lookout in Shadow Hills. She's got Easton there and he can help."

I pressed my lips together and darted a curious look toward my best friend. He and Easton, the gnome shifter still trying to get a handle on his powers, had been spending a lot of time together lately. Stormy was convinced something romantic was going on between them. I couldn't help being curious. I also didn't want to overstep my bounds. Evan had gone through a trauma when I'd repaired his fractured soul. Despite his bravado, he was still recovering from it. If he was taking tentative steps in a relationship with Easton, I might cause him to end that relationship if I wasn't careful, and that was the last thing I wanted.

"Bonnie is going to go under, at least for a few days," I said. "Our problem is that we don't know who else she's drawing to her side. We've got dwarves and Arachnids that we know about. It could be a whole heckuva lot more of them, though."

"So, I'll send out feelers," Rooster said. "We won't waste time on small jobs right now. We'll respond to the big ones ... and go from there."

. . .

WE SPENT A FEW HOURS AT THE CAULDRON putting out potential fires. Gunner and I even headed out to a cabin because the neighbors were convinced there was weird activity happening there. Turned out, the new homeowners just liked getting freaky in front of the huge bay windows and the busybodies next door were judgmental monsters.

By the time the sun was starting to set, I was tired and all I wanted was to curl up to sleep in my own bed. Gunner stopped at our favorite gas station for chicken, fries, and potato salad, and we took our dinner into the bedroom after feeding Merlin.

"I can tell that you're thinking hard," Gunner said as I changed into a pair of comfortable flannel sleep pants and an oversized T-shirt before attacking the chicken. He'd gotten enough for four people, but we were gluttons when the opportunity arose. "Maybe it will help if you start talking about it with me."

I sent him a fond smile. "Are you worried I'm internalizing things too much?"

"Maybe a little," he conceded. "I just want to know what you're thinking. After last night ... well ... I have a lot of things on my mind too."

"Let's start with your things," I suggested as I tore into a chicken thigh. Gas station chicken in Hawthorne Hollow was a thing of beauty. I'd been suspicious the first time Gunner suggested it. Now it was my favorite.

"Well, okay, my first problem is that I panicked when that plane door closed out at the cabin and I had no way of finding you. I've been thinking that maybe we should put one of those air tags on you."

My eyebrows lifted. "Are you being serious right now?" I couldn't believe he was actually considering that. "That's not going to work on another plane."

"No, but you weren't on another plane. You were just in a

different part of Hawthorne Hollow. I could've found you if I knew where to look."

"Would an air tag even work underground?" I was honestly curious.

"I have no idea. I freaked out, though. How would I have found you if Bonnie managed to take you prisoner?"

"You would've called the Winchesters and let them cast a locator spell. Evan probably could've found me on scent eventually, too."

Gunner frowned. "I didn't even think of the Winchesters."

"That's because you were panicking." I patted his forearm with greasy fingers. "Just remember, that if things go sideways, the Winchesters are badasses."

"Yeah." He managed a smile. "Why do you think Baron took you to them?"

I'd been thinking about that too. "Honestly? I believe part of him just wanted to meet them. You saw how he was with Tillie. They are a unique pairing ... and they clearly had fun. He likely just knew they would be able to fix my issues."

"I guess." Gunner rolled his neck. "When we got the call from Winnie, I was relieved and angry."

"Why were you angry?"

He shrugged. "I just didn't like thinking of someone else swooping in and rescuing you. That feels like my job ... and if I'm busy, then it should be Evan's job."

It took everything I had to hold back a smile. "That is ... such a you thing to say. Don't feel too guilty, though. I would feel the same way."

He smirked. "We do have that alpha thing in common."

"We do."

"I am glad he took you to the Winchesters, though," Gunner said. "I trust them more than I trust just about anybody else."

"Even though your father might marry into the family?" I teased.

He shrugged. "I like Marnie. I think she's good for him. After my mother..." He trailed off before shaking himself out of his reverie.

"It's weird. I know it's weird to be that invested in my father's love life. I just don't know how to adapt. I'm just used to the way things are."

I chose my words carefully. "I think for a long time it was just you and your father, and the two of you had a very rough go of it. Even when you were fighting—which I think is how you two showed you still cared—you had a very specific relationship.

"I changed that relationship," I continued. "I made it easier for you in some respects and harder in others. Graham also changed because he realized that he was too crusty. You needed him to be a bit softer."

"I don't need him to be something he isn't," Gunner argued. "I just ... I don't know. We just have a weird relationship. I can't explain it."

"You don't have to explain it. Look at my relationship with my parents. It's weird too."

"It's getting better." His voice was soft. "You're starting to accept them. I think the best thing that they ever did was start to push you but not in a really stringent way. They're amping up their efforts, but they're not coming at you like a freight train. They recognize you would've shut them down immediately if they'd tried that."

I nodded. "Yeah. I would have. Do you know what my biggest problem is with them?"

"You want to hate them and you can't," he answered without hesitation.

"I *do* want to hate them. They kind of make it impossible, though. I see myself in them, which is weird, right? They didn't raise me. I shouldn't be like them."

"Do you think I want to be like my father? That stuff just happens."

"I know, but I really want to hate them, and I can't pull it off. Even Emma is making me like her more."

"She does seem happier without the magic, doesn't she?"

"It's like a burden has been lifted from her shoulders," I agreed. "She's lighter ... and freer ... and she smiles way too much."

Gunner snorted. "Maybe you and she can come up with a relationship that works for both of you eventually. In a weird way, she reminds me of Bonnie. Just the Bonnie we thought we used to know."

When he said it, a flip switched in my head. "Crap. That is who she reminds me of."

"You miss Bonnie," Gunner said. "I see it sometimes. She was your girly friend, and even though you're not girly, occasionally you still like to chat about things like moisturizer and shaving."

I shot him a dirty look. "That is a very sexist thing to say."

He smirked. "It's true."

"I have Poet for that," I reminded him.

"Yeah, but it's not the same as having someone who lives in the same town, someone you see every single day."

"Except now Poet and I can see each other every single day if we feel like it." I turned to him and reached for a fry. "Do you think it's weird we have similar abilities now?"

"Are they that similar? She can teleport and you open plane doors. To me, that doesn't feel like the same sort of magic. Yours feels a little bigger."

"The outcome is the same, though." The next part was hard for me to get out. "Rick and I were talking about routes earlier. Routes to get places. Seeing the loas with Cernunnos, I can't help but wonder if it was all part of some bigger plan by them."

Gunner opened the potato salad. "What was part of a bigger plan?"

"Me and Poet. What if we didn't end up in the same home for those few months by chance? What if they wanted us to meet?"

"Because they knew you were going to be important to each other?"

"Because they knew that they needed us to forge a bond if they were going to get the outcome they wanted."

"That's quite the conspiracy theory."

"And yet I can't help feeling that it's true."

He shoveled in some potato salad and methodically chewed and swallowed. "Maybe it is true," he said finally. "Does that change how you feel about Poet?"

"No. I held onto her memory for a reason. She was one of the few bright spots of my childhood."

He nodded in understanding. "Maybe you two found each other because you were always meant to find each other. You guys held on to a great amount of love for each other because it's real love. So, even if they wanted you to meet because they knew your friendship was going to be important, that doesn't make your friendship any less important."

I agreed with him, wholeheartedly. "My mind has been all over the place today," I admitted. "Bonnie is clearly trying to build up her army. What if, maybe, we stop focusing on her and start focusing on getting rid of her army?"

Intrigue lit in the depths of Gunner's eyes. "We could hamper her without actually going after her. I like that. It's not going to solve our problem in the long run, though."

"It's not, but it could make her second-guess herself, which will allow us to formulate our own plan."

"I do like that."

I beamed at him. "Right? I'm a genius."

"You're my little genius," he agreed. When his lips brushed against my cheek, he left grease behind. I didn't even care. "I think that's going to be my goal for tomorrow. If we take out her nests of helpers, then she's going to have to figure out a different plan."

"I don't want to see the spider people again." Gunner involuntarily shuddered. "I'll take on a whole army of zombies before I deal with the spider people a second time. They're just ... so wrong."

I laughed and turned to the wall, just as our resident ghost, Tim —Peeping Tim, because he had a penchant for watching women undress through windows—made an appearance. "What are you doing here?" I asked before attacking my chicken again. "You already missed the show. I'm in my pajamas and bedding down for the night."

"Believe it or not, I've seen you strip so many times I don't get the same thrill I used to," Tim replied dryly. "I mean ... you're fine. Unfortunately, when you get naked, he usually gets naked too." He jerked his ghostly thumb toward Gunner. "That dampens the effect."

"I'll have you know that I look my best when I'm naked," Gunner replied dryly.

Tim didn't look convinced. "Not everybody thinks bulging muscles are to die for. In fact, I've had more than a few women—this was when I was still alive mind you—tell me that a leaner man is preferable to ... whatever it is you are."

"They were lying to you," Gunner replied. He flexed his left arm so Tim could see his bicep pop. "Women much prefer this."

"Except the way you eat means all that muscle is going to turn to mush in five years," Tim argued. "Where will you be when that happens? Do you really think Scout is going to want to give you a slap and ride the wave to utopia every night?"

Gunner blinked twice, then looked at me. "You don't think I'm going to get fat, do you?"

I thought about the heavy breathing that had accompanied the hike out to the cabins and lied. "Of course not."

His lips curved down. "You *do* think I'm going to get fat."

"I think I love you and not your body," I replied. "If you want to hear the truth, though, you're a freaking glutton. You're going to have to up your workouts now that you're in your thirties if you expect to keep that body and still eat as much as you do. I don't make the rules of aging, but that's a pretty basic one."

Gunner's mouth fell open. "That is probably the worst thing you've ever said to me."

I shrugged. "It is what it is, my friend. Bay is trying to rein in Landon's eating, too. He's not taking it well either."

"This is just crap."

I left Gunner to stew and focused on Tim. It was rare for him to actually wander into our bedroom. He preferred watching from afar. If he had something to say to us, he caught us in the yard. If he was here, there had to be a reason. "What's up?"

"There's been a lot of activity in the woods," he replied. He was busy glaring at Gunner, so he wasn't all that engaged in the conversation. "I just thought you should know."

"What sort of activity?"

"Not spider people, right?" Gunner demanded. "I don't want spider people hanging around our house."

"I don't know who it is. I just know I've sensed various paranormals in the area," Tim replied. "I've been out and about a lot lately. I'm not often here."

I chewed as I thought about it. "Have they managed to cross the wards?" I asked finally.

"No, they have not. That doesn't mean they won't find a way across eventually."

"Yeah." I nodded. "Thanks for the heads-up. I'll take a look around beyond the wards in the morning, when it's light out."

"If you want, I can drop in more frequently too," Tim offered. "You know ... just to make sure you're safe. I might be bored with seeing you naked, but that doesn't mean I want anything bad to happen to you."

"That's possibly very flattering," I said. "If you can drop in more frequently, that would be great. I wouldn't mind knowing who is lurking in the trees. If you can't manage it, though, I'll figure out something myself."

"I aim to please." Tim winked at me. "And I rarely miss."

He was so creepy at times that he gave me the shivers. He was also helpful, so I didn't tell him what I was really thinking. "Well, keep it up. Things are tense around here right now. I don't look for things to get better for quite some time."

He saluted. "I'm on it." With that, he was gone.

"I'm not going to get fat," Gunner said when I turned my attention back to him. "I'm just going to up my workouts."

"Okay." I patted his shoulder. "I'll love you no matter what, though. Extra love handles make for easy gripping. I'm good with that."

If looks could kill, I would be dead. "I don't do love handles."

"Good to know."

"Just eat your chicken," he barked. "Maybe we should build a gym out here or something."

"Whatever makes you happy, baby. I'm here for all of it."

11
ELEVEN

I slept hard, which I probably needed to shake off the final dregs of the cave collapse, but I didn't wake up to Gunner's snores. No, he was talking. Sure, it was in a low voice, but he was having a conversation with somebody, and when I rolled to focus on him, I realized he had the tablet on his lap, and he was having a video conversation.

"What in the hell?" I complained as I stretched. "Are you and your dad going to start video calling now that he's spending nights at The Overlook?"

Gunner, shirtless and with his morning stubble on full display—he could almost grow an entire beard overnight thanks to his shifter genes—sent me a dark look. "I'm not video chatting with my father. Can you even imagine that?"

"Then who are you talking to?" Something dark and insidious infiltrated my still sleepy mind. "Are you talking to another woman?"

"I am," Gunner confirmed. "It's one you would approve of, though."

Confused, I shifted so I could look at the tablet screen. There I found Poet and Kade—also in bed—staring back at me. "What's going on?" I asked, suddenly suspicious.

"We were having a threesome behind your back," Poet replied without any hesitation. "It was Gunner's idea."

Gunner made a loud protesting sound. "They're lying."

I absently patted his chest. "There, there. Don't freak out for no reason. They're messing with you." I turned to the people on the tablet screen. "You should be nice to him. He just found out last night that he can't keep eating five thousand calories a day if he wants to maintain his eight pack, and he's mad at the world."

"Ah." Poet nodded in understanding. "That had to be crushing."

"Just work out more," Kade suggested. "That's what I do."

"Thank you, Mr. Universe," Gunner drawled. "I don't want to talk about this."

Something occurred to me. "Aren't you guys in California?"

"We are," Poet confirmed. "Why?"

"What time is it there?"

"It's six o'clock," Poet replied. "We're up too early. We haven't adjusted to the time change yet."

I did the math in my head. "That makes it nine o'clock here."

"It does," Gunner confirmed.

"You let me sleep until nine o'clock?" I pinned him with a dirty look. "What's wrong with you? I had plans for world domination today."

He sent me a "step back" look. "You were down and out. There was no way I was going to wake you up. That's why I took Poet's call. You needed your sleep."

"Yeah, but I slept for like ten hours."

"You needed it." Gunner dragged his finger down my cheek. "Your bruises are basically gone now."

That was good news. Still... "I don't want to sleep ten hours. That makes me feel like a slug."

"Do you feel better than you did?" Gunner challenged.

"I'm not answering that."

"Because you feel better."

"No, because it's a trap, and I'm not walking into it." I rested my head on his shoulder and focused on the tablet camera. "How are you guys?"

"Pretty good," Poet replied. "It's San Diego. We have stuff going on here because we always have stuff going on. Nothing major, though."

I thought about digging into the nitty-gritty of it, but I didn't. If she had something she needed my help on, then she would ask me for help.

"How is Baron?" she asked instead.

"I don't know. We went out on a job yesterday. When we came back, he was gone."

"Do you think he's up to something?"

I shrugged. "I think they're all up to something. I'm just not sure that they're up to no good."

"Scout thinks they had a hand in the two of you crossing paths when you were kids," Gunner volunteered.

"I've thought that myself a few times," Poet admitted.

I stuck my tongue out at Gunner. "See. I wasn't being a conspiracy theorist."

"I'm not saying it's for sure true," Poet cautioned. "I just don't know that I believe we magically found ourselves in the same home when we were teenagers. I mean ... there were hundreds of homes for kids our age in that general area. How did we get put under the same roof?"

"And right before both of us took off on our own adventures," I added. "It's as if someone knew we were both going to leave the system of our own volition."

"Well, I think kids in our position take off on their own all the time," Poet countered. "I know for me, being on the street was ten times more stable than being in a home."

"Yeah." I played with Gunner's bellybutton, causing him to squirm as he struggled to suck it in. "It's something to think about."

"Oh, I always think about things like that," she agreed. "It doesn't change anything, though. I think we were always meant to cross paths. If they arranged it so we crossed paths before we originally would have, I can't hate them for it."

"No, but I don't totally trust them."

"I don't either," Poet agreed. "The thing is, I've been with them when they could've done real evil. That's not the route they chose. I have to believe that they've got the greater good in their sights. Now, does that mean they're perfect? Absolutely not. I don't think they want to hurt people just to hurt them, though."

I was right there with her. "I don't know where he's at. I think he could just be wandering around or something."

"He does tend to wander," Poet agreed. "The thing with Baron is, even when you don't believe he has his eye on the prize, he proves you wrong. He was helpful in Phoenix. I think he's going to be helpful there. That doesn't mean he won't stir up trouble—especially if he's allied himself with Tillie Winchester—during the interim."

"He does really seem to like Tillie," I agreed.

"You really like Tillie," Gunner pointed out.

"Well, she's funny. As long as I'm the one who doesn't have to pick up her mess. I can't help but feel, if she gets Baron cranked up, that I'll be the one who has to clean up her mess this time."

"I don't think you can stop whatever they're going to do," Poet said. "Hopefully it's just mindless stuff."

That was definitely the hope.

"What about Bonnie?" Poet asked. "Have you seen her since the cave collapsed?"

"No. We did run into some Arachnids yesterday." I told her about the run-in with the spider people. All the while, Kade made faces on the other end of the call, and Gunner emitted ridiculous gasping noises next to me. "Gunner says he refuses to even look at the spider people again," I volunteered as I was finishing up.

"Do you blame him?" Kade challenges. "That's disgusting. And I thought the snakes were bad."

"Kade is terrified of snakes," Poet explained.

Kade shot her a withering look. "Some fear is smart. Snakes are dangerous."

"I've got it, babe." She patted his arm, making me grin. When she turned back to me, she was serious. "What are you going to do? Bonnie is obviously amassing an army."

"She is," I agreed. "I think, rather than search for Bonnie and try to get ahead of her, I'm going to focus on destroying her army instead."

"How are you going to do that?" Kade asked.

"Well, she's obviously not amassing them in the same place. I think she's doing that because she believes she's flying under the radar. I'm going to try to find her clumps of smaller soldiers and kill them."

"That sounds like a good move." Poet bobbed her head in agreement. "At the very least, that will keep her busy. She'll stop bringing soldiers in because she'll be focused on trying to protect the ones she already has."

"That is the goal."

"Well, it's a solid plan." Poet flicked her eyes to Gunner. "Just keep the spiders away from him. The whining gets to be a bit much if you let things snowball."

"I heard that," Kade complained. "Snakes can be deadly. It's a legitimate fear."

Poet shot him a loved-up look. "I get it. I was just teasing you."

"I don't think you understand how deadly snakes can be," Kade argued. "I've done some research. I can show it to you."

Poet's sigh was long and drawn out. "I should probably go."

"Yes, you have to charm the snake," I agreed. "I'm hungry anyway." I glanced at Gunner. "What's for breakfast?"

"Dad is bringing it," Gunner replied. "He texted a few minutes before you woke up. He says he has something to talk to us about."

"That doesn't sound good. You don't think he knocked up Marnie, do you?"

Gunner glared at me. "Say goodbye to your friend."

I waved at Poet. "I'll keep in touch. If I get any information on Baron, I'll send it your way."

"I'll do the same," Poet said. "Even though he seems fixated on you, something tells me he'll be dropping in here, too."

That made sense. "They have investments in both of us. They're not going to waste them."

"No, they definitely are not."

GRAHAM SHOVED THE BOX OF BREAKFAST containers into Gunner's hands the second he crossed the threshold and headed straight for the cat.

"How is Grandpa's little man?" He lay down on the floor with Merlin, who was washing his face next to his empty food bowl.

We'd showered quickly after disconnecting the call with Poet. I hadn't bothered drying my hair. The air was parched because of the winter weather, and I knew it would air dry before we had to leave. I didn't much care what it looked like.

"What did you bring?" I asked as I sniffed the containers in the box.

"What do I always bring?" Graham kissed the top of Merlin's head—something the cat did not allow Gunner or I to do—and stood. "You'll be happy." He lightly grabbed my chin. "Your face looks ten times better, kid."

"See, if I were a lesser person I would point out that was a rude thing to say."

"Good thing you're not a lesser person." Graham planted a surprising kiss on my forehead to match the one he'd given the cat and then took the box. "Let's eat."

My stomach growled with enthusiasm. "Yeah. I could eat."

For the next few minutes, the only sounds consisted of coffee sips and opening food containers. Once we'd all had a few bites, the conversation sparked up.

"Your loa was over in Hemlock Cove last night," Graham volunteered.

I stilled with my fork halfway to my mouth. The news wasn't surprising. It was, however, annoying. "He should be focused on Bonnie."

"He's made it pretty clear that he's not going to take out Bonnie," Gunner countered. "He wants us to do it."

"I don't think he can take out Bonnie," I clarified. "The same rules apply to him as they do to me. If I kill Bonnie, I get her powers. The problem is, I can't absorb her powers on top of the powers I already have. That makes it a death sentence."

"What about someone else?" Graham asked. "Like ... me. If I were with you, could I take her powers?"

I shook my head. "No, because you're not a lamia. She wasn't even a strong enough lamia to actually absorb the powers. They were killing her until she stole Emma's powers and managed to balance herself out.

"When I saw her, there were splits in her skin," I continued. "That tells me that the power was stretching her to the point of no return. You wouldn't even be able to make it the few weeks she did. I think you would die instantly."

"Well, then scratch that." Graham made a face. "I'm too young and pretty to die."

Gunner gave his father a sidelong look. "You've let yourself go and still snagged a woman," he said out of the blue. "Are you unhappy about your current waistband size?"

Surprise had Graham blinking. Then anger had him scowling. "I let myself go?"

"You're rounder than you were when I was a kid," Gunner persisted, clearly not reading the room. Or perhaps it was that he didn't care. "You managed to snag Marnie anyway. Do you think you would be happier if you were still ripped, or do you prefer being mushy around the middle?"

Graham's eyes flashed with fury. "I am not mushy around the middle!"

"Well, you're way mushier than when I was a kid," Gunner argued. "Come on. Just tell me."

Rather than respond, Graham lifted his hand so he wouldn't have to look at his own offspring. "I can't stand him sometimes," he said to me.

"Sorry." I didn't mean it. In truth, I adored watching Graham and Gunner go after one another. It was their love language as father and son, although neither of them would admit it. "I think he's kind of cute. Plus, well, this is my fault."

"And what did you do to cause this?" Graham demanded.

"I might have agreed with Peeping Tim when he told Gunner that his muscle was going to turn to fat in a few years if he didn't start working out more or eating less."

"Well, that's true." Graham lowered his hand and flicked his gaze to his son. "I'm just as ripped as I was when I was thirty."

Gunner and I snorted in tandem.

"I am," Graham insisted. "I don't like that you're pretending otherwise. I am a lean, mean, law enforcement machine."

I bit into my bacon. "Do you tell that to Marnie when you're about to do the deed?" I asked after I'd swallowed. "I only ask because your son tells me he's a lean, mean, witch loving machine, and it's obvious he got all of his moves from you."

"I did not," Gunner fired back.

I cocked an eyebrow.

"I didn't," he insisted. "I am a self-made man."

"Yeah." I flicked my eyes back to Graham, suddenly curious. "Do you watch yourself in reflective surfaces when doing it?"

Graham looked confused. "When doing what?"

"You know."

"I..." He realized what I was getting at and glared. "That is not funny, young lady."

"It wasn't meant to be funny. Gunner likes to catch his reflection in the windows at night. I'm wondering if you do the same thing."

"Of course not." Graham's response was a little too quick. Even Gunner picked up on the fact that he was lying.

"Crap," Gunner muttered. "I really have turned into my dad."

"We're done with this conversation," Graham said. He was firm. "We're just ... done with it." He shook his head. "I have something else to talk to you guys about."

"You can't have the cat," I replied without missing a beat. "I know he likes you better than us, but he's still mine."

"I'm not taking the cat ... at least not yet." Graham managed a smile. "There was a fire last night, though. It was out on Rasputin Road."

I lifted my chin. "There's a Rasputin Road? Why have I never heard of this?"

"Because it was renamed Folgers Road before you came to town," Gunner replied. "Everybody thought Rasputin Road was a terrible name, especially because a lot of bad things have happened on it."

"That's not because of the name of the road," I argued.

"Definitely not," Graham agreed. "Everybody local still calls it Rasputin Road. That's not the point, though."

"What is the point?" Gunner asked. He leaned closer to me to whisper the next part. "I don't tell a story like him. I'm much faster and better when it comes to that. At least give me that."

I could only shake my head and wait for Graham to get done glaring at his only son.

"Anyway," Graham said after an extended beat. "There was a fire out there in the overnight hours. It was a weird fire, though. I thought you two could head out with me after breakfast and check it out."

It was rare for Graham to need help with his job. I'd volunteered my help a few times, of course, but he rarely took me up on the offers. If he was asking, there was something wrong. "What is it about this fire that has you so concerned?"

"It started in the middle of the night, in the middle of nowhere, and went out without any outside intervention," Graham replied. "It was a big fire. The house was fully engulfed on the second floor."

"But?" I prodded.

"But the first floor is largely okay."

There was more. I could tell. I just waited.

"The house is owned by Tiffany and Brandy Beechwood," he continued.

Gunner jerked up his chin. "What now?"

"Who are Tiffany and Brandy Beechwood?" I asked.

"Witches," Graham replied.

"New age witches," Gunner corrected. "They're not magical as much as mystical."

That was a distinction I wasn't certain I understood.

"I'll show you when we get there," Graham said. "Right now, the fire is out, even though we didn't stop it and it didn't rain last night. The sisters are gone, too."

Well, that didn't sound good. "Are you thinking Bonnie did this?"

"Not everything paranormal in this town can be blamed on Bonnie. It's not normal, though."

That was all he needed to say. "We'll go with you. It can't hurt to check things out."

"Thank you." Graham returned his focus to his food. "Now, as for the reflective surface thing, he totally came up with that on his own."

I didn't believe him. I smiled anyway. If Gunner grew up to be just like Graham, I would consider myself a lucky woman. Sure, neither of them wanted to admit how similar they were. It was all right there for anybody who wanted to take a good look, though.

There were no ifs, ands, buts, or lean machines about it.

12

TWELVE

Being in a vehicle with Gunner and his father was an exercise in patience. They fought like Gunner was still twelve and making his armpit fart.

"What did I say about rummaging through my glove box?" Graham demanded. I'd wisely sat in the backseat because I was used to their shenanigans. "Nothing I have in there is your business."

"See, the fact that you don't want me to go through your glove box suggests there's something in here worth finding." Gunner came back with a heart-shaped box of candy. "Is this for me?"

"No. Put that back!" Graham's face flushed with fury.

Despite myself, even I was invested in this fight now. "Is that for Marnie?" I asked.

"I like candy," Graham growled. "Who doesn't love candy?"

"Everybody loves candy," Gunner readily agreed. "This candy is in a box that's shaped like a heart, though." He flipped it over to get a gander at the price tag. "Wow. You didn't go cheap either." He didn't put the candy back in the glove box and instead clutched it tighter. "Why are you buying Marnie candy? You're not ... like ... going to propose to her, are you?"

The look Graham shot his son was withering. "Why would I propose with candy?"

"Candy is romantic," Gunner replied, unruffled by the little growls coming from his father. "I know I would say yes if somebody proposed to me with candy."

Was that supposed to be pointed at me? There was no way I was responding to that.

"Why do you care what I do?" Graham hissed.

"I'm just curious." Gunner shoved the candy back in the glove box. "You and Marnie have been spending a lot of time together lately."

"We just started dating."

"I know." Gunner sounded defensive. "It's just ... you were at the inn."

"So were you."

"The circumstances were not the same."

"I thought you liked Marnie," Graham challenged, changing tactics.

"I *do* like Marnie. I just ... am figuring things out."

Graham let loose a heavy sigh. "I like Marnie. We're nowhere near getting married. I bought her the candy and then decided it was hokey and took her out to dinner instead."

"Does that mean I can eat the candy?"

"No!"

"You're such a tyrant," Gunner complained.

From my spot in the backseat, I studied Graham's profile. He looked to be as uncomfortable with the conversation as his son. That told me Graham wasn't taking marriage off the table. He just wasn't ready for it to be a reality yet.

Interesting.

"Is this about your mother?" Graham asked after a few seconds of uncomfortable silence. "Because, if it is, I said goodbye to my feelings for your mother a long time ago."

"It's not about Mom," Gunner said. "I don't expect you to remain loyal to the memory of a dead woman who tried to kill us all."

"Then what is it?"

Gunner didn't answer. I wasn't surprised at the firm set of his jaw. I also wasn't going to let this conversation fester.

"He's afraid that the breakfasts we have at the cabin are going to dry up," I volunteered.

"Scout!" Gunner barked my name with a soupcon of angst.

"He likes our little family meals," I continued. "He wants to make sure they don't go away."

"Why would they go away?" Graham demanded.

"Well, if you move into The Overlook..." I trailed off and held out my hands.

"Why would I move into The Overlook?" The mere thought looked to be freaking Graham out. "I live in Hawthorne Hollow."

"And Marnie lives in Hemlock Cove." I eyed him closely. "Have you really not considered the logistics? I can't see her moving away from the inn. Their power base is tied to the land. Plus, well, there's Tillie. Winnie is not going to like it if she's the only one babysitting Tillie."

"I guess I didn't get that far," Graham admitted. "I don't ... I mean ... I don't think I can live with that many people." Suddenly, he looked panicked. It was enough to make me feel bad for him.

"I don't think you have to worry about it this early in the relationship," I assured him. "Plus, in a few years, Landon and Bay will be living in their new house. That will leave the guesthouse open. Maybe you and Marnie can move in there."

Graham perked up. "I've only seen the guesthouse from outside. It looks nice, though."

"What about me?" Gunner complained. "What about our breakfasts?"

Graham shot his only son an annoyed look. "What exactly is stopping me from bringing breakfast when I arrive in town? I'm still going to be working in Hawthorne Hollow. You guys can come out to the inn on weekends, too. We'll have our breakfasts."

"It won't be the same," Gunner muttered under his breath. His disgruntlement was a thing of beauty ... for a twelve-year-old. Still, I had to give him credit for sticking to his guns on this one. He wasn't letting it go. It was something I would do. That meant I was rubbing off on him.

"This is not something we need to be planning for right now," Graham said as he turned onto a street. Right away, my interest was piqued by the flashing lights a few doors down. I could make out a house through the haze, and it had clearly seen better days. "I promise I'm not going to rush into anything."

He looked so perplexed, I had to take the edge off the conversation with an ill-timed joke. "Daddy won't forget you when he gets his new family," I promised Gunner.

"Knock it off," Gunner snapped.

"Yes, knock it off." Graham shot me a dirty look. "You're not helping."

"I didn't know I was supposed to be helping." Rather than continue the conversation, I unfastened my seatbelt and hopped out. The first thing that hit my nose was the scent of sulfur. It was positively oozing out of the damaged house. "Well, that can't be normal." I looked to Graham for confirmation.

"The smell?" Graham shook his head. "It's not. There's more, though." He motioned for us to follow him.

As we passed several firefighters, who appeared to be resting ... or maybe waiting for something, Graham nodded in greeting. He didn't explain our presence or anything. He just took us around back.

"So, the wires are fine." He pointed toward the wire that connected to the back of the house. "That is not what started the fire. We have a fire inspector coming from the county, but the fire only touched the top floor. It didn't go down. The only damage on the main floor came from smoke."

"No water?" I asked as I scanned the back of the house for clues.

"The fire was out before we got here. They didn't even have to throw water at the problem just in case. Everything was already over with."

"I've never heard of a fire stopping when it still had fuel."

"That's why I want you to take a look."

I nodded, allowing my eyes to flick to the pots on the back patio. It was winter, so the flowers inside were dead. I recognized some of the plants, though. It wasn't pansies or tomatoes. No, it was something else.

"You say the women who live here are witches?" I asked as I snapped one of the dead stalks and lifted it.

"They're new age witches," Gunner countered. "Like ... they do tarot readings at festivals. I think they make their own wine. That's as close as they get to the Winchesters, though."

"Okay, but do you know what this is?" I held up the plant.

"A weed?"

I shook my head. "Agrimony. It's for shielding and hex breaking. You use it in a lot of reversal spells."

Gunner's forehead creased. "Okay."

"That over there." I pointed toward a different pot. "It's blackthorn. It's mostly used in wards and exorcisms."

"So, there are real witch herbs here," Graham said.

I nodded. "Are you sure they're not real witches?"

Graham's hesitation was enough to tell me all I needed to know. "I'm not. They keep to themselves. This fire is weird. Given everything else we have going on, I think it's best we try to figure out what actually happened here."

"Yeah." I moved toward the door. It was open to allow the smoky smell to waft away. "Is it safe?" I asked.

"It is," Graham confirmed. "Most of the time, when a house is deemed unsafe after a fire, it's because of water damage. That is not a problem here."

"Right." I touched my tongue to my top lip, then headed inside. "Let's see what we've got."

I didn't look over my shoulder to see if Gunner and Graham were following. I knew they were. The first room was the kitchen, and it looked like most normal kitchens, except for the fact that there were at least thirty cookie jars on the counters and shelves.

"What in the world?" I cocked my head as I looked at the nearest one. "Is that what I think it is?"

"Erotic cookie jars," Graham confirmed. "Apparently Brandy made them. She has a potting wheel in the back barn and in the summers she sells her art."

I couldn't stop staring at the cookie jar. "It's very ... stimulating."

Gunner moved closer to me. "You like that? I can make it happen in the real world now that you don't look hurt any longer."

"You can't do that." I shook my head.

"What do you mean I can't do that?" Gunner was outraged. "I was born to do that."

"You're not that bendy."

"I'm totally bendy."

"Can you two pretend you're adults and not have this conversation in front of me?" Graham growled. "Also, you're not that bendy, son. Nobody is that bendy."

"I could totally be that bendy," Gunner muttered under his breath.

I took the time to look at a few of the other cookie jars and found one odd detail that I couldn't just shake off. "What is with the birds?"

"How can you focus on the birds where there are little penises as far as the eye can see?" Gunner challenged.

"Because each and every one of these scenes has birds in it." I was creeped out. "You don't find that weird?"

"We have a Peeping Tim ghost who watches us do it on the regular," Gunner replied. "The birds are not abnormal compared to that."

"I guess." I moved to the stove and touched the empty pan on the burner. There were no ingredients out on the counter, but there was a cookbook opened to a page for a shrimp pasta. "It seems they were in the middle of something," I mused.

Graham nodded. "Yes. I can't figure out where they are, though. Why would they run once the fire was out?"

"You're sure they're not upstairs?" I asked.

"Pretty sure. There are no bodies as far as I can tell ... and I would be able to smell them."

"Right. You have shifter genes." I cracked my neck. "What about vehicles?"

"They have one pickup truck they share. It's in the front of the house."

"Horses? I mean ... this is a big parcel of land."

"No horses. They could have snowmobiles I guess. I can send someone out to the barn to check."

"We should probably do that," I agreed. I rested my hand on the cookbook, hoping to get a flash, or some sort of idea what had happened. There was nothing, though. "What are your people saying about the fire?"

"That it burned hot and then burned itself right out."

"Yes, but do they have a ballpark on the time?"

"Oh, they think around midnight. The neighbors called it in about twenty minutes after midnight."

"How close is the nearest neighbor?"

"Half a mile. They were driving past when they saw the fire. They stopped, called us, but there were no signs of life in the house. They didn't go in."

"You can't really blame them for that," Gunner hedged. "If nobody was inside, would you risk running into a burning building?"

"I don't know," Graham replied. "I would probably check. I don't blame them for staying outside. It would've been a wasted effort."

"But if the truck is here, and they don't have snowmobiles, where did they go?" I pressed.

"I don't have an answer for you, Scout." Graham looked frustrated. "I've told you everything I know."

"And I'm not giving you a hard time," I assured him. "I'm merely curious. I don't understand this scene. It's just ... there's something off." I left them in the kitchen to keep perusing the pornographic cookie jars and walked into the living room. There I found their coffee table had been turned into an altar of sorts, complete with obsidian runes and a deck of well-loved tarot cards. I picked up the runes, expecting to find designations for the four elements, but instead I found a strange drawing.

"What's that?" Gunner asked as he moved up behind me. "That's not the sign for earth, air, fire, or water."

"It's not," I agreed. The design wasn't fancy. It featured several squiggly lines, as well as four circles that appeared to have crosses, and even symbols that looked suspiciously like pineapples to me. "I've seen this before," I said more to myself than them. "Not exactly like this, though." Without thinking, I put the runes in my pocket. When I turned, I found Graham watching me with an upturned eyebrow.

"I'm not stealing them," I assured him. "I'm just holding onto them until I remember. If the sisters come back, I'll return them."

"But you don't think they're coming back," Graham surmised.

"I didn't say that." I vehemently shook my head. "I don't actually believe that. It's just ... this feels off."

"Was it the pornographic cookie jars that sent your antenna twitching or the altar?"

"The altar isn't all that surprising," I said on a laugh. "If they're new age-y like you say, then this would be the sort of altar they would build. The runes are weird. I want to figure out what the design is. The altar doesn't get me going, though."

"If it's the cookie jars, we can go home and I'll show you just how bendy I really am," Gunner offered.

"You're sweet." I patted his arm. "You're never going to be that bendy, though. And, as weird as the cookie jars are, I think they're a cover."

"For what?" Graham asked, his eyebrows moving toward one another. "What are they trying to cover for?"

"I think maybe they're the real deal."

"But … they get dressed up and read tarot cards at festivals," Graham argued. "I don't know anybody real who does that."

"Maybe that's their cover." I moved to one of the bookshelves. "See, these are all superficial books. It's the sort of thing you can get at any bookstore these days. These, though, are different." I pointed toward a weathered set of books on top of the fireplace. "They're real magic books."

"Maybe they think all the books are the same," Gunner said. "They could've lucked into real ones."

"Maybe, but that doesn't feel right." I stopped in front of another shelf. It was scattered with gazing globes, small cauldrons, more candles than I could count, and even an herb chest. It was the spot right in front of the herb chest that caught my eye, though. "What do we think was here?" I asked, pointing.

Graham moved closer. He seemed confused when he saw the spot I was referring to. The shelf was in bad need of a good dusting and there was a round clear spot right in the middle of it. "Something is missing."

"Yeah." I glanced around the room again. "I can't help thinking it was removed recently, too."

"What makes you say that?"

"Because the smoke created soot and dust," I replied. "There's nothing in the circle."

"Suggesting that whoever took the item from the shelf did it after the fire," Graham realized.

"Or close to the end," I agreed. "My question is, were they here when it started? Actually, I have more than one question. If they weren't here, where are they now? Were they taken? Did they flee because they recognized they had an enemy?"

"That's a lot of questions," Graham agreed. "Where do you think we're going to find the answers?"

"We need to talk to the neighbors." I was grim as I looked up and down the street. "We need to figure out if Brandy and Tiffany were the real deal. We also need to know if they had any visitors recently."

Realization registered on Graham's face. "You're wondering if this has something to do with Bonnie."

"Do you blame me? These two feel as if they could be real witches. Bonnie is trying to build an army. These two might make good recruits."

"But?" Graham prodded. "There's something you're not saying."

"But ... this seems like a really weird way to recruit fighters. What if Brandy and Tiffany told her no and took off? They could be in trouble."

"And, what, either they or Bonnie removed the item from the shelf because it's somehow important?"

"Can you think of a better theory?"

"Sadly, I cannot." Graham was rueful. "We'll talk to the neighbors. You should know that a few of them are odd too."

"Odder than the cookie jars?" I had my doubts.

"Let's just say that the paranormals like this road. If Tiffany and Brandy were real, then they fit in with at least half of the other neighbors. Nobody is going to be happy seeing us coming up their walk."

"They'll survive." I was ready to get to it. "Let's hit the neighbors."

"Okay." Graham dragged a hand through his hair. "Don't say I didn't warn you, though. Even the humans are oddballs."

13
THIRTEEN

One thing I'd learned about neighbors in Hawthorne Hollow was that they were all up in each other's business. Even though the Beechwood sisters didn't have neighbors who could regularly look out their windows and spy, that didn't mean the people who lived on their street didn't know what they were up to.

"They're sex fiends," Althea Johnson announced when Graham told her why we were knocking on her door so early in the morning.

"With each other?" Gunner asked, caught between intrigue and disgust.

Graham and I accidentally slapped hands when we both went in to cuff him at the same time. Graham sent me a small, encouraging smile, before turning his attention back to Althea. "Why is it that you think they're sex fiends? I've never known them to do ... stuff like that."

"Only a sex fiend would say something like that," Althea complained. "How do you know they're not sex fiends if you're not one yourself?"

"Let's just call it a hunch," Graham said.

Althea's eye roll was a thing of beauty. "Yeah, they're sex fiends. They have visitors all the time."

"What sort of visitors?" I asked.

When Althea looked at me, her distaste was obvious. "People like you. They would show up at the front door, go inside for no more than ten minutes, and then they would leave. We all know what they were doing."

Actually, I had questions. "Um ... what is it that you think they were doing?"

"Sex," Althea hissed.

"So, you think that strange people—I'm guessing we're talking men and women here—would show up at the house, go inside, and then leave ten minutes later and you believe they were having sex for money in that time period?"

"What else could it be?"

"Just off the top of my head, I'm thinking they were selling the cookie jars."

Graham nodded. "That makes sense. Did you ever see the visitors leave with packages, Althea?"

"Sometimes," Althea replied. "I just assumed that those harlots were giving them sex stuff in a bag."

Gunner shifted. "What sort of sex stuff would one give in a bag?"

"How should I know?" Althea barked at him. "I obviously don't get sex stuff in a bag. That would be more your speed."

"Oh, I would totally love to get sex stuff in a bag," Gunner agreed. "I just can't imagine what that would look like."

"Perhaps you should go to one of those shops with the lingerie in the window and the neon up front that's meant to distract you, to look around," Graham suggested tightly.

"How do you know what's in those shops?" Gunner shot back. "Is Althea right? Are you a sex fiend, Dad?" Gunner was calm when turning back to the older woman. "I tried to be a good boy growing up but there was abject filth surrounding me. Why did this happen? Why?" He shook his fist at the sky.

"That was the worst bit of acting I've ever seen," I complained. "It was almost painful to watch."

"I thought he was sincere," Althea countered. "The boy wants to live a good, clean life. He should have that option. His daddy never gave it to him."

Graham murdered Gunner with a glare but managed to hold it together. Mostly. "We're just trying to figure out what happened to the Beechwood sisters. Their house was damaged in a fire, but we can't find any sign of them."

"Do you think they were kidnapped?" Althea bobbed her head. "That's why you're here, isn't it? You think someone broke into their house—or they let them in because of all the sex—and then that someone kidnapped them." Her eyes moved to me, catching me off guard with their intensity. "I saw a *Dateline* on human trafficking and that's what this is."

"Hold up." Graham raised a hand. He looked legitimately worked up. "Don't spread that rumor around town because we have no idea if it's true."

"Of course it's true." Althea shot him a deadpan look. "What else could it be?"

"I think it's likely a magical snake woman who is looking to bolster her paranormal army for a war," I replied without thinking. "That's just me, though."

Althea's eyes went wide. "What?"

"Yeah, what?" Graham pinned me so hard with his glare I was surprised I could breathe.

"She's crazy, Graham," Althea complained. "How can you allow a crazy woman to hang around with your son?"

"It's something I'm going to have to deal with," Graham replied firmly. The look he lobbed at me promised retribution. "She's been a problem for months now."

"You could do better," Althea said to Gunner.

"Oh, it's cute that you think that," Gunner said. "I couldn't do better, though."

"Definitely not," Graham agreed. "That's why the situation is so difficult. That's not why we're here, though. Gunner's issues will have to be dealt with at a later date. We're here about Tiffany and Brandy. You must know something that can help us."

"I don't." Althea held out her hands. "I didn't know them very well. They kept to themselves."

"Except for all the sex fiends that visited them, right?"

"Well, that goes without saying," Althea groused. "I mean ... come on."

I waited until we were outside to voice my opinion. "Althea needs to watch less *Dateline* and get out more. Isn't there a senior center downtown?"

"Yes, but nobody likes her," Graham replied. "She's been there before, but she ticks everybody off with the judgmental crap."

I could see that. "She shouldn't be out here alone. She's going to go even more crazy."

"I'll put some thought into it," Graham promised. "What were you thinking with the paranormal talk?"

"It's not as if she's going to believe me," I countered. "She was predisposed to think I was a kook."

"That's true," Gunner said. "She disliked Scout on sight."

"She's lost in her own little world where everything is black and white," I said. "She can't help us. There has to be somebody else."

Graham thought about it for just a second. "There's Bubba Watkins."

I managed to keep a straight face, but just barely. "Bubba?"

"That's a nickname. His real name is Brad."

"And he chose to go by Bubba?" I just couldn't get over that. "Wow."

Graham extended a warning finger. "I know he helped the sisters when they wanted to do some home repairs. That means he was inside the house."

"And where does he live?" I asked.

Graham pointed toward the hill, to where an aged house looked down on us.

"Well, he would have the angle to see things," I mused. "Is Bubba going to be happy to see us?"

"Not even a little."

"I didn't figure. Let's do it anyway."

"Yeah. This time, you let me do the talking," Graham stressed.

"I let you do the talking last time."

"No, you and Gunner ran your mouths like you always do."

"See, I think you're remembering it wrong."

"Just ... let me be the one in charge. It's important."

"Fine. You can be in charge. I won't say a thing." I mimed zipping my lips.

"Why do I think this is going to be more trouble than last time?" Graham complained.

"Because you've ticked her off now," Gunner replied. "She's going to drive you crazy for the next hour ... and she's going to like it."

Graham looked resigned. "That's exactly what I was afraid of."

ONE GLANCE AT BUBBA TOLD ME HE wasn't what I was expecting. He wore khakis, was thin as a rail, and his button-down shirt was open and allowed me to see the tattoos he had covering his body.

Oh, yeah, he was a phoenix too.

"What in the hell?" I didn't bother to hide my surprise.

Bubba arched an eyebrow behind his wire-rimmed glasses. "Is something wrong?" he asked in a thin and reedy voice.

"I think Scout just got a lesson in preconceptions," Graham replied as he extended his hand. "How are the experiments?"

"They're coming along." Bubba smiled. "I think I'll be able to have the pack up and running this spring."

Okay, I was beyond confused. "What sort of experiments are you doing with the pack?"

Graham shot me a quelling look. "What did I say about me doing the talking?"

Oh, right, like I was going to keep my mouth shut. I sent him an eye roll.

"This is Scout Randall," Graham said. "She's got a mouth on her."

Rather than wrinkle his nose or feign offense, Bubba grinned. "I've heard many a story about Ms. Randall." He extended his hand, and I readily took it to shake. The second I touched him, I could feel the power rolling off of him.

I was shaken when I pulled back. "Again I say, what the hell?" I was annoyed when I fixed my gaze on Graham. "Why haven't I heard about this guy until now?"

Graham shrugged. "It didn't come up."

I switched my glare to Gunner and waited.

"Bubba minds his own business," Gunner explained. "He keeps to himself. He does, however, come up with some interesting experiments to help the town. In exchange, we don't bug him unless we have no choice."

"That *is* the trade-off," Bubba agreed.

I was dumbfounded. "You're a phoenix."

"You picked that up from one shake?" Bubba arched an eyebrow. "I'm impressed."

"I picked that up the second you opened the door," I countered. "I've seen phoenixes before. I know you guys are rare now—and you keep on the down-low by choice—but I've worked with a few of your kind."

"You came from Detroit," Bubba said. "I was made aware of your presence when you first arrived in town. Your parents have been waiting for you for a long time. I'm glad you finally made your appearance."

I didn't know what to say. When I looked at Graham again, I found he was equally surprised.

"I didn't know." Graham held out his hands as an apology. "If I'd known..." He trailed off.

We both knew that if he'd known, he might not have told me. It was clear he had a strong relationship with Bubba.

"I wouldn't have put you in the position where you had to lie," Bubba assured Graham. "I know that you're fond of her. Scout cohabitating with your son makes for a stressful situation all around. I'm just glad Scout finally found them." He beamed at me. "You're where you're supposed to be."

Was he telling me that because he thought I might run? "I like it here," I assured him. "Sure, I miss being able to walk out the door of my apartment building and cross the street to get a coney at midnight if I have a hankering, but this is my home now."

Bubba nodded. "I'm glad." He turned to Graham. "I'm assuming this isn't a social visit. I've told you more than once that I don't want to get involved in the town's problems."

"You just said you had a fix for the pack," I argued. "What?" I complained when Graham glared at me again. "He's the one who said it. I want to know what sort of experiments he's doing to help the pack. Everything going through my head is weird and dirty."

"That's because you're a sex fiend," Gunner offered.

Bubba's chuckle was light. "I don't care if the two of you know about my plan for the pack lands. I expect discretion, but Scout here has had to keep so many secrets over the course of her life that I don't doubt she's adept at keeping things quiet.

"As for what I'm working on, for years, the pack has had trouble raising healthy crops in their current location," he continued. "The soil is nutrient poor. I've managed to come up with a fix for that problem, which means the pack will be more self-sufficient going forward."

And less likely to have to hire out their males as muscle to make a living, I realized. "That's pretty cool. Do you have a laboratory out here or something?"

"The barn." Bubba pointed toward the structure at the back of the property. It looked as if it were one stiff breeze away from falling down.

"Really?" I was dubious.

"It's different inside. I purposely keep it looking rundown on the outside, so looky-loos don't come poking into things that don't concern them."

"That's probably smart."

He nodded. "Why is it you're here, Graham?" Bubba pressed. "I wasn't expecting you. Normally, you give me a heads-up before dropping in."

"I'm sorry," Graham offered. "I truly am. This couldn't be helped. Are you aware of what happened to the house down the way?"

Bubba shook his head. "I haven't been paying attention. Are you talking about Althea or the Beechwood sisters?"

"The latter," Graham replied. "Their house caught fire last night."

"I see." Bubba's face contorted in confusion. "Are they dead?"

"They're missing," Graham replied. "Given some other things that have been popping up in town, we can't help being concerned."

Bubba might've had a poker face that could've won him millions, but he couldn't hide the ripple that passed through him from me. "You know something," I blurted.

"I don't know anything about the fire," Bubba assured me. "I'm just ... can you tell me why you think this has anything to do with your lamia problem?"

"You know about that?" I challenged.

"I keep my finger on the pulse of this town even though I'm desperate to keep away from the day-to-day activities," Bubba replied. "People think I'm a loner, maybe a little bit of a freak. I would be the first person they pointed at if there was some sort of shooting because I keep to myself, and in a town like this, that makes them uncomfortable.

"That doesn't mean I tell other people's secrets," he continued.

"If I feel that what I know is important, then I will give you the information."

He was blunt. I had to give him that.

"I'm just going to lay this out for you," Graham said. He had his cop face firmly in place. "In the past few days, we've had run-ins with loas, spider people, dwarves, and ghouls. They've all been situated in outlying areas."

"Loas?" Bubba looked flabbergasted. "What would loas be doing here?"

I raised my hand.

Bubba gave me a long once-over. "Interesting," was all he said.

"I have a friend who is in tight with the loas," I volunteered. "We believe they're working with Cernunnos and have some big plan for all of us. That's actually not one of our primary concerns right now, though."

"What a weird little world we live in that that's not one of our primary concerns," he said on a small smile. "What do you think is happening?"

"We think the lamia apex is trying to build an army, and she's bringing in outsiders to do it," I replied. "Now, my understanding is that the Beechwood sisters—who I've never met—are witches. It's been said they're not real witches, but I saw a few things in their home that suggest to me they might be the real deal ... just masquerading as the fake deal."

"Your instincts are interesting," Bubba said. "I'm not saying you're right, but do you believe Tiffany and Brandy are helping the lamia apex? What could they offer her, even if they were the real deal?"

It was a question I struggled with. "I don't know. Something was taken from one of their shelves."

Bubba heaved out a sigh, looked back inside his house, then shook his head. "I don't want to tell their secret, but I believe that they could be in trouble and you're their only way out. They're not witches."

I deflated a bit.

"They're harpies," he said.

I stilled. I'd heard about harpies—you couldn't go through the Spells Angels program without learning about them—but I'd never actually crossed paths with one. "Harpies?"

"Harpies are bird people, right?" Graham asked.

I nodded.

"First spider people," Gunner complained. "Now bird people. This town is going to Hell in a handbasket."

I ignored him and tried to run the new information through my head. "Why are harpies pretending to be witches?" I asked finally.

"Why not?" Bubba asked. "Why are you still calling yourself a witch when you're so much more?"

"I think that's a little different."

"Because it's you?"

I didn't like his attitude. "Just tell us what you can about the harpies. They're either helping Bonnie, or she's taken them for some reason."

"How can you be certain of that?"

"I just am. It fits what we've been dealing with."

"Well, the truth is, I don't know much about them," Bubba replied. "I've watched them from afar. They have magic, but they seem much more interested in chasing human endeavors."

"Like their cookie jars?"

Bubba smirked. "They gifted one of those jars to me. I happen to think they're lovely."

"Yes, and there are birds all over them." I sent Graham a triumphant look. "I told you that was weird."

"Yes, you see and know all," Graham replied dryly. "You're gifted, one of the great thinkers of our time."

"Nobody needs the sarcasm. I just need to know about what to expect." I pointed my gaze at Bubba. "Are they going to work with us or against us if I try to find them?"

"I can't think they would willingly join forces with the lamia,"

Bubba replied. "What I know of them suggests they would fight her. They just want to do their own thing."

"So, they had something Bonnie wanted and she took them," I surmised. "Maybe she's trying to force them to do something."

"It's possible they fled," Bubba argued. "They have a cairn somewhere in the woods, not far from the nexus. I don't know the exact location, but they mentioned it once."

"What's a cairn?" Gunner asked.

"It's like a big pile of stones," I replied.

"In this case, it's a second home built out of stones," Bubba explained. "They described it to me. It's where they go when they want a break from this world. They can charge their magic near the nexus and enjoy privacy when they do it."

And that, I realized, was the answer to the riddle. "Bonnie is looking for a new lair since her last one was destroyed."

"It's fixed now, though," Gunner argued.

"It is, but she won't use it again. We know where it is."

"And this cairn is obviously hidden," Graham said. "It makes sense."

"My guess is that Bonnie has them there." I exhaled heavily. "We're going to have to find it. I don't suppose you have a spot for us to look, do you?" I asked Bubba. "The nexus is big. That means the area surrounding it is big."

"I can't help you." Bubba held out his hands. "I wish I could. You'll have to do the next part yourself."

"Great." I blew out a sigh. "There's nothing I like better than doing things myself."

"Then you should be a happy girl."

Then how come I was anything but happy?

14
FOURTEEN

We didn't head out alone. That wasn't the smart way to handle things. Instead, we contacted Rooster, and he met us out there with Marissa, Rick, and Andrea in tow. To my surprise, he also had Doc with him.

"What are you doing here?" I asked the most science-minded member of our group.

"I heard there's a harpy lair out here," Doc replied as he used his middle finger to push up his glasses. It seemed deliberate, telling me that I could F-off for questioning his presence. He wasn't even field-rated—we'd tried—so it was rare to actually bring him along for the ride when we were doing something dangerous.

"That's the rumor," I agreed. "Are you actually going to help?"

The look he shot me was disdainful. "I always help."

"Whatever." I shook my head. "The first order of business is finding it," I said to Rooster. "Then, when we know exactly what we're dealing with, we'll go in."

Rooster nodded. "What about more backup? Like ... what about Stormy? I can't help thinking some firepower might be good right about now."

I didn't disagree with him. "I don't want to bring them in on this," I replied. "It's our fight."

"You've helped with their fights." Rooster eyed me, his expression unreadable. "Why is it that you're willing to put yourself at risk for others but not ask for help in exchange?"

"Because Stormy just got engaged and is happier than I've ever seen a person," I replied. "If she were to get hurt helping me..." I trailed off.

"You're a martyr is what you're saying," Rooster surmised.

"She's definitely a martyr," Graham replied. "Let's find this cairn first and see what we're dealing with. If we think it's too big of a job, I'll call Marnie myself and see if she can get Bay out here."

"Where's Evan?" Gunner asked.

"He's already in the woods looking," Rooster replied. "He'll definitely come in handy if we have to engage."

I could tell by the look on his face there was something he wasn't saying. "What aren't you telling us?" I asked.

"I'm just concerned that if Bonnie's here and we don't have anybody in place to absorb her powers that maybe we shouldn't be doing this," Rooster admitted.

"I get it." I'd already thought about that myself. "The thing is, we don't have a choice in the matter. We can't do nothing."

"I know." He forced a smile that didn't touch his eyes. "Let's just find the cairn first. We'll go from there."

I DIDN'T KNOW WHAT I WAS LOOKING FOR. All I could picture was a big pile of rocks. That's why I allowed my magic to do the walking and chased it to a babbling brook. The scene was beautiful ... and serene ... and when I turned, I realized I was looking at what could only be described as a small cabin made out of rocks. It was built into the side of a small cliff, almost completely camouflaged thanks to the way it had been built. It was the bird sculpture that had been made out of rocks in front of it that told me we'd found our destination.

"Text Rooster," I said in a low voice, drawing Gunner's attention away from the brook. "I think I found what we're looking for."

He glanced in the direction I was staring and nodded. "Yup. That's definitely what we're looking for." He pulled out his phone.

So as not to draw too much attention to ourselves, we moved away from the cairn. We could still see it, but the running water was enough to drown out our voices as we waited for the cavalry to arrive.

Evan was the first. He dropped out of the trees overhead and tilted his head. "I wouldn't have even thought about that being what we were looking for until you pointed out the obvious," he admitted.

I nodded. "Yup."

Rick and Andrea joined us next. Andrea's eyes went wide as she first looked at the bird sculpture and then took in the house. "It looks as if it's part of nature and yet somebody clearly made it," she said.

"Yeah. Somebody clearly made it," I agreed. Birds. Human birds. I knew from my studies that harpies looked like humans until they went into attack mode. Then their wings, which were only visible when they wanted them to be, took shape and their faces transformed. It was that way for a lot of paranormals. "There's only one entrance."

"How can you be sure?" Evan challenged. "There might be a back way in on the other side of the cliff." Rather than wait for me to argue with him, he took off to look. His speed was so great that he turned into a blur before disappearing.

"He sucks," I complained to Gunner.

"You just wish you could run that fast."

I did wish I could run that fast. Rooster, Doc, and Marissa had joined us by the time Evan returned.

"I can't find another entrance," Evan supplied. He looked annoyed when I sent him a triumphant look. "That seems like shoddy craftsmanship to me."

"I'm pretty sure they weren't looking at it as a place they would have to escape from," I said. "That's what makes it such an appealing lair for Bonnie."

"So, what do we do?" Rooster asked. "If anybody is asking my opinion—and I know that's folly at this point—I think we should call in the Winchesters."

The suggestion rankled. "Why would we call them in? There's one entrance. Too many people will be unwieldy."

"Yes, but we don't know how many people are in that thing," Rooster argued. "For all we know, it's huge in there and she has an entire army waiting for us."

That was an option. It didn't feel right, though. "She wouldn't be having her soldiers amass at other places if she was traveling with them," I argued. "At the most she's got four or five dwarves in there with her."

"And the harpies," Rooster said pointedly.

"Yes, but ... I don't happen to believe that the harpies are working with her. I think she's holding them hostage." *Or worse*, I silently added, *they're dead*. There was no point in saying that part out loud, though.

"Okay, but what if she took them to make a deal with them?" Rooster challenged. "What if whatever item she stole from their house somehow turns them into slaves?"

I made a face. "Would you keep that sort of item out in the open at your house?"

"No, but they were openly pretending to be witches, so we already know that they don't approach things from a normal perspective."

I scratched my cheek. He wasn't wrong. "I'm going in."

"No, you're not." Graham was the one who grabbed my arm. "We're coming up with a plan. You're not getting hurt again on my watch."

"It's not your watch, though," I said softly. "This is my deal. I'll go in and see what we're dealing with. If I don't come out in five minutes, you guys can call the Winchesters and get backup." I wasn't keen on the idea, but it was the best thing I had.

"We're not doing that, Scout." Graham was firm. "You can't go in there and face off with Bonnie without backup. It's just not going to happen."

I stared at him for several seconds, then pressed my lips together. He wasn't going to back down, and it wasn't as if I could force him to my way of thinking. "What if we try something different?" I suggested. "What if Evan goes in through the front door and I go in through a plane door?"

Graham opened his mouth, then shut it. The gears in his mind were clearly working overtime.

"It's just a thought," I added quickly.

"It's an interesting thought." Graham darted his eyes to Evan. "Are you okay with that plan?"

"Actually, I was going to suggest that myself," Evan said. "I can draw Bonnie's attention to me when I go through the door. She'll be confused as to why I'm there and hopefully will forget to watch for Scout."

"Except her whole goal is to beat Scout," Gunner countered. "I don't like that plan. I think I should go in with Scout so there are three of us in there."

"We don't know how much space we're going to have to maneuver once we're inside, though," Evan argued. "I mean ... it's not that I don't think you'll be helpful. If there are a lot of dwarves in there, we're going to need to handle them. If there's only limited space, we could find ourselves in a very sticky spot."

Gunner touched his tongue to his top lip, seemingly debating. "I get what you're saying, but I refuse to be cut out of the action."

And there it was, his line in the sand.

"What if Gunner goes in with me?" I said to Evan. "If we make Bonnie believe you're the scout, she might not be expecting Gunner and me to move in at her back when she's engaged with you."

Evan's face was impassive for several seconds. Then he nodded.

"Okay, I think I can live with that. If you get in there and realize that we're in a closet-sized room, though, I want you to back up and let me do my thing."

I had one problem with that. "What if your thing results in Bonnie killing you?"

"Better me than you."

"I happen to disagree."

"Well ... you've already been on the front line with her once." Evan refused to back down. "This is my show. I'm in charge this time."

"I think that's smart," Graham offered.

I shot him a dirty look.

"I already told you that I'm not going to be okay with you getting hurt on my watch," Graham argued. "Just ... let's do this Evan's way for a change. You can make the plans next time."

"Whatever." I shook my head. "We don't have time for this. We'll follow Evan's plan. If I feel I'm needed in there, though, I'm going to stay."

Evan opened his mouth, likely to argue, and then snapped it shut. "Fine. Let's just do this."

"Yes, sir." I mock-saluted him.

The corners of Evan's lips curved up. "You really are a pain in the ass."

"And don't you forget it."

GUNNER STUCK CLOSE AS WE MOVED to the side of the cliff. If Bonnie had sentries, they would be near the opening. Because Evan was more than just a vampire—so much more—I wasn't all that worried about him taking on a few dwarves. Heck, even if she had a cadre of Arachnids in there, he would be okay.

If it was just Bonnie, though, then she would be the one taking him on. I was less certain of Evan's abilities when it came to facing down the lamia apex.

"He'll be okay," Gunner assured me, his mouth close to my ear. "You cannot let fear for Evan—or fear for me—take you over. Just focus on what needs to be done."

He was right, of course. Evan could take care of himself. He'd been without me more than with me over the past few years, and he'd managed to survive just fine. His powers were enhanced now, making him an absolute dynamo when it came to a fight.

Still—*still*—the thought of losing him a second time was almost too much to bear.

Gunner seemed to know where my head was at because he rested his hands on my shoulders and squeezed. "Do not get trapped in your own head."

I sucked in a breath and nodded. "Evan will be fine." I meant it. "We're going to be fine, too."

"Of course we are. I have you on my team. That means I can't lose."

That was a bit of a stretch, but I didn't argue with him. Instead, I flashed a smile I didn't feel and nodded. "Let's go." I took his hand before he could object and tell me to wait—the plan was to give Evan a few more minutes to assess the situation—and opened a door. We were already through it before Gunner could say a single word, and once on the other side I dropped his hand and prepared to fight.

The room—another cave, proving that Bonnie had a specific type of lair she wanted to coil up in—was empty except for two individuals in the middle of the space. Their backs were pressed together, their faces bruised and battered, and they looked to have been tethered together with some sort of magical rope.

"The Beechwood sisters I presume," I said in a low voice.

The one facing me raised her puffy and bruised face and frowned. "What..." She trailed off.

"Hey, Tiffany." Gunner spoke in a low voice as he dropped to his knees. His first instinct was obviously to reach out and untie them, but he didn't. He could see the magical rope as easily as me.

"What are you doing here?" Tiffany shook her head. Her eyes

were cloudy and unfocused. "You shouldn't be here. You're the one she wants."

Since that was hardly earth-shattering news, I offered up a tight smile. "We've got everything under control." At least I hoped that was true. "Is there another room to this place?"

Tiffany inclined her head toward the door.

"I pretty much figured." I considered my options for a beat, then reached for the magical tether.

"Don't," Gunner protested, slapping at my arm. "You could end up hurt."

"It's fine," I assured him. "I'm going to free these two, and then you're going to take them out through a plane door."

Surprise and fury lit in Gunner's eyes. "No, that's not what's going to happen."

"It is. It's the smart move."

"She's draining us," Tiffany said. "She's been at it for hours. She wants our powers."

"Well, she's done draining you." There was no hesitation when I grabbed the magical rope. I poured as much pixie power into it as possible and it snapped in two seconds.

Tiffany fell forward and I caught her. Gunner grabbed Brandy, who was unconscious but still breathing.

"Can you take them both?" I asked him.

"I can," he confirmed. "I don't want to, though, Scout. I don't want to leave you."

"It's the smart move. Get them out." With little fanfare, I opened a plane door and helped him get an arm around both harpies. "Get them help. I'll go after Evan."

Gunner wanted to argue—it was written all over his face—but he didn't. Instead, he merely nodded. "Fine. I'll get them out. If you get hurt, though, I'm going to be mad."

"Great. I love it when we fight." I faked a bright smile that I didn't feel and pushed him through the door. The second he disappeared from sight, I closed the door and turned. Now it was just Evan and me.

And Bonnie. I couldn't forget Bonnie.

There was no hesitation as I strode through the door. I could hear voices on the other side, and when I emerged, I found quite the sight. Evan stood in the middle of the space—which wasn't any larger than a small apartment bedroom—and stared down Bonnie, whose back was to me. There were several dwarves on the ground next to him. They were either dead or wished they were dead. And Evan, cool as ever, was smiling at the freshly minted lamia apex. He didn't acknowledge that I'd joined the fray.

"You can't win, vampire," Bonnie hissed. "You've sealed your own doom."

Evan's expression didn't change. "I wouldn't be so certain of that."

"I wouldn't either," I said.

Bonnie practically came out of her skin when she heard my voice. Her fingers were sparking to life as she turned, and my instincts kicked in before my brain did. Her magic flew at me, and I deflected it. Again.

"Scout!" Evan sounded furious when he realized what I was doing. It was already too late, though.

The cairn might've been well constructed, but the meeting of lamia and pixie magic made for an explosion. Evan raced to me rather than Bonnie and threw himself over me as a shield as the rocks began to fall.

I had a split second to eye Bonnie and then she disappeared through her own door. It wasn't nearly as good as the doors I'd managed to erect, but she was gone all the same.

Evan made sure my face was covered as the cairn collapsed. He could withstand a cave-in better than me. "I can't believe you did that twice," he growled.

He wasn't the only one. Still, I felt the need to stand up for myself.

"This isn't my fault," I complained as the rocks stopped falling and the dust took over. "When somebody throws magic at you, the natural thing to do is to make sure that magic doesn't hit you."

Evan was incredulous when he pulled back, his face streaked with dirt. "Yes, but once you've survived one cave-in, you would think that a different plan might be in order. I mean ... couldn't you have aimed for the floor?"

"I just reacted."

"You are too much." Evan released me, and when we looked around, we found that the front of the cairn was completely gone. We were exposed to the elements, and our team had rushed in to make sure we were okay.

"Bonnie?" Rooster asked when he snagged gazes with me.

I shrugged. "Gone. Where are the Beechwood sisters?"

"Graham and Gunner are loading them into Graham's truck. They're taking them to Hemlock Cove."

That made sense. "Well, I guess my work here is done." I was prim when wiping at the dirt on my face. "Is it lunchtime yet?"

"Geez." Rooster turned his attention to the sky, as if praying to some deity to come smite me. "You are just so much freaking work, Scout."

"Yes, but I'm worth the effort."

"I'm not sure I believe that right now."

"Yes, you do."

And, because I was right, all Rooster could do was shake his head. "Seriously, just so much work."

15
FIFTEEN

We all went to The Overlook together. Once I'd destroyed the cairn and Bonnie had made her escape, there really was no reason to stick around. The dwarves Evan had slaughtered to get inside the structure remained under the rubble. There was nothing we could do for them. Tiffany and Brandy were another story, though.

"I don't have wings that I can remove and loan to you," a testy voice barked as I made my way to the second floor of the inn. "That's not how it works."

"You could at least try," a voice I recognized as belonging to Tillie complained from somewhere inside the room to my left. "I mean ... I'm not asking for the world here. You're being a defeatist, though. How do you know you can't do something until you actually try to do it?"

When I moved into the open doorway, I found Tiffany in the bed. She looked exhausted. Her skin was almost translucent, veins popping from beneath what looked to be some very thin skin. There were bruises everywhere. Despite that, there was a fierceness in her eyes.

"Would you rip off your arm and try to loan it to me?" she demanded of Tillie.

"Of course not," Tillie scoffed. "That's not the same thing."

"Do you have magical wings?"

Tillie shook her head.

"Then how do you know it's not the same thing?" Tiffany challenged.

"Whatever." Tillie flicked her eyes to me. "Did you get her?"

I didn't have to ask who she was referring to. Instead, I just shook my head. "I did not get her. She managed to get away." I flashed a smile for Tiffany's benefit as I sat. Unlike the last time a roof had fallen in on me, I was mostly okay. Evan had taken the brunt of the damage—something we were going to have to talk about because I didn't want him sacrificing himself for me—so I was mostly okay except for a couple of stray aches.

Tiffany was another story.

"You look rough," I said without thinking.

Winnie made a tsking sound as she walked into the room with a tray. The look she shot me was dark. "Did you like it when people said similar things to you when you were recuperating?" she barked.

"No, but I'm me." I flashed her a smile. "People find me entertaining."

Winnie turned to Tiffany. "Do you find her entertaining?"

To my surprise, Tiffany was smiling when I glanced at her. "Actually, given what she did when she swooped in, I think she might be the most entertaining person I know."

I straightened and shot Winnie an "I told you so" look.

Winnie being Winnie, she was not impressed. "Sit down," she ordered. "I want to make sure you're not hurt again. As for you, leave her alone about the wings." She pinned Tillie with the darkest look in her repertoire. "You're being needlessly obnoxious, and she needs her rest."

"You're not the boss of me," Tillie fired back.

Winnie's nostrils flared, reminding me of a bull that was about to charge. Bay had once told me that her mother was the only person in the world who could control Tillie with any regularity. She didn't look happy about that fact today.

"Don't you have a new friend to play with?" Winnie challenged in a clipped tone. "You and Baron said you were heading into town to torture Margaret again. Doesn't that sound like more fun than torturing me?"

"Not really," Tillie replied dryly. "Believe it or not, you're my favorite person to torture."

"I thought that was Thistle," I interjected.

"Well, that's true." Tillie cocked her head. "There's always Landon too." She bobbed her head, as if making up her mind. "Okay, you've convinced me. I'll go downstairs and use my powers of annoyance on others. We're not done with this conversation, though," she said to Tiffany.

"I'm sorry," Winnie offered Tiffany as soon as her aunt had disappeared. "She just does what she wants whenever the mood strikes."

Tiffany looked amused despite herself. "That's how my sister is. I'm used to it. You don't have to worry."

Winnie didn't look convinced, but she forced a smile all the same.

"How is my sister?" Tiffany asked. She appeared to be struggling with asking the question. It was almost as if she didn't want to hear the answer.

"She's a little worse off than you," Winnie replied. She looked resigned as she settled in the chair next to the bed. "We've given her some potions. She needs to rest, though. We're going to watch her overnight."

"But you think she'll be okay?" Tiffany pressed.

Winnie hesitated, then nodded. "I do. I'm obviously not an expert on harpies. I think she's going to be okay, though." Her eyes moved to me. "All thanks to you, of course. I don't think that Brandy had a full twenty-four hours left to survive without your help."

I hated it when people drew attention to me the way Winnie often insisted on doing it. I was no hero. "I did what was necessary," I stressed before flicking my eyes to Tiffany. "You probably won't want to thank me when you hear what I did to your cairn."

To my utter surprise, Tiffany burst out laughing. "A cairn can be rebuilt. In fact, Brandy and I have been talking about redecorating for more than a year. When she's back on her feet—when the weather breaks—we'll handle that." She sipped the water Winnie provided for her and then leaned back against her pillows. "Don't feel guilty over it, Scout. You did what had to be done."

"Actually, I knew better than deflecting Bonnie's magic into the ceiling." I was rueful. "It was only a few days ago when I did the same thing and a cave fell in on me. I reacted without thinking. I just ... made a boneheaded move."

"They're alive, Scout," Winnie chastised. "You saved two sisters. I think you should take that as a win."

"Maybe." I was feeling restless, so I didn't sit. Instead, I strode to the window and looked out. "Can you answer a few questions?" I asked Tiffany, my back to her.

"I can try," Tiffany replied. "I think you've earned the proper answers."

"Great." I rolled my neck. "Tell me what happened."

"I actually don't a hundred percent know." Tiffany's expression was rueful when I turned back to her. "We were asleep. Our bedrooms are at opposite ends of the house. We woke up to the smoke alarm going off.

"At first I thought we left the oven on or something, but then we realized there was an actual fire," she continued. "It wasn't a normal fire either. It was raging but not spreading naturally. It crept through the house with a purpose."

She took another drink of water.

"We managed to make it to the first floor," she explained. "We got to the stairs at about the same time. I think... I think that she was trying to herd us so we came down the stairs together."

"What makes you think that?" I asked.

"She was waiting for us." Tiffany was grim. "She had two of the dwarves with her. They were ransacking the main floor of the house. They seemed to be looking for something. I never got a chance to figure out what that something was, though, because the snake was on us with her magic before I could even ask a single question.

"We went down together and didn't wake up until we were in the cairn," she continued. "I didn't know what was happening at first. I felt weak, drained. I still didn't realize she'd tried to absorb our powers until she came back and did it a second time."

Now we were getting somewhere. "Did she say why she was trying to absorb your powers?" I asked.

Tiffany shook her head. "Not really. I think I know why, though."

"I'm all ears."

"She's trying to balance her powers."

I was caught off guard. "I thought she already balanced her powers. Wasn't that what absorbing Emma's powers was all about?"

"I can't answer that for you," Tiffany replied. "I just know that she was fluctuating some when she was with us. You could see it under her skin. Occasionally, she would get a power surge and have to tamp it down."

Well, *that* was interesting. "Maybe she's not as stable as we assumed," I said to Winnie.

Winnie held out her hands. "It's possible that she stabilized some when she absorbed Emma's powers. Then maybe the cycling she was dealing with started again and she decided that what she needed was more powers to balance herself again."

It was an interesting theory. "I don't think she's all there any longer. She could be telling herself anything."

"She could," Tiffany agreed. "You're right about her not being all there. She is struggling to understand her part in the world. She seems desperate to stop the cycling, but she's losing her mind in the process."

"And there's nothing worse than fighting a crazy person because that means you can't predict what they're going to do." I dragged a hand through my hair and sighed. "Did she say anything about me?" I asked finally.

"Oh, she's obsessed with you." The smile Tiffany shot me was sympathetic. "She thinks there's some all-powerful force at work that has pitted you two against each other. She says she's the force of light and you're the force of darkness."

"Oh, well, I always wanted to be the force of darkness. That's actually what I put down as a career goal in high school when they made us take those aptitude tests to decide what we should be when we became adults."

Winnie frowned. "I don't like those tests. They're designed to pigeonhole kids and not allow them to reach their full potential."

"Actually, I think they're designed so kids with limited means are pointed toward trade schools," Tiffany replied. "Scout grew up in the system if I understand correctly. She wouldn't have had the option of a liberal arts degree anyway. They would've wanted to direct her at plumbing or something."

"Ah, I would've made a great plumber," I lamented.

Winnie smirked. "I still don't like those tests. You're more than the little bubbles you fill out."

"You're my biggest cheerleader, aren't you?" I grinned at her.

"Actually, I think Evan and Gunner are your biggest cheerleaders, but I'm not too far off," Winnie confirmed. "Where are the others?"

"Downstairs. They didn't want to overwhelm Tiffany and Brandy. They left that for me to do on my own."

"You're not overwhelming me," Tiffany assured me. "I simply don't know what I can tell you."

"I just want to know what she said when she was interacting with you."

Tiffany sucked in a breath as she searched her memory. "She didn't interact with us a lot. She didn't like the cairn though. She thought it would be bigger. She kept complaining that you stole her other lair."

"How Batman of me," I mused.

Tiffany's lips twitched. "She said that you were getting all the glory—that's how it had been since you came to town—and she was getting all the crap. She was sick of getting all the crap."

What an interesting way of looking at things. "What glory did she think I was getting?"

"I'm not a hundred percent certain. She rambled."

"Just tell me whatever. I'm not going to make you swear to it in court."

Tiffany laughed, but it was hollow. "She talked a little about how when you came to town that she was excited because she knew you were the one, but that excitement only lasted a few days because she discovered quickly that you were an idiot."

Tiffany sent me an apologetic look right away. "That's what she said. I don't happen to think that you're an idiot."

"Thanks for that, but I'm not surprised she believes I'm a moron," I assured her.

"Of course not," Winnie agreed. "You go out of your way to make others believe you're an airhead at the very least. You go off on tangents."

"Hey!" I jabbed a finger at her. "Those tangents are who I am."

She smirked. "I'm just saying, your personality is colorful. You embrace that to avoid dwelling on the darkness of your childhood."

"Um ... I wouldn't go that far," I hedged.

"No?" Winnie arched a challenging eyebrow. "You might not want to admit it, but you're the class clown, Scout. You make fun of yourself and put on a show to entertain others ... and all because you don't want to risk deep conversations."

"You're a peacock," Tiffany countered. The way she said it made me wonder if it was an insult. Seemingly reading my mind, she laughed. "Peacocks are smart," she assured me. "They're also the models of the bird world. They distract their enemies with their beauty. It's all a mirage, though, because they're determined and deadly."

"Huh." I lifted one shoulder. "I guess I don't mind being a peacock."

"You're more than just that shell, Scout," Winnie assured me. "The thing is, Bonnie might never have realized that."

"Because Bonnie was never more than her shell," I surmised. "I get it. Bonnie doesn't understand that I'm more than the sum of my parts."

"She definitely doesn't," Tiffany agreed. "She went on and on about how you were the favorite and she was always the one left picking up the scraps of leftover affection."

"I was the favorite of whom?" I asked. Now I really was confused. "Was she talking about Gunner? Oh, maybe she wasn't really a lesbian and she's angry that Gunner didn't show her any attention."

"Yeah, I don't think that's it." Tiffany wrinkled her nose. "She mentioned Rooster. I think she was jealous of the fact that you became Rooster's go-to girl right away. That seemed to put her nose out of joint a lot. She also mentioned the Winchesters and how they practically adopted you after your first meeting."

"I wouldn't go that far," I hedged, suddenly uncomfortable.

"I would," Winnie replied. "We loved you from the start, Scout. You fit right in with us."

And maybe that was Bonnie's true problem, I realized. "She was here before me. For years. What if she had a plan to rally everybody behind her cause when she and Zeno finally moved on me? I mean ... isn't it possible she doesn't see herself as the bad guy?"

"The villain rarely does," Winnie agreed. "You see it in television and movies all the time. Like ... Aunt Tillie is obsessed with *The Walking Dead*. That character played by Jeffrey Dean Morgan, he was a bad man who bashed people's heads in with a baseball bat and forced women to be his sex slaves and yet he still saw himself as the hero."

I was familiar with the character. "Do you think that's Bonnie?" I asked. "Do you think she believes she's doing the right thing?"

"I don't think anybody sets out to be the villain," Winnie replied. "Nobody looks at themself and sees abject evil."

"So, if she doesn't see herself as bad, what's the ultimate goal here?"

"I can't answer that." Winnie shook her head. "I have no idea."

I tapped my fingers on the bedpost, then nodded. "She thinks I'm the one working against her."

"Well, you technically are," Tiffany said. "It's important that you not get caught up on the hows and the whys though. That woman ... well ... she is not all there. She hears voices."

I jerked up my chin. "What sort of voices?"

"If I'm not mistaken, she's speaking to someone named Zeno. She seems to think that he's inside of her."

That's when reality smacked me across the face. "Holy crap!"

"What is it?" Winnie asked, properly reading my sudden excitement. "What have you figured out?"

"She *is* hearing voices," I replied. "She's not making that up."

"So, she's not crazy?" Tiffany looked disappointed.

"The voices are likely going to make her crazy," I replied. "That and a few other things. She is hearing a real voice, though."

"How?" Winnie challenged.

"It's Zeno's voice. He was the apex. She killed him and absorbed his powers. It's no different from me hearing Agnes's voice."

"Except she did things in the proper order," Winnie realized. "Her essence passed on to the book and you only hear her voice from the book."

I nodded. "The Wix. She's in there. When I need to talk to her, I can. Zeno wasn't prepared to die ... and Bonnie didn't understand the intricacies of what she was doing when she killed him. Zeno's essence didn't pass on to a book. It's inside of her."

"Slowly driving her mad," Winnie surmised.

"Yup." I nodded.

"Do you think you can use that?"

"I don't know. I need to think on it." I flicked my eyes back to

Tiffany. "Just one more thing and then I'll let you rest. When we got to your house, it was obvious something had been taken from one of your shelves." I described the location to her. "Do you know what that would be?"

"A channeling rune," Tiffany replied. "She tried to use it on us to take our powers. It didn't work how she wanted it to work, though."

"I'm starting to think that nothing is working how she wants it to work," I agreed. "She's got a pile of magic at her disposal, and yet none of it is working correctly."

"And she's aware of that," Tiffany said. "She knows that she's not as powerful as she should be. She doesn't like it. That was one of her complaints. She kept saying things were so easy for you and hard for her."

"She's jealous," Winnie said. "That's her biggest problem. She's jealous of you."

"Yeah, but it's more than that," I said. "She thought getting Zeno's power would make her important. It's not happening yet."

"No, and she's bitter about that, too," Tiffany agreed. "She said that the other lamias weren't falling in line. I think she plans on making them."

Well, wasn't that interesting? "Thanks for your time." I shot Tiffany a soft smile. "Rest. I'm probably going to have more questions. I'm done for now, though."

"I could use the rest," Tiffany said. "Hopefully, when I wake up again, Brandy will be up."

"I expect her to sleep all night," Winnie said. "If she's not awake tomorrow morning, we'll reassess. I think she's fine for now, though."

"Then I'll sleep, too." Tiffany closed her eyes. "Tomorrow is a new day, and that snake bitch has a fight coming for her."

I wanted to warn Tiffany about going after Bonnie, but there was no point. In her shoes, I would want to do the same thing. "I'll check in later," I promised.

She didn't even wave. She was already asleep. That was for the best.

16

SIXTEEN

D ownstairs, there were people everywhere, and Marnie and Twila were happily setting the table.

"It's pot roast night," Gunner said when he saw me, excitedly rubbing his hands together.

"I guess that means we're staying," I deadpanned. "Although ... I was thinking about whipping up some canned pasta when we got home. I guess you'll have to suffer through the pot roast instead, huh?"

"Oh, you're such a kidder." He poked my side, then turned serious when he gauged my expression. "Is something wrong?"

"No." I shook my head. "Nothing is wrong. I'm just ... thinking."

"About what?"

"Tiffany said Bonnie was hearing voices ... and talking to Zeno. I think she hears his voice in her head, like I do Agnes's when it comes to the Wix."

"Is that important?"

"I don't know. It just has me thinking." I squeezed his wrist and then moved around him. "I don't suppose you've seen Baron, have you?"

"He's on the back patio with Aunt Tillie," Twila volunteered. "I just saw him about five minutes ago."

"Thank you." I left the others to their discussions in the dining room and cut through the kitchen. The scent of the pot roast was heavenly, and I didn't realize how hungry I was until my stomach let loose a growl. I grabbed a roll from the counter and bit into it as I walked into the family living quarters, which was cut off from the guests by design. Right away, I saw three figures on the back patio. Evan looked to have joined Tillie and Baron.

"How is Tiffany?" Evan asked when I walked outside. He seemed relieved that I'd interrupted whatever conversation was transpiring.

"She's okay," I replied. "She needs to sleep. She already fell out. Brandy hasn't regained consciousness yet, but Winnie believes she will tomorrow morning. Bonnie was trying to suck their magic from them."

"Why?" Tillie asked. "Oh, wait, I bet she wanted the wings too."

It took everything I had to keep from laughing. "Maybe, but I think that she wanted the magic because she's still unbalanced." I flicked my eyes to Baron. "What do you think?"

The loa should've looked out of place in the snow—and he did to a certain extent—but he didn't appear to be worked up about the new development. Instead, he appeared content. "I think you're a bright girl and will have no problem figuring things out," he replied, not missing a beat.

"You don't have a theory on what's going on with Bonnie?" I pressed.

"No."

He was starting to irritate me. Okay, he'd passed "starting to" days before. "You could've come out to the cairn to help."

"You seemed to have things under control." Baron pinned me with a serious look. "When you truly need my help, I'll step in. Until then ... it's my choice," he said. "I'm going to do what I want to do. You understand that, right? You don't get to boss me around and tell me what I am and am not going to do."

His tone rankled. His stare was annoying to the nth degree. He didn't back down in the face of my fury, though. "This is your fight. If I can help, I will. That's for me to decide, though."

I stared at him a beat longer, then shook my head. "You are a very obnoxious individual," I growled.

That earned a smirk. "I've been called much worse." He held my gaze a beat longer. "Now, what's for dinner? I'm starving."

"Pot roast. The whole crew is getting ready to eat inside."

"Lovely." Baron turned on his heel and retreated into the inn, leaving me staring in his wake.

"I loathe him," I complained.

"He's up to something," Evan agreed. "I'm just not certain he's up to what you think he's up to."

That didn't make me feel any better. "What about you?" I asked Tillie. "Have you managed to get more out of him?"

"Right now, he's just serving as my third sidekick," she replied. "He's fun ... and he likes to drink. He's not here for me, though." Was she disappointed about that? She didn't look it. "He's here for a specific reason. He's not going to tell us what it is until he's good and ready, though."

That wasn't what I wanted to hear. "He makes me itchy."

"You can't control him," Tillie warned. "It's like trying to control you. It's just not going to happen."

There was a compliment buried in there. I didn't like it, though. "Let's eat dinner. I'll figure out a way to bug him again before the night is out."

Evan's eyes twinkled. "Won't that be fun?"

That was not the word I would've used. "Or painful. Either way, he's going to offer up some answers ... whether he wants to or not."

THE DINING ROOM TABLE WAS BURSTING AT the seams. I sat on the same side as Bay, although I was separated from her by Terry, who sat across from Winnie and laughed at something she said. They were engaged, planning a wedding even though they would've been happy going to City Hall. Bay, however, wanted a big celebration ... and she wasn't going to take no for an answer on this one.

Graham sat across the table, next to Marnie. Twila was in the corner chatting away happily with Rick and Andrea. Tillie was at the head of the table on one end. Baron was on the other. Rooster and Doc were on the other side of Gunner. That's when it hit me that Marissa had gone missing.

"Where did Marissa go?" I asked Rooster, suddenly suspicious.

"She decided that she preferred having dinner with her aunt," Rooster replied.

Since Marissa's aunt was Margaret Little, the mere idea of that meal made me shudder. "How is she getting home?"

"She said she would handle it." Rooster held out his hands and shrugged. "I didn't argue with her."

"It's not as if she would've been comfortable here," Gunner pointed out around a mouthful of food. "We're better off without her."

I didn't disagree. Still, I couldn't help feeling a little sorry for her. We were a family. Everybody at this table—well, except Baron—had opted to join together to fight the good fight. That meant we were joined by more than circumstances. There was a lot of love here. Marissa didn't have that. And, after listening to Tiffany, I realized Bonnie didn't have that either. Would things have been different if she had?

"Switch places with me," Bay instructed Terry out of the blue, causing me to look in her direction.

"What?" Terry appeared baffled. "We always sit in the same seats."

"I know. I want to talk to Scout."

Terry studied her face, perhaps searching for something, then nodded. "Okay." He switched with her, ignoring the way Landon protested being separated from his wife.

I turned my full attention to Bay as she got comfortable. "Is something wrong?" I asked finally.

"That was going to be my question." Bay's gaze was searching. "You know, I haven't really had a chance to talk to you much in the past few days. How are you?"

Bay wasn't subtle. I didn't have to think hard about what she was asking. Despite that, I decided to go for the safe answer. "I'm fine. I'm back to full strength. Evan protected me with his body during the cave-in today."

"Where is Evan?" Gunner asked.

That was a good question. "He's probably getting some air. I think being around too many people makes him uncomfortable."

"Or he's doing something else," Bay surmised.

Now it was my turn to stare at her. "What else would he be doing?"

"Well, it's not my place to spread gossip." The twinkle in Bay's eyes told me that's exactly what she was going to do. "But Evan tends to occasionally meet up with Aunt Tillie's second sidekick out on the bluff. I've seen them out there twice."

Oh, well, that was interesting, wasn't it? "He meets Easton on the bluff?" I made sure to keep my voice low. I didn't know what to make of that. "Why?"

She shrugged. "You'll have to ask him that. I'm not a busybody."

Next to her, Terry snorted. "Oh, sweetheart, you're a great many things. I include being a busybody in that statement."

Bay scowled at him. "I mind my own business ... most of the time."

"Right." Terry chuckled. "That's what I think when I look at you. *There's my girl. She's so not interested in what everybody else is doing.*"

I choked on a laugh, which was wrapped around a hunk of pot roast. Gunner had to thump my back to make sure I didn't choke.

"Okay?" he asked me.

I nodded as I swallowed the pot roast. "Just got a little over-stimulated."

His eyes fired with flirty intent. "I'm going to overstimulate the crap out of you later."

"I heard that, Junior," Graham barked from across the table. "Be respectful at family dinner."

"Yes, *that's* the Winchester motto," Bay agreed blandly. "We're nothing if not respectful. Right, Aunt Tillie?"

For her part, Tillie looked to be concentrating on something else. I couldn't quite decide what it was, though. She had something in her lap, and that was garnering the bulk of her focus. "What?" she asked when she heard her name, blinking like an owl. "I didn't do anything. It was Bay."

Bay glared at her. "Why are you blaming me?"

"Because Thistle isn't here," Tillie replied. "I mean ... isn't that a given?"

Bay muttered something I couldn't quite make out under her breath.

"How are things with the loa under your roof?" I asked, turning the conversation to something different. If Bay got a full head of steam where Tillie was concerned, she wouldn't stop ranting and raving.

"He's not technically under our roof," Bay replied. "I mean... I've seen him with Aunt Tillie a few times. Apparently, he made Mrs. Little's unicorns poop chicken feet this morning. That was quite the mess."

"What?" I had to have heard her wrong. "How does a pewter—or porcelain or plastic for that matter—unicorn poop chicken feet?" Something else occurred to me. "Wait ... were they real chicken feet? Because that is just gross."

"They were real chicken feet." Bay bobbed her head. "I saw them."

"But ... how?"

"I have no idea. I think it's something he and Aunt Tillie thought of together. Or ... maybe she wanted the unicorns to poop, and he threw in the chicken feet because that's a voodoo thing."

"What does voodoo have to do with it?" I asked.

"Well, he's a loa." Bay lifted one shoulder. "He talks about New Orleans nonstop, to the point where Aunt Tillie is insisting we visit suddenly. She doesn't even like traveling to Detroit, so I can't see her going to New Orleans. I would have to think that voodoo is part of his schtick."

I wanted to kick myself because it hadn't occurred to me. When I turned, I found Baron watching me with gleaming eyes. "Do you practice voodoo?" I blurted.

Everybody at the table stopped talking and focused on us.

"I have a working knowledge of voodoo," Baron replied as he reached for his wine glass. It was obvious he was being careful when responding to me. "My powers are beyond what the queens in the Quarter can manage, however."

Was that an answer? It didn't feel like an answer. "I'm just curious. Voodoo is one of those things that can take on many forms."

"Yes," Baron agreed.

"What about voices? Like ... do you hear voices when dealing with voodoo?"

"I believe voices can be heard no matter what tenets you follow," Baron replied. "Why?"

"Tiffany mentioned that Bonnie was talking out loud to Zeno, as if he were talking inside her brain and she was responding."

"Yes. You mentioned that outside." Baron cocked his head. "Why are you so caught up on that tidbit?"

"Because she's either hearing voices that aren't there, which tells me she's crazy, or she's listening to a voice that's going to drive her crazy," I replied. "Either way, she's in trouble."

"And what do you think we should do about that?" Rooster asked.

That was the question I'd been rolling over in my mind. "Before we got distracted today, I made a decision to go after the small armies Bonnie was trying to amass to forge her big army," I explained. "My plan was to start weeding out those armies and eradicating them."

"That sounds like a good plan," Winnie enthused.

"Totally," Tillie agreed. "I want to weed out some armies."

I wasn't surprised. There was little Tillie loved more than a fight. "I think we need to check our various communities for signs of invaders," I said instead of encouraging her. "Don't move on them. Just get locations. I'll handle taking them out."

Tillie made a protesting sound. "Um ... what fun is that for me?"

"It's not about fun. It's about making sure you guys don't get hurt fighting my battle," I fired back.

"It's not just your battle," Bay replied. She was deadly serious. "We're all fighting this battle, and there's nothing you can do to stop us from helping, so you need to get over that martyr thing right this second."

I rolled my eyes. "I'm not being a martyr."

"Yes, you are." Bay didn't back down. "We're used to it. We're not going to just accept it, though."

"Bay is right," Winnie interjected, drawing my eyes to her. "There's no way we're going to let you do this alone. So ... knock it off."

"Geez," I muttered under my breath.

"Tomorrow we'll start searching," Bay said. "I'll have Stormy and Easton start checking Shadow Hills, too. If it were me, I would be looking for cabins and vacation homes that are cut off from civilization and buried behind the snow. That doesn't mean all of them will be out there, though."

I nodded. It made sense. "Don't take on an enemy unless you're certain you can beat them," I warned. "If you're not certain, call for help."

"So far, Bonnie hasn't managed to lure any big armies to her side," Rooster noted. "Are we expecting that to change?"

I darted a look toward Baron, but he didn't respond. "I am concerned that the disgruntled lamias might come here in the hope that Bonnie can help them in her apex role. They want to be able to keep feeding on humans and paranormals. Bonnie might lie and tell them she can make it happen."

"And a slither of lamias coming to town might be detrimental to us all," Rooster surmised.

"I can't see how it would be a good thing," I agreed. "On the flip side, it's winter in Michigan. I don't know a lot of snakes that like that sort of weather. It's possible the lamias aren't going to come until the weather breaks."

"But we expect them to eventually come."

I held out my hands. "I don't know. It makes sense to me, though."

"We'll be on the lookout," Bay promised. "We'll figure it out." She lowered her voice. "You're not doing this alone, so don't even try."

I was both gratified and worried by her response. I needed her. I felt that to my very marrow. On the flip side, I would never get over losing her in one of my battles. How was I supposed to balance my needs with that knowledge? It wasn't something I couldn't wrap my head around. I would have to, though, because we were running out of time.

WHEN IT WAS TIME TO LEAVE, I WENT looking for Evan. He hadn't shown his face for dinner, and I was starting to get worried. His house was in Hemlock Cove. His aunt and uncle had left their farm to him, and that's where he holed up when he needed downtime.

He spent a lot of time at The Overlook, something he seemed to enjoy, but he'd been missing since I saw him on the patio. That didn't concern me as much as it piqued my curiosity. Because of that, I stretched out my magic, and found Evan on the bluff.

He wasn't alone.

I wasn't a dainty stepper, and yet the way Evan and Easton were focused on each other told me they hadn't heard my approach. I was careful not to breathe too loudly—I didn't want to get caught eaves-dropping or anything, because that would be undignified—and watched them interact.

I wasn't close enough to hear them talk to one another, but it was obvious they were having a serious conversation. Nothing about the way they interacted suggested a romantic relationship ... and that was what I was looking for. It wasn't until I'd been staring for a good three minutes that they finally touched.

It was a simple brush of the arm. Easton touched Evan. Then they smiled.

I knew in that moment that they were at least attracted to one another. Bay and Stormy were convinced they were about to embark on a love story for the ages. They tended to get worked up about stuff like that, though. I was more of a pragmatist.

My pragmatic heart did a long, slow somersault when Easton said something to Evan and they both burst out laughing. They were in their own little world. They hadn't even registered me. As much as I wanted to question them about what they were doing, why they'd snuck out to the bluff to be alone, I didn't. Instead, I showed my friend the respect he deserved and backed away.

When Evan was ready to talk about what was happening, he would talk about it. Until then, I had to be a good friend and stay out of his business. No matter how torturous it felt.

17
SEVENTEEN

I was tired when we got home—Rooster dropped us off—but I still waded into the snow to check the ward lines. I hadn't forgotten what Tim had told us the night before.

Gunner didn't comment when following me. Instead, he kept close and watched as I tugged on the ward lines to make sure they were holding. They were still as strong as ever. That didn't stop me from frowning at the prints on the other side of the lines.

"That's a lot of footprints," Gunner noted as he stood next to me.

"It is," I agreed. "It's a whole lot of ... something." I knelt down to get a better look. "Small feet here." I pointed.

"Dwarves," he surmised.

"Regular footprints there." I pointed toward a different set. "I bet those belong to the ghouls."

"I forgot all about the ghouls," he admitted.

"Those over there belong to the spider people." I pointed one last time.

"Did you have to remind me about the spider people?"

I didn't crack a smile when I looked over my shoulder at him.

"Baby, what is it?" he asked as he moved closer. "You're clearly upset."

"I'm not upset. I'm ... contemplating."

"What?"

"You're not going to like it."

"Then stop contemplating it."

That elicited a harsh laugh from me. "I can't. I'm afraid."

"Of what?"

"I'm afraid that this fight will kill people I care about."

"You're not contemplating doing something stupid to fix that, are you?"

"Define 'stupid.'"

"If you sacrifice yourself in a one-on-one with Bonnie, I'm going to be mad forever," Gunner warned. "I can practically see that idea going through your head. That's not allowed."

"I don't want to sacrifice myself. I don't exactly have a giving nature. But what if that's the way to save the most people?"

"That's not the way to save the most people."

"How do you know?" I was genuinely curious.

"Because there are a lot of people out there who you will be helping in the future. I guarantee you're not taking them into account."

"Probably not," I agreed. "Others could swoop in and save them, though."

"No. It has to be you." For once, there wasn't a hint of a smile on his face. "I'm going to be really angry if you seriously consider this as an option."

"I'm not considering it," I assured. "Well, mostly. My issue is what I did today. I knew that deflecting that magic into the ceiling was a bad idea, but I felt it was my only option because I can't go on a full attack against her."

"I can see that." The air was cold and crisp and yet neither of us made a move to head to the house. "What were you supposed to do?"

"I don't know. If I'd killed her, though, then even if I died after the fact, at least it would be over with. Nobody else would fall victim to her."

"Let's say you had done that." Gunner's tone was deceptively mild, telling me he was close to exploding. "What would've happened if Evan was the one to absorb the lamia magic instead? He was still in there, and an option for the magic to jump to."

It was something I hadn't considered. "Huh." I rubbed my cheek, absently noticing that my skin was freezing to the touch. "I wonder if Evan could survive it."

"Actually, I'm kind of wondering that too." Now Gunner did smile. "That would solve a lot of our problems."

"But would it work? Evan is already multiple things."

"Yes, but the vampire in him makes him practically unstoppable. It's a thought."

It was indeed a thought. "I won't risk him unless I know for certain he could survive it."

"Well, we won't risk you. We're going to have to come up with a solution." He held out his hand to me. "It's not happening tonight. You need sleep, and I need to feel you sleeping next to me. Tomorrow is a new day."

"I guess." I allowed him to tug me along. There was a heaviness hanging over us that I didn't often feel. I decided to lighten the mood. "When we were leaving The Overlook, I went looking for Evan."

"Did you find him? I wondered where he went."

"I did find him. He was out on the bluff. With Easton."

"Really?" Gunner's tone turned lascivious. "What were they doing?"

"Talking. Laughing. Touching."

"Touching? Like ... in a gross way?"

"No, in a way that two people touch when they're connecting on more than a physical level."

"Ah." Gunner nodded. "So, the rumors of their love match are not as exaggerated as we thought."

"Definitely not," I agreed. "There's something going on."

"I can't wait to give him grief about this."

I turned my glare to him. "You're not giving him grief."

"Oh, but I am. He gives me grief all the time. He says I'm whipped."

"You are whipped. There's nothing wrong with that."

"Since you're the one whipping me, why am I not surprised that you believe that?"

I couldn't hold back my smirk. "I'm not whipping you. That sounds kinky."

"I'm giving Evan a hard time about this," Gunner insisted. "It's happening."

"No, it's not." I was firm on that. "For now—just for now—you're going to let them find their own way and not say anything."

"And why am I going against my baser instincts?"

"Because Evan needs peace. He's slowly getting there. If he knows we're watching him and Easton too closely, then he'll pull away. He won't be able to stop himself."

"Oh, you're being dramatic," Gunner complained. "I can't see Evan pulling away simply because we give him a hard time. He likes busting my chops, and I like doing the same to him."

"I know, but I still want you to wait. Evan deserves some time to figure it out."

"He didn't give me time."

"We were already set in stone by the time he showed up on the scene."

"He didn't know that, though."

"I knew it. That means he knew it."

"Aw, so cute." Gunner pulled me close for a hug when we reached the front door of the cabin. "I knew it too."

"Is this you bucking for romance before bed?"

"No. I'm fine just cuddling up next to you. I'll even tolerate your frigid feet on mine tonight and not say a word."

It was a sweet offer. There was just one problem. "I had my heart set on romance. What a bummer."

He chuckled. "Well, now that you've brought it up, my heart is set on romance, too."

"Fancy that."

"It is a truly amazing development."

FALLING ASLEEP WAS LIKE PLUNGING DOWN A deep hole. I slid into the darkness and was content to stay there until I woke up. Instead, what had been a cave dream turned into a beautiful bluff overlooking an ocean I didn't recognize. When I looked around, I found a familiar face waiting for me.

"Seriously?" I planted my hands on my hips and glared at Agnes. "What are you doing in my head?" I recognized I was wearing overalls and frowned. "More importantly, why am I dressed like this?"

"It's your head," Agnes replied. I'd become accustomed to the sound of her voice, because when I asked the Wix questions, it sounded just like her when it answered. "You should ask yourself why you're wearing overalls."

"Yeah, there's no way I dressed myself like this." I vehemently shook my head. "This is all you."

"If you say so." Even though she was clearly intent on denying it, Agnes had a wide grin on her face as she regarded me. "You look tired."

"It's been a long few days." I moved to stand next to her on the bluff. "Where are we?"

"Nowhere. Everywhere." She shrugged. "This is what I always pictured Heaven looking like."

"Ah."

"Is this what you picture Heaven looking like?"

I didn't have to look around to debate my answer. "No. No

offense to you, but Evan and Gunner aren't here. Besides, I don't think I believe in Heaven."

"You don't believe in an afterlife?" Agnes cocked an eyebrow. "How can you of all people not believe we go on after everything you've seen?"

"I didn't say we didn't go on. I just said that I wasn't certain I believed in Heaven. Because—and hear me out—how would Heaven work? Say you want to surround yourself with all the people you love. Okay, fine, poof. There you go. There's everybody you love, including your ex-husband Joe who you never got over."

"You have an ex-husband named Joe?"

"No. It's just a 'for instance.'"

"Ah. Continue."

"What if Joe doesn't like you, though?" I challenged. "What if Joe's idea of Hell is you being in his Heaven? So ... what happens? If Joe isn't in my Heaven, then is it really Heaven? On the flip side, if Joe doesn't want me in his Heaven, what does that mean for him if I'm there?"

Agnes blinked. "You've given this a lot of thought," she said finally.

"These are the things I think about," I agreed. "I can't help myself."

"You have issues."

"I think it's a pragmatic approach."

Agnes waved her hand and a comfortable bench appeared. "Sit. You seem to be having a manic episode."

"I'm not manic." I sat even though I wasn't in the mood. I figured this was one of those dreams I wouldn't be able to control, so there was no point in not being comfortable. "I'm simply ... thinking."

"It's a dangerous thing when you think."

"Thanks for your support."

"Do you know why I'm here?"

"Probably because I've been doing a lot of thinking this evening about voices ... and books ... and what happens if we kill Bonnie and we don't have a replacement lined up. You're here to make sure I don't make a stupid decision and sacrifice myself."

When I risked a glance at Agnes, I found her watching me with unreadable eyes. "That's actually a pretty good overall assessment as to why I'm here."

"Well, you don't have to worry about me sacrificing myself," I assured her. "I said that in a moment of weakness. I'm far too pretty to sacrifice myself."

"You can cover all you want," Agnes said. "I know your heart, though. If it comes down to it, you're going to sacrifice yourself to save those you love. If you think that's your only shot, then you'll pull the trigger."

"Wouldn't you do the same?"

"Maybe, but there's something else you need to consider."

"And what's that?"

"You might not die."

I frowned. "If you're trying to deter me, that's not going to work. Not dying is the goal."

"Yes, but what happens if all that magic interacts badly with the magic you're already boasting? What happens if the magic, all that evil Zeno and Bonnie have been using it for, takes you over?"

My mouth fell open as the ramifications of what she was suggesting became a little too obvious. "Oh, crap."

"Yes, crap," Agnes agreed. "The loa might've told you he was afraid you would die, but that's not all he's afraid of."

"What about one of them?" I asked. "Could a loa absorb Bonnie's powers and survive?"

"In theory, yes. In practice? I can't be certain. Either way, we would be facing the same question if Baron Samedi absorbed all that power. It could change him. That power wasn't meant for him."

"Who was that power meant for?"

"That I can't answer. I don't know. Although, I do have an interesting idea."

"What's that?"

"Your friend Poet, she has a lamia friend."

"I've already thought of it," I said. "I don't think Raven is going to want the job."

"Oh, I don't either. Raven has made her choice. She's going to walk into mortality with her beloved. She's earned the right to pick her end, and she's done it."

"Okay." I cocked my head. "If you think Poet can absorb that much power, she can't. She's already absorbed a load of power."

"She has, and that type of power was never meant for her. She can't absorb another powerful being. The same with Charlie Rhodes."

"Then what are you getting at?" Something occurred to me quickly. "I am not putting one of the Winchesters in harm's way."

"The Winchesters have cultivated their own form of magic. It's relatively new in the grand scheme of things. They couldn't possibly survive taking in the lamia magic. And, even though hellcat magic is old, Stormy couldn't either."

"So ... what are my options?"

"Raven might not be your savior, but that doesn't mean someone in her family can't be."

I immediately started shaking my head. "No. I don't want another male apex. That will undo all the good Poet just did in Phoenix."

"I didn't say you should give the power to a man." Agnes pinned me with a dark look. "Ask Poet about Raven's mother."

I stilled. "Raven's mother is dead. I don't know much about her, but I know that."

"Or, perhaps, that's simply a story that Raven told people to protect her mother when she escaped."

I opened my mouth to shut down the idea, then closed it. "Huh," I said after a few seconds. "I can see Raven protecting her mother. How does that work in our favor, though?"

"Because Raven's mother has more reason than just about anybody to want to take over the lamia orders. She's also smart, dedicated, and she spends most of her time helping others now. That wasn't always her way, but she's done a lot of growing.

"She once fled to save herself," she continued. "I believe it's entirely possible that she can be convinced to return to save us all."

"Well, *that* was a bit dramatic," I said on a laugh.

"Just a little bit," Agnes agreed on a chuckle. "It's true, though. Raven's mother could take the power and then ride into Phoenix and take control of a floundering community. It would be in the best interests of us all."

"Wow." I didn't know what to say. "I'll talk to Poet."

"Good. Don't sacrifice yourself in the meantime. You dying would be bad enough. You living and hurting those you love because the magic changes you would be something else entirely." Agnes was serious as she leaned close to stare directly into my eyes. "That magic wasn't meant for you. Don't take it."

"Okay." I held up my hands. "I won't take it." I glanced down at the overalls again. "Can you please change my outfit? I seriously can't take another moment of this conversation if I have to be dressed like this."

Agnes laughed as if I was in the middle of a standup routine. "I happen to think the outfit suits you. Is there anything else you would like to discuss before I leave you to get your rest?"

"Just one thing." I tried to look chill and cool in my new outfit, but it was impossible, so I abandoned the effort. "I want to know about you. Did you sacrifice yourself?"

"Of course."

"Why is it okay for you to sacrifice yourself, but it's not okay for me?"

"Because I was sacrificing myself to make you stronger. The others in this area—actually, the others in this world—need you to be the strongest pixie apex you can be. Your strong witch genes enhanced what you're capable of. You haven't even touched on everything you can do yet, but you will in time."

"How did you know it was supposed to be me, though?" This was the question that had been bugging me ever since I'd become the pixie apex. "How did you know it wasn't supposed to be Emma? Or my parents? Or even Ezekiel?"

"Because they lack the strength you naturally possess." Agnes's expression was carved out of granite. "I know you want to be angry because you believe they left you behind—"

"I don't actually want to be angry about that."

She shushed me with her hands. "You might not want it—perhaps that was a poor choice of words—but you're angry. I get it. You believe all the hardships you would've gone through wouldn't have been so terrible if they'd kept you.

"Here's the thing, though," she continued. "You would not be as strong as you are if they'd kept you. All of you would likely be dead. If by some miracle you'd made it out, the loss of your family would've emotionally crippled you."

She wasn't saying anything I hadn't already considered. "Then there's the Poet factor," I added.

Now a small smile did make an appearance on Agnes's features. "Then there's the Poet factor," she agreed.

"Did they set it up? The loas I mean. Did they arrange it so we would find one another?"

"I can't answer that. They didn't confide in me, and rightly so. I have a big mouth and can't keep a secret."

I was amused despite myself and nodded. "I have that problem too."

"And yet, earlier tonight, you took a big, bold step into adulthood and didn't give Evan grief. You recognized he is trying to grow, too, and instead realized that it would be better if he came to you with his big news when it was time."

"I just want him to be happy."

"And I want you to be happy. As for your relationship with Poet, despite what you believe, the loas and gods can't control everything. Sometimes the universe makes the decision, and I think that's what happened with you and Poet."

It made me feel better to hear that. "Other than asking Poet about Raven's mother, what should I be doing?"

"Following your instincts. They won't let you down. When it's time, you'll know what to do."

"You have more faith in me than I do."

"That's because your greatest fear is letting down those you love. I don't have that fear where you're concerned. You will do what needs to be done. You *will* win. That's why I sacrificed myself. There will be other sacrifices, too. Just make certain you don't make the wrong one."

That was easier said than done, but I nodded all the same. "Can I go now?"

"You just want to get out of the overalls."

"You have no idea."

18

EIGHTEEN

G unner was spooned up behind me when I woke. His body was warm—he slept hot—and his arm was heavy as it rested over my hip. I was careful not to wake him as I thought about the dream.

A dream that wasn't really a dream.

As if to prove it, I heard a laugh from the other room. It was light and playful. I didn't bother going to check out the noise. I knew what it was. The Wix was letting me know that it wasn't a dream.

"Yeah, yeah, yeah," I muttered as I shifted in Gunner's arms. I'd thought I was sly, but he stirred.

"Why are you up?" he muttered in a sleepy voice.

"Because it's morning." I traced my finger over his beard. "I think the better question is, why aren't you up?"

"Shh." He pulled me against him. "It's quiet time."

He likely thought he could lull me back to sleep. That was unlikely, though. I was up and the day was in front of us. "Do you ever wonder where you would be if I hadn't come to town?"

He opened one eye. "Why are you starting the day with deep thoughts?"

I shrugged. "I'm just thinking."

"And what is it that you're thinking about?"

"I'm thinking about how things had to line up perfectly for us to get here."

"I happen to think we were meant to find each other."

"That's just it, though." I shifted so I could stare into his eyes. "How would we have found each other if I hadn't decided to take the opening up here?"

"We would've found a way."

"I only came up here because I was lost and floating. To get to the place I was at when I agreed to come up here, I had to lose Evan. To become as strong as I want, though, I had to get Evan back ... and find you ... and make friends with the Winchesters ... and reconnect with Poet."

"Actually, to reconnect with Poet, you had to make sure you could connect with her in the first place."

"Yeah ... and all of it feels as if someone was giving me nudges along the way to make sure I made it to this place."

Gunner stared at me for a beat, then shook his head. "Wow. You're really getting into the thick of things now, aren't you?"

"Yup." I bobbed my head. "I had a dream last night."

"Was I naked?"

I told him about it. When I was finished, he no longer looked as if he wanted to go back to sleep.

"Do you think that she was right?" he asked.

"Which part?"

"All of it, although we'll start with Raven's mother."

"Yeah, I found that part interesting." I rolled away from him and grabbed my phone.

"What are you doing?"

"What do you think?" I texted Poet. It was early. I didn't expect her to get back to me right away, but when the little dots popped up to tell me she was typing, I was secretly relieved.

"I don't like my morning cuddle being interrupted," he groused as I opened the laptop.

"You'll survive."

Poet answered quickly when I placed the video call.

"Why are you up so early?" I asked her by way of greeting.

She shrugged. "It's hard to keep constantly adjusting my internal clock so I tend to stick to East Coast time."

"That sounds horrible."

"I like seeing the sun rise on the water. It's fine." Her gaze was serious as it roamed my face. Next to her, there was a misshapen lump under the covers. It had to be Kade. "You look better."

"Yes, only a beauty such as mine can shine through the bedhead."

"I don't remember you being so cheery in the mornings. When did that happen?"

"I'm a cheery person regardless."

Gunner and Poet snorted in unison.

"You're obviously calling for a reason," she said when she'd recovered. "What's up?"

"We've had a few things happen." I caught her up. When I got to the dream, I was careful. "I know it was the real Agnes in the dream."

"I should think so," Poet agreed. "It's kind of neat that she can still annoy you from the great beyond."

"Yes, that's exactly what I was thinking," I replied dryly. "She mentioned something that I'm trying to wrap my head around."

"That doesn't sound good." Poet propped herself up on her pillows, ignoring Kade's disgruntled growl from beneath the covers. "What is it?"

There was no way I could get to the heart of matters without asking the obvious question, so I went for it. "Is Raven's mother alive?"

Shock rippled across Poet's features, then her forehead creased in concentration. "The first story Raven ever told me suggested her mother is dead."

I had to give her credit. That was a masterful way to talk around the question I'd asked. She didn't want to lie to me. She also didn't want to betray Raven. "I'm going to assume that's a yes," I offered. "You can continue to deny it. Agnes wouldn't have made that up."

Poet licked her lips, and I could practically hear the gears in her mind working. "Why would Agnes bring up Raven's mother?"

"Because she seemed to think that Raven's mother—she didn't mention a name—would be the perfect fit as the new lamia apex."

Poet opened her mouth, then shut it. Then she cocked her head. "Huh."

"Talk to Raven about it," I said. "She might give you the go-ahead to confirm to me that her mother is alive. At the very least, I'm betting she has a way to contact her mother."

"I can talk to Raven," Poet said. "I'm not sure this is going to turn out the way you want it to turn out, though. If Raven's mother is still alive—and I'm not saying she is—but if she is, why would she want to ruin all the work she put into making herself disappear?"

"I don't know. Just off the top of my head, though, as the new apex, she would be able to order around the male-dominated slithers. Didn't you tell me Raven's father is the head of one of those slithers?"

Realization flashed on Poet's face. "Oh, wow. That might be funny."

"Not that Raven's mother is alive or anything," I teased.

"Definitely not," she agreed. "I'll talk to Raven, though, and get back to you."

"Awesome." I leaned back, some of the weight I'd been carrying dissipating. "What's up with Perky McPerkison next to you? Does he not like getting up before the sun?"

"Not really," Poet replied. "He likes to sleep in."

"You could join him. Get another few hours of sleep."

"I might." Poet flashed a smile. "You're okay otherwise, though, right?"

I couldn't lie to her any more than she could lie to me. "Other than the fact that I can't seem to stop thinking about the way the loas and gods have likely lined us up like dominos."

"If you think about that stuff too much, you're going to drive yourself crazy," she warned. "You can't change the past. You have to move forward. So what if they arranged it so we would meet?"

"Doesn't that bug you?"

"You've always let the little things in life bug you. That's not who I am."

"I don't let the little things bug me," I argued.

Gunner snorted again. Then he had the gall to adopt an innocent expression when I glared at him. "Baby, I love you, but come on. You spent an entire week obsessing about the fact that the witch you were fighting was wearing dress slacks."

"You do not wear anything that has to be dry cleaned to a witch fight," I insisted.

He held up his hands in supplication. "I'm just saying."

They were right. I did tend to obsess about the little things in life. When the big things happened, I just reacted. When the little things cropped up, I turned into an idiot. "I'll do my best to keep looking forward," was all I could say.

"You're smart, Scout," Poet said. "You're loyal. There's a reason I never forgot you. Don't lose yourself in all of this. Just ... keep looking forward. If you second guess all the things the loas and gods might've done, you'll go crazy."

"And we already have Bonnie," Gunner pointed out. "We don't need any more crazy."

"I know. I just feel that we're about to get buried."

"Because Bonnie is going to keep bringing in people to distract you?"

"Yup."

"Well ... can you do anything about it?"

"Just kill her allies."

"Well, maybe you should focus on that."

"You read my mind."

. . .

WE SHOWERED, DRESSED, FED THE CAT, and then headed into town for breakfast. Graham hadn't texted to say he was coming, which meant we were on our own. Since I wanted something big—eggs and hash browns were a must this morning—that meant we had to go to the local diner.

It was bustling with activity when we went through the door, and one of the first things I noticed was Graham sitting at his regular table. He had his reading glasses in place and looked to be studying something on his phone.

"Oh, well, this is just crap," Gunner complained as he started in Graham's direction. "Seriously?" he snapped when he got to his father. "I assumed you were over in Hemlock Cove. I mean...why wouldn't you deliver breakfast otherwise?"

Graham slowly lifted his chin and regarded his son. "I am not your errand boy."

"You're supposed to love me so much you want to bring me breakfast." Gunner sat down in front of Graham. "I mean ... I'm your bouncing baby boy."

"I kind of want to bounce your head off a wall right now," Graham muttered.

I sat next to Gunner and glanced around the diner. It was one of the first places I'd eaten at in town, and the food was typical for this sort of place. I was a fan of grease, so I fit right in. For some reason, the vibe I normally got from the diner wasn't there this morning, though.

No, something was off.

"How long have you been here?" I asked Graham.

He shot me a dirty look. "Since when are you the breakfast police?"

"I'm not asking because I'm being a baby like your son," I replied. "I just ... don't you feel that?"

Graham's eyebrows moved toward one another. "Don't I feel what?"

"That."

"That what?"

How could I explain what I was feeling to him? "I don't know." I looked around one more time. Nothing seemed out of the ordinary. I couldn't shake the feeling that something was off, though. I didn't like it in the least. "I guess it's nothing."

Graham kept his eyes on me a beat longer. "Did you sleep okay?" he asked finally. "You're a little pale."

"I had a weird dream."

"Was Gunner naked in it?"

That had me choking on a laugh. "You guys are way too much alike," I complained. "I mean ... geez. Do you know that's the exact same thing he said to me?"

"Great minds," Gunner teased, poking my side. My gaze was on him, so I saw when he looked up to greet whoever was coming over to take our order. His smile disappeared too fast for my liking, and I swiveled.

Mindy, the daughter of the diner owner Mable, looked as if she'd been through a war. Mable insisted on her workers wearing uniforms—the sort that I'd only ever seen in ancient television shows—and Mindy's had rips on each side. Her face was also pale and bare of makeup. Since I'd never seen her with anything other than three layers of makeup, it was jarring.

"Hey, Mindy," Gunner said as he took her in. Obviously, he realized there was something wrong with her too. "How are things? Were you out partying last night?"

Mindy eyed him with about as much interest as I reserved for cold carrots as an entree. "What do you want?" she asked blandly.

I exchanged a quick look with Graham. He seemed to be watching Mindy with as much trepidation as I felt.

"Are you feeling okay, Mindy?" Graham asked, drawing her

attention to him. "Maybe you should rest if you're not feeling well. I'm sure your mother would understand."

"No she wouldn't," Mable barked as she moved toward our table. "There's nothing wrong with that girl that a good swift kick in the behind wouldn't fix. She was out late last night. Actually, she's been out late three nights in a row. She did this to herself, and I don't feel sorry for her."

I attempted to muster a smile for Mindy's benefit and came up empty. "Well, if it was a good party, maybe she thinks it was worth it," I said.

"Oh, it definitely wasn't worth it." Mable waved her hand in front of her face. "Seriously, you smell like gas. Go wash yourself down or something. I'll take their order."

Mindy didn't react to her mother, which was something I couldn't ever remember seeing. From the first moment I'd met Mindy, she'd been a bubbly mess. On top of that, she'd been completely and totally in love with Gunner. To the point where she actually swooned whenever he smiled at her. She had barely reacted to him today.

Mindy stared at her mother for what felt like a really long time and then turned on her heel and walked away. It wasn't anger fueling her, though. There was no energy—good or bad—to be found. Mindy was just there. Not really living.

"That girl, I swear, is turning into her father." Mable didn't look happy as she held up her order pad. "I've never seen her act like she has been."

I was careful when venturing forward. "Just out of curiosity, was she acting normally up until three days ago?"

Graham shot me a sharp look but didn't speak. He just watched me.

"Normal for her," Mable replied. "I mean ... the girl is hardly what I would consider a go-getter. She whines a lot. Sometimes she whines about you."

"About us?" Gunner made a face. "Why would she whine about us?"

"It's Scout mostly," Mable replied. "She believes that Scout came in and stole you right out from under her nose."

Gunner looked appalled. "But..."

"Oh, you don't have to explain yourself," Mable assured him. "I get it. You always flirted with her a little bit—in a respectful way—because you knew she had a crush on you. Her nose has been out of joint since Scout came to town. She thinks Scout stole you from her or something."

That might've explained some of Mindy's attitude. There was more bubbling beneath the surface of that previously happy young woman than her nose being out of joint, though. Rather than say that, I waited.

Mable took our orders, and as soon as she was gone, I drew Gunner and Graham closer. "Mindy is possessed."

Graham rubbed his cheek. "Like in *The Exorcist*?"

"More like she's been infected by some sort of creature. She's under the thrall of something."

"Like Brandon with the vampires?"

I nodded.

"How can you be sure of that?" Gunner asked. "I mean... I'm not saying you're wrong, but she's young and still lives with her mother. It's entirely possible that she's just in a bad mood because she's too old to be living with a parent. I mean ... that is like a slow death."

"Thanks, son," Graham said dryly.

"You're welcome, Dad," Gunner shot back, his grin sunny.

"No, it's more than that." As much as I wished this was just a case of an annoyed daughter wanting some space from her mother, I knew better. "I told you there was something wrong when we got here. It's Mindy."

"Okay." Graham held out his hands. "What is it?"

"I don't know." I looked over toward the counter, to where Mindy was standing. She stared into nothing, as if waiting for prompting. I was just about to turn back when I saw something. It was a shadow working from inside Mindy ... and it had a very specific shape. "Wait."

I pulled out my phone and started typing.

"Who are you texting?" Gunner asked.

"Are you worried she's got another pretty boy whiner boyfriend you don't know about?" Graham challenged.

"Oh, please." Gunner was haughty. "I'm so much more than a pretty boy whiner. I'm also a gifted lover."

"I cannot believe you just said that in front of your own father," Graham complained.

I was right there with him. I didn't engage in their conversation, though. Instead, I just messaged Doc for confirmation on my suspicion. It didn't take long to get it.

"Mindy is definitely possessed," I said after I read the message.

"By the devil?" Gunner wrinkled his nose. "I'm not in the mood to fight the devil."

"Well, you're going to wish you weren't just being so flippant because this is clearly karma for you."

Gunner waited, confusion knitting his eyebrows.

"I saw a shadow a few minutes ago," I explained. "She's got an entity squatting inside of her."

"Well, don't drag it out, Scout," Graham said. "What's the entity?"

"It's the spider people. I forgot that they can take humans over and turn them into mindless drones. Doc just confirmed it for me, though."

Gunner visibly blanched. "They can take people over?"

"Yup. If they were to take you over, for example, they would make you eat bugs and live in a web."

"Ugh. Why did you tell me that?" Gunner whined. "You know I'm going to turn into a big baby now."

I *did* know that. Sadly, it was the least of my worries. "We need to eat breakfast as if it's a normal day. Then we need to come up with a plan away from Mindy."

"Do you think we can save her?" Graham asked.

There was no hesitation before I answered. "Yes, but it's not going to be easy."

"Well, we have to do what we have to do. We can't just let them take her."

At least we were on the same page there. That was something. It didn't feel like enough though.

19
NINETEEN

G unner picked up the tab for breakfast and then we moved outside, leaving Gunner's truck behind so we could move Graham's truck to a side street. There we had a clear view of the back door in case Mindy left. That's when I told them what I'd double checked with Doc.

"I had a vague memory from all the book work we had to do when I was tested for the group," I explained. "I remembered something about the spider people. They have a queen. She can control actual spider people ... and anybody they bite."

"I think I'm going to need more than that," Graham said. "Are you saying Mindy was bitten?"

"That's exactly what I'm saying," I confirmed.

"But ... how?"

"I'm guessing that Mindy went to a party or something. That's basically what her mother intimated, right?"

"Mindy is young," Gunner replied from the passenger seat. He opened the glove box and eyed the candy that was still in there. "There's not a lot to do in this town if you're young and not hunting monsters." He shot an imploring look toward his father. "Can't I please have the candy?"

"No." Graham reached over and shut the glove box. "I bought that for Marnie."

"Then give it to her and stop torturing me."

To my surprise—although not really when I thought about it a little bit—Graham reached into the console between the two seats and came back with a bag of peanut M&Ms. They were one of Gunner's favorite snacks. "If I give you these, will you stop making all that noise so I can talk to your girlfriend?"

"Yes," Gunner replied.

"You shouldn't be eating candy this early." Graham relinquished the bag. "You just had breakfast."

"Thank you, Daddy," Gunner said in his prettiest voice.

Even though he was clearly annoyed, Graham's lips curved. "You be quiet. Scout and I have adult things to talk about." He angled himself so he could meet my gaze in the backseat. "If there's a queen, where was she when you guys were out at the cabins?"

That was a good question. "Maybe she doesn't stay with the drones. Maybe her lair is separate, as an added layer of security."

"Okay, I can buy that I guess. Does that mean there are more of those spider creatures you guys took out running around?"

"I don't know." I shrugged. "That would be my guess, though."

"No more spiders," Gunner muttered as he chewed his M&Ms. "They're gross and freaky."

"I'll handle the spiders," I assured him. "They're easy to kill. Throw some fire at them and that's all she wrote."

"What about the queen, though?" Graham asked.

"I've never actually seen a queen," I admitted. "Evan and I took on a nest in Detroit but there wasn't a queen. I think that's why I forgot what I read."

"What does Doc say?" Gunner asked as he happily munched.

"He says that if we can take out the queen, then we can save Mindy."

"What's the point of taking over Mindy?" Graham asked. "Not that I'm not happy to be able to save her—she's not a favorite, but Mable is—but I'm curious what she could possibly do for this queen?"

"She can act as a sentry. Spy on us. We noticed there was something wrong with her, but only because she's normally so bubbly and chipper."

"Plus she tries to rub herself all over me whenever she sees me," Gunner added.

"That too."

"I forgot about her crush on you." Graham smirked. "You always were popular with the ladies."

"I get it from my Dad." Gunner winked at him.

"Oh, geez. You guys run hot and cold on each other like nobody's business." I shook my head. "Let's focus on the problem at hand, because if Mindy has been infected, I'm guessing whoever she was partying with was infected too. We need to get her isolated so we can look inside her head."

"And what do you expect to find there?"

"I don't know. I wouldn't mind a location for the queen."

"If we kill the queen, that will be a blow to Bonnie," Graham surmised.

"Yup, and if we upset Bonnie, she might stop bringing in minions and try to protect the ones she currently has."

"Do you think that's probable?"

I shrugged. "It can't hurt to try, right?"

"Definitely not."

THE BREAKFAST SHIFT ENDED AT ELEVEN O'CLOCK. Mindy was the first one out through the back door when it was time to leave. She got in on the passenger side of a truck I didn't recognize and they took off like a shot.

"Who is driving that truck?" I asked as Graham started to follow.

"Bart Buckley," Graham replied. He didn't look happy. "He's quite a bit older than Mindy."

"Is he paranormal?"

"No." Gunner shook his head. "He went to school with me. He was two years older. He was a bully. You know, one of those guys who gets off trying to give other guys wedgies."

"Yeah, that's totally a guy thing," I said. "Girls don't do that to each other."

"No, but girls throw tampons at each other and stuff."

I frowned. "I've only ever seen that in the movie *Carrie*."

"That doesn't mean it's not true."

"Oh, it's sad that all your knowledge of girls comes from movies," I said. "It's just ... really, really sad. For the record, we don't freeze each other's bras at sleepovers either."

"Don't crush his dreams and tell him the pillow fights aren't real," Graham warned.

"The pillow fights aren't real?" Gunner sounded anguished. "That is just not fair. How am I even supposed to continue knowing this?"

I didn't want to laugh—it would only encourage him after all—but I couldn't help myself. "I think I need to give you a crash course on reality versus fantasy."

"Oh, my little boy is going to be forced to grow up," Graham teased. His smile didn't last long when Bart's truck turned down a side road. "Where are they going?"

I focused on the neighborhood we'd found ourselves in. "What's out here?"

"Not much," Graham replied.

"That's not true," Gunner countered. "There's the trailer park."

Graham and Gunner exchanged weighted looks.

"What sort of trailer park?" I asked when neither of them said anything else.

"It's the sort of trailer park people live in," Graham replied. He looked to be choosing his words carefully. "A lot of the people who live out here are just trying to get by. They don't want to cause trouble."

"But?" I prodded.

"But a lot of the other people are looking to cause trouble," he replied. "We're called out here at least three times a week."

"There's a lot of partying," Gunner explained. "I wouldn't say we have a prostitution problem, but there are a few people who like to make their rent by turning their trailers into mini brothels."

"There's drugs too," Graham added. "They don't cook it out here —that would be a death sentence if there was ever a fire because the trailers are practically on top of one another—but they package it and sell it out here."

I considered what they were telling me. "Okay, but why would the spider queen be out here?"

"How do you know she is?"

"It's just a feeling."

Graham didn't say anything for a long time, then he sighed. "Well, I've learned not to argue with your feelings. Should we call in the others?"

"Yes," Gunner said around his half-chewed M&Ms.

"No," I replied. "I very much doubt Bonnie is out here. I can take on the spider people myself. You guys can wait here."

Graham's eyes went wide, his mouth slack. Then he started shaking his head. "I'm not just going to leave you to handle everything on your own, Scout. That's not who I am."

"She can totally take the spider people," Gunner argued. "She's good at it. In fact, we should call Evan. He likes ripping their heads off."

"Let's call Evan," Graham agreed.

"I don't need Evan," I said as Graham's truck rolled to a standstill near the entrance to the park. "I've got this." I unfastened my seatbelt and opened the door. "You guys wait here. I won't be long."

"Scout!" Graham looked perplexed. He didn't exit the truck, though. Instead, he turned to Gunner and started yelling.

Gunner yelled right back—that was their way after all—but I didn't focus on them. I didn't have to. The magic emanating from this park was through the roof. I was completely surrounded. So were they, although it was best they didn't realize that.

I moved to the middle of the main road. I didn't want anybody being able to jump out of the bushes—not that there was a lot of landscaping in this particular park—and reached out with my senses. I could feel eyes crawling over me. So many sets I couldn't even count them. They were all around me, telling me that they'd taken over the entire park.

When I heard crunching on the gravel behind me, I didn't turn around. I knew from the heavy way they walked that it was Gunner and Graham. They might not have wanted to tangle with the spider people. They loved me too much to let me do it alone, though. That's simply how they were built.

I cleared my throat. "Is there someone in charge here?" I called out. "I would like to have a discussion."

"Take me to your leader," Gunner muttered under his breath. It wasn't even worth chastising him because he wasn't wrong.

I could hear scrambling inside the trailer directly in front of me. When the door opened, I held my breath, and wasn't disappointed. The creature that came out was taller than the others. She wasn't broader but was obviously stronger.

The queen. Given the rundown state of the trailer park, however, this wasn't much of a kingdom.

"Hey." I offered up an awkward wave as I took in her ankle-length black skirt and white top. It made for a striking combination on her statuesque figure. "I'm Scout Randall."

The queen looked at me, then stared behind me at Graham and Gunner, and then turned her attention back to me. "You shouldn't be here," was all she said.

"Yes, well, I'm not great at following rules. I don't often do what I'm supposed to do."

"Isn't that the truth," Graham muttered from behind me.

"I am here, though," I continued. "I would like to have a discussion with you."

"A discussion?" The queen let loose an eerie laugh. "You don't strike me as the sort of person who likes to discuss things. You're more of a 'shoot first, ask questions later' witch."

"I don't really deal with guns, so that's not an apt analogy."

"You shoot your magic, don't you?"

She wasn't wrong. "Let's get to the discussion," I pressed. "I need you to release all the humans you've enslaved. I also need you to tell me where I can find Bonnie. If you do that, I'll let you and your drones leave."

To me, it sounded like a great offer. The queen obviously thought otherwise. "So, we get what exactly?" she challenged.

I didn't back down or change my tack despite her tone. "You get to live. Trust me when I say, if this comes down to a fight, I'm going to have no choice but to kill you all."

"And do you really think you're capable of that?" She looked dubious. The fact that she had multiple eyes in her chin wasn't doing much for my distraction level either.

"I know I'm capable of killing you all," I replied. No hesitation. No regrets. "I don't want to unless I have no choice. I do have another question, though."

"And what's that?"

"Can you see out of the eyes in your chin? Because that's just gross. Actually ... it's gross whether you can see out of them or not. Why do you have so many eyes?"

"Spiders have eight eyes," Gunner volunteered out of nowhere. It was impossible to miss the sound of Graham swatting him. "What? They do. I did some reading after our first encounter with them. They have eight eyes and yet still can't see very well."

"Thank you for that National Geographic special report," Graham said dryly. "Now ... shut up."

"Fine. I thought I was helping, though."

It took everything I had not to turn around and admonish them. I knew that I would be attacked if I showed the queen my back, however, so I remained focused on her.

"What if I don't believe you're capable of killing us?" the queen challenged.

I could've responded with words, but I went right for the big power flex instead and threw my magic at two of her drones as they tried to creep up on my right. They burst into flames immediately, their screams lingering for a few seconds, and when the fire dissipated, they were gone.

"I can do that to the whole park," I explained. "I can do it to you."

"And the people of this town who have joined my team?" she asked. "Will you sacrifice them too?"

"Yup." I dipped my chin. "I'm not Superman you see. I can't save everybody. It's not possible. That means I have to save the greatest number of people, and to do that, I have to end the threat you pose. If that means I have to lose the people in this park to save the whole town, I'll do what I have to do."

"Just like that?"

"Just like that." I was firm. Somehow, I even managed not to shudder when all of her eyes zeroed in on me. "What do you say?"

"I say that I want you dead."

That was pretty much what I thought she would say, and yet I couldn't help being a little disappointed. "Fine." I tossed more pixie fire magic at the group of Arachnids that were trying to sneak between two trailers. They kept low to the ground but against the snow, they were impossible to miss.

The queen jerked when they screamed, rage rolling off her in waves. When she turned back to me, her hands were gripped into fists at her sides.

"Listen up," I said when she just stood there and seethed. "I can do everything that I promised. As gross as I find you guys—you're pretty freaking disgusting—I still don't want to kill you all. It feels destructive to me, and I'm trying to draw a firm line in the sand between Bonnie and me.

"Now, I don't know how you hooked up with her," I continued. "It doesn't matter to me in the grand scheme of things, though. I don't care if she threatened your people. I don't care if she paid you. I care that you're gone.

"You *are* going to release the people you've bitten and enslaved," I promised. "If not, I'm just going to kill you and see what happens. I think, under those circumstances, that whatever spell you've cast over these people will die with you. If I'm wrong, it's going to suck, but nobody else is going to get hurt.

"Your only option here is to release them yourself and tell me what I want," I said. "There isn't going to be a negotiation. That's your only option. Period."

The queen's eyes narrowed—all eight of them, including the ones in her chin—and if hate was next to a photo in the dictionary, it would be her photo. "How is it that you think you get to make the decisions here?"

"Because I'm the true queen," I replied. "You might be queen of the spider people, which actually isn't any better than being queen of the monkey people, but I'm the queen of everything else. Bonnie and I are on a crash course to oblivion. I'm sure she didn't tell you that. She probably offered up some vague promise she's never going to fulfill. That doesn't matter either, though. What matters is that you're going to give me what I want."

"You can't kill us all," she spat.

I burned more spiders between trailers to prove her wrong. I didn't know where they'd come from. I didn't care. Even if she had a hundred soldiers, though, I'd managed to wipe out a decent chunk of her army without breaking a sweat.

"So, do we have a deal?" I asked.

"No," the queen spat back. "We don't have a deal. I don't know where the lamia is."

"Fine. Release the townspeople, give them to us, and then find out where Bonnie's lair is. I'll trust you long enough to do that."

"You probably shouldn't trust them," Graham said in a low voice. "Just burn it all and be done with it."

I knew the queen had heard him by the way her breath came out in a gusty hiss. I managed to hold back a smile ... although just barely. "Do you think you can do as I've requested?" I asked her.

"We'll release the minions," she said finally. It looked as if it took a lot of effort for her to say it. "I will see if I can find the lair."

"Great." I shot her a thumbs-up. "You have twenty-four hours. If you don't provide me with the location of the lair between now and then, I'm going to burn your whole kingdom to the ground. Do we have an understanding?"

"Yes."

"Awesome." I was triumphant when I flicked my eyes to Gunner and Graham. "See. I was calm, cool, and collected. You guys doubted me, and I came through without killing them all. I think that deserves a reward."

"The day isn't over yet," Graham countered.

"No, but I'm going to win."

"I do like your healthy sense of competition." He squeezed my shoulder. "We need to get these people out of here."

I nodded. "Yeah. Then we'll figure out our next move."

Graham winked at me. "I'm looking forward to it."

20
TWENTY

Our next stop was the Rusty Cauldron. I had to catch the others up on what I'd done. I thought I'd acted appropriately. The surreptitious looks Gunner and Graham kept slipping each other told me they believed otherwise.

When I strode up to Rooster in the bar, I was determined to present my case like a pro. Unfortunately, Gunner had other plans.

"She made a deal with the spider people, and now we can't kill them," Gunner lamented. "The town is going to be overrun by Friday. We're all going to have eyes in our chin and live in webs."

I tracked my eyes to him. "Really?"

"What?" Gunner shot back. "It's true."

"You're so freaking dramatic." I shook my head. "The town is not going to be overrun. In fact, we have five members of the town currently sitting in the jail recovering."

"Why are they in jail?" Rooster asked. His expression was impossible to read.

"Because we wanted to make sure that the queen didn't activate them a second time," Graham replied. "Marnie and Twila are on their way over here with a potion that will ensure that."

"Okay." Rooster nodded. "Fair enough." His eyes moved back to me. "And you made this deal because ... why again?"

"Because we need to know where Bonnie's lair is," I replied. I refused to back down. "They don't know—and, quite frankly, it makes sense Bonnie wouldn't be keeping them updated with her current whereabouts—but they all have eight eyes each. If somebody can find Bonnie's lair, it's them."

"Uh-huh." Rooster rolled his neck. "I thought the plan was to kill everybody Bonnie was bringing into town to add to her army."

"I can still kill them."

"Wouldn't we all be happier if you'd already killed them, though?" he challenged.

"I know I would be." Gunner hopped up on a stool and tapped the bar. "I need something to obliterate the image of the queen and her six-eyed chin, please."

Whistler nodded. "You've got it."

Next to him, a head appeared out of nowhere. Tillie, dressed in a purposely distressed shirt with angel wings on it and her bra visible through the slits, made her presence known. "I think what Scout did was spot-on," she said.

I smiled. "Thank you."

"I mean ... they're spider people. They're not that smart. I'm sure she cast a spell to make sure they didn't turn around and double-cross her."

Now I faltered. "Well..."

Tillie arched an eyebrow. "Come on. You're the pixie apex. You could've forced them to do your bidding. Why did you trust a spider queen to follow the rules? That's just sad."

I made a face. "I killed like twenty of them."

"Yes, and from what I understand, you could've killed all of them without breaking a sweat," Rooster said. "I mean ... how do you know they only had the five townspeople under their control? They could have another thirty of them out there and we have no way of knowing."

He wasn't wrong. "I still think I did the right thing. She's going to come through."

"Uh-huh." Rooster shook his head. "You know what, Scout? I didn't expect you to be the one to go soft."

Was he purposely poking me right now? If so, the stick was sharp. "I did not go soft. I just don't want to wipe out an entire pack of spiders—are they called a pack?—if I don't have to."

"Clutter," Doc volunteered from his regular booth.

I turned my narrow-eyed glare to him. "What?"

"A pack of spiders is called a clutter," he replied, not looking up.

"Well, thank you for that tidbit. I appreciate it." That was only kind of true. "As for the queen, I think she's going to come through."

"And if she doesn't?" Rooster challenged.

"Then I'll kill her."

"She could already be dead."

He was on my last nerve. "While I get that you would prefer that I do things your way, you're not the one killing everything in sight," I shot back. "Maybe I don't want to kill constantly. It's not going to hurt anything to see if they do what they say they're going to do. I gave them twenty-four hours. At worst they're going to run. At best, though, they're going to give me what I want."

Rooster looked taken aback. "I didn't mean that I thought it was easy for you to kill," he started.

"That's exactly what you meant." I shook my head. "All of you basically think I should be the one doing the killing. I get that. Maybe you guys should go out and kill the entire cluster of spiders."

"Clutter," Doc corrected.

I shot him the finger and turned away, focusing on the window. I knew they were trading looks behind my back. Was I being a bit of a baby? Yes. I just didn't want to wipe them all out until I had no other choice. There would be a lot of killing in my future—*a lot* of it—and I didn't want to embrace the dark side if I didn't have to.

"Scout, I think maybe you have a point," Rooster said after

several seconds. "I didn't realize how much pressure I was putting on you."

"I'm fine," I replied. "I'll kill them if I have to."

"Okay, but ... I don't just want you here because you're good at killing."

"That's exactly why you want her here," Marissa volunteered. She was seated at a different booth from Doc. "We all know it. What's more, she knows it. Personally, I'm hoping when this prophecy thing is finished, that she goes. There won't be as many things to kill here once it's over with, and she'll be bored."

"Shut up, Marissa," Gunner snarled.

"Yes, shut up," Rooster agreed. "Scout isn't going anywhere. If anybody is going anywhere, it's you. In fact—" Whatever Rooster was going to say was drowned out by his ringing phone. He answered right away, and when I turned back to him, he looked far too apologetic.

"I don't need people feeling sorry for me," I said when Gunner moved closer. "Just ... don't."

The door behind me opened, but I didn't look over my shoulder to see who was entering. I already knew.

"Why does this room feel as if it's about to explode with anxiety?" Evan asked.

"Scout basically told everybody she's not their personal assassin, and now everybody feels bad," Marissa explained. "I don't feel bad, mind you, but everybody else does. Scout regrets saying anything because she hates being pitied more than being looked at as a killing machine. It's all very *Days of Our Lives*."

"Huh." Evan moved closer to me. "Do you want to take a walk?" he asked in a low voice.

Not really. It was cold out. "I'm fine," I insisted.

"Yes, I can tell by the rigid way you're carrying yourself that you're fine." Evan looked up when Rooster viciously swore under his breath and disconnected the call. "What's wrong?"

"It's Raisin," Rooster replied, making a face. Ruthie "Raisin"

Morton was essentially his surrogate daughter. He hadn't legally adopted her, but he handled most everything a father would for her. "Apparently she's in the principal's office."

"What did she do?" I asked, forcing myself to focus on something other than my issues.

"The secretary said that she was caught sneaking a weapon into the school," Rooster replied. "Someone needs to sit down with the principal, but I'm expecting a call from the main office regarding these spiders."

I didn't think on it long. "I'll go," I offered.

Rooster immediately started shaking his head. "It's not your responsibility."

"I thought we shared responsibilities around here."

"Yeah, but ... Scout, I don't want to pile more pressure on you," Rooster admitted. "Whether you meant everything you said or not, it's obvious that maybe you need a bit of a break."

"I'm pretty sure I can handle a high school principal."

"Yeah, but—"

I cut him off with a shake of my head. "I've got it. Don't worry about it, okay?" I turned to walk out the door. Of course, it didn't occur to me that I didn't have a vehicle until I was in the parking lot.

Evan was the one who found me standing in the same place two minutes later. He smiled—that same arrogant, insufferable smile that used to drive me nuts years ago—and shook the keys in his hand. "Graham gave me the keys to his truck."

I wasn't expecting that. "Why? He doesn't even let Gunner drive his truck."

"I think that's why he gave them to me. Gunner is whining."

"About the truck or you telling him you would be the one going with me?"

"Both," Evan replied. "He wants to comfort you but isn't sure how. I said I would handle it."

"So, you're going to the school with me?"

"Yup." He spun the keys around his finger. "And we're taking Graham's truck because that makes Gunner want to cry."

It took everything I had to hold back a sigh. "Fine. I don't want to talk about anything serious, though."

"That's okay. You don't have to talk. We'll just sit together in uncomfortable silence."

"I'm fine with that."

"Yeah, we'll see how long that lasts."

IT LASTED EXACTLY THREE MINUTES. THAT'S WHEN I let loose a sigh as Evan navigated us toward the high school.

"I shouldn't have said what I said."

"Why not?" Evan didn't look nearly as worked up as the others had. "If you're feeling stressed because everybody looks to you for answers, I think you should be able to express your feelings."

"I'm fine."

"You say that even when you're not fine."

"I'm always fine."

"No, you're not. You're not fine right now. You have too much going on inside that head of yours. Tell me what's got you riled up, and I guarantee you'll feel better when you're finished."

"You guarantee it, huh?"

"I do."

"Fine." I kept saying fine. Was I really fine, though? It seemed I wasn't. I hadn't realized I wasn't fine until I was already careening over an emotional cliff. "If I just keep killing to get my way, what keeps me from turning into Bonnie?"

Other than a slight eyebrow hop, Evan didn't respond.

"I thought we were going to talk," I complained after a few seconds.

"I didn't realize that you were voicing a real concern," Evan replied. "The thing is, Scout, it's impossible for you to turn into Bonnie. I don't understand why you're suddenly worried about this."

"I keep thinking about the time I spent with her. It's been said that some of what she showed me had to be real, because otherwise it's just too much to keep up on. So, at what point did the real stuff give way to the evil stuff? Would I even notice if it was happening to me?"

"I'm pretty sure the evil stuff took over when she realized she was going to die. She opened herself up to it and that was that. You always try to do the right thing, Scout. Bonnie never did. Stop second-guessing yourself. It bugs me."

"How can you be so sure?"

"Because you healed my soul, Scout. Evil can't do that."

I slid my eyes to him. "Are you sure you're not just saying that because we're besties?"

He smirked. "I'll always stand by you. I don't ever worry that I'll be doing evil again when that happens, though. Just take a breath. You're dealing with a lot right now."

"Yeah." I scratched my cheek. "I still can't figure out why I volunteered to deal with the principal. If I'm so overwhelmed, why did I add more to my plate?"

"Because you love Raisin ... and it was a way for you to escape. You didn't want them all coming up to you and apologizing. You can't deal with that. It irritates you."

He wasn't wrong. "Why do you think Raisin brought a weapon to school?"

"Who knows. That kid is around a lot of weird stuff. She might've decided she needed a weapon to protect herself."

"I guess."

"We'll find out soon enough."

"I hope I don't have to kill the principal."

"I would say odds are low for that."

THE SECRETARY SEEMED CONFUSED WHEN I introduced myself and explained why I was there.

"I thought Mr. Tremaine was coming." The secretary's name-plate read Susan Sutton. She looked as if she'd been sitting behind her current desk at least ten years too long. She had that strained thing going on, a tight smile that she whipped out for annoyed parents while secretly wishing she could retire.

"He has other business," I replied. "I'm here to deal with the matter."

"And your relationship with Ruthie is what?"

"I'm her big sister." It wasn't that much of a stretch. I did often feel like Raisin's big sister. I had a better relationship with her than Emma. Plus, for some reason, Raisin reminded me of me. I wanted to protect her for that reason alone.

"Um..." Susan looked at her computer screen, then back at me.

"Listen, most kids can't get one person here to deal with their crap when they act up," I said. "Ruthie has a bunch of people willing to show up for her. Just show me into the principal's office, and I'll handle it."

Susan looked dubious, but she nodded all the same. "You may enter. Principal Jacobs ran to the lavatory. He won't be long."

"Awesome." I shot her a sarcastic thumbs-up before walking into the office.

Raisin, her head hanging low, sat in one of the chairs across from the huge desk. She looked as if she were waiting for the firing squad to show up. "How much trouble are you in?" I asked as I sat next to her.

Hope warred with worry when she jerked up her chin and real-ized it was me. "Where is Rooster?" she asked, her lower lip trem-bling. "He didn't want to come?"

Seeing the fear in her eyes gave me pause. "He wanted to come," I assured her in a gentle voice. "The home office expected him to be there for a call, though, so I volunteered."

"Oh." Raisin relaxed a little bit. "I don't think this should be such a big deal."

I looked around to make sure nobody had entered the office

without us realizing it. "Tell me what happened. Keep the story short. I can't get you out of this if I don't know what you did."

Evan cleared his throat to draw my attention.

"What?" I demanded.

"I don't think you should be promising to get her out of trouble until you know what she did," Evan argued. "She might need punishment."

"I don't," Raisin said hurriedly. "I was just minding my own business."

I slid my eyes to her. "Tell me what happened. Be quick about it."

"I had a stake in my locker. They think it's a weapon for people, but I told them it's not. When I told them it was for vampires—not you, Evan—they decided that I was showing signs of aggression and called you guys."

I scratched the side of my nose. "Just out of curiosity, why did you think you would have a reason to stake a vampire at school? I mean ... school happens during the day. There's only one vampire I know out during the day."

"Two," Raisin corrected. "That other vampire we met could be out during the day, too. I just figured it was better to be safe than sorry."

I glanced at Evan and found him smirking. "She was just trying to be prepared."

"You're going to be the softest parent ever one day." Evan shook his head. "Seriously, I think you're going to be worse than Gunner."

"I've got this," I assured him. Because I was so certain of that, I got to my feet when I heard the office door open. "Listen, Ruthie watched a few too many *Buffy the Vampire Slayer* episodes and made a stupid decision. It's not a big deal. I'll make sure she's properly punished, and she won't bring a stake to school again."

When I turned, I found a spider person staring back at me. "Oh, crap." I grabbed him by the throat before he could launch himself at me. "Seriously?" I shook my head as I pulsed magic through him, wrinkling my nose when the creature exploded and spider bits landed everywhere in the office.

That's when—of course—Principal Jacobs joined the fray. His eyes went wide when he saw the explosion, and I swear there was a moment where I actually watched his eyes roll back in his head before he began to fall backwards.

"I've got him." Evan caught him before he hit the ground and held him about a foot from the floor. "You can still kill him if you want."

I made a face. "We can't kill him. Although ... you don't think he's working with the spider people, do you?"

Evan lifted an eyebrow as he considered it. Then he proceeded to tug at the principal's shirt until he found what he was looking for. "Bite." He pointed at the man's shoulder.

I pulled out my phone and searched for Graham on my contact list. "We're going to have to check everyone at this school."

Evan nodded. "We can't risk the kids."

"This is not going to go over well."

"Are you second-guessing not killing the queen?"

"What do you think?" I barked. I looked down when Raisin tugged on my coat sleeve. "What?"

"Does this mean I'm not in trouble?"

"I think you're probably safe."

"Awesome." Raisin rubbed her hands together. "Can we get ice cream when we're done here? Rooster always gets me ice cream after a visit to the principal's office."

"And you think I'm the soft one," I said to Evan.

"I think we're all soft where Raisin is concerned," he replied.

There were worse things, and what was coming next was one of them. "I'm sure you'll get your ice cream," I said. "We have a mess to clean up first."

Her smile was pretty. "I can wait."

Of course she could.

21
TWENTY-ONE

To Rooster's credit, he didn't say "I told you so" when he came to the school. Instead, he quietly helped us round up Arachnids so they could be locked away until we were ready to deal with them. There were also three members of the school staff—thankfully, no children—who had been bitten and taken over. They were transported to Graham's jail until the spell could be reversed.

"You can say it," I offered Rooster as he allowed Raisin to lean in and hug him. Her mouth was going a mile a minute about what had happened, but Rooster was more interested in stroking her hair and glaring at me than talking.

"I'm not saying anything," Rooster replied blandly.

"I know you want to," I insisted.

"Oh, we're not playing this game, Scout." Rooster's expression was torturous. "You, young lady, can't have it both ways. You can't yell at us that we expect you to kill for us in one breath and then get mad at yourself for not killing in the next."

"Actually, I think that's fairly normal," Evan countered. "I mean … it makes sense to me."

Rooster extended a warning finger in his direction. "Don't. I'm not mad at her."

"You seem kind of mad," I hedged.

"Well, I'm not." Rooster was firm. "I am concerned." He released Raisin and planted his hands on his hips. "Obviously, they were trying to take me over," he started.

My mouth fell open. "Crap. I hadn't even gotten that far yet."

Rooster pinned me with an "oh really" look. "What did they say when you were the one who showed up for the meeting?"

"Well, Susan—who it turns out was being mind controlled but was way more put together than Mindy—seemed flustered. She was expecting you, and in hindsight, it's likely she was thrown by my appearance."

"Scout was kind of mean to her," Evan volunteered. "She said that Raisin had a lot of people willing to show up for her and then basically told her to stuff it."

"They had to know that you wouldn't fall for their plan," Rooster insisted. "You've seen the Arachnids before. You've been around the infected. They still moved on you."

"They didn't really have a choice," I replied. "I wasn't going to sit in there forever."

"I guess not." Rooster shook his head. "This was one heckuva way to get out of trouble," he said to Raisin, who looked genuinely amused. "I guess this means you aren't going to get a lecture, huh?"

Raisin was the picture of innocence. "I think it's best for everybody concerned if I don't get punished," she agreed. "It's not my fault they were spider people. I'm going to have nightmares as it is."

"You and me both, kid," Gunner offered as he walked behind her and ruffled her hair. "I know this makes me seem like a punk, but I'm really glad it was you with her and not me," he said to Evan.

"Yes, well, I don't think you screaming like a banshee as you clung to her and wailed that she needed to save you would've made things easier on her," Evan agreed.

"I don't wail," Gunner replied. "Why would you assume I wail?"

"Oh, I don't know," Evan deadpanned. "Just call it a hunch."

"I don't wail," Gunner said to me. "I manfully yell."

"Well, at least you understand the distinction." I reached over to pat his arm and then surprised us both by placing my hand in his.

"Everything is okay," he said, forgetting for a moment that he was arguing with Evan. "You have a lot on your plate right now. It's all right to feel overwhelmed."

"I just want an entire day in bed with nothing but chicken," I admitted.

He made a face.

"And you," I added.

"You'd better include me in that." He gave me a quick hug and then released me. "What are we going to do here? Do we have the authority to shut down the school?"

"You don't, but I do," Graham said as he strolled into the office. His gaze moved to me first, then to Rooster. "I'm saying there's an outbreak of something. What should it be an outbreak of?"

"Why are you asking me?" Rooster challenged. "Say it's an outbreak of spider people."

"Right, because that won't cause a panic." Graham rolled his eyes. "I need something else."

Raisin was the one who came to his rescue. "RSV."

"What's that?" Graham stroked his hand over her hair when he focused on her.

"RSV," she repeated. "It's a respiratory virus that spreads really easily and can make people sick. They shut down the elementary school for three days because of it last month."

"I didn't realize that." Graham bobbed his head. "That's a very good suggestion."

"Plus it's already been done," Rooster said. "You've checked all the kids and teachers, correct?" he asked me. "There's no more spider people, right?"

"I checked them all," I confirmed.

"Then you need to go home."

It was not the tack I was expecting him to take. "What do you mean?"

"Take your day in bed." Rooster was firm. "Eat your chicken. Do whatever you do with this putz when you want to unwind." He gestured toward Gunner, who didn't appear bothered to be called a putz. "You need to decompress."

I immediately started shaking my head. "No, I do not need to decompress."

"Yes, you do."

"No." I pinned him with the same glare I'd seen Winnie use on Bay a multitude of times to force her hand. "What I said earlier ... forget it. I was just feeling sorry for myself. It was a momentary lapse, and it's passed."

"It hasn't passed, Scout," Rooster shot back. "You feel as if we put too much pressure on you. And, quite frankly, we all agree that we haven't been taking your needs into account."

"What is that supposed to mean? What needs?"

"You need a break. You cannot carry the weight of the world on your shoulders."

"I'm pretty sure that's not what I'm doing." That was true, right? "I just had a bad moment."

"No, you've been having a lot of bad moments and keeping them to yourself," Rooster countered. "We've been putting too much pressure on you."

"This is worse than you putting pressure on me."

"Oh, yeah?" Rooster cocked an eyebrow. "And what do you think this is?"

"You ... thinking I'm weak."

"I can guarantee nobody thinks that."

"Well, that's how I feel when you expect me to go home and go to bed. I don't have a case of the vapors. I'm fine." I mostly meant that. "I'm just ... a little persnickety."

"You're not a little anything," Rooster countered. "You're struggling, and I need you to get some rest, so you don't continue to struggle. Even your parents realize that they're putting too much pressure on you."

It was only then that I realized Rick and Andrea weren't present. "Where are they?"

"They went to have a meeting with the family so everybody understands that it's not okay to keep pushing you."

I threw my hands in the air. "I don't want everybody looking at me and feeling sorry for me."

"Nobody feels sorry for you."

"Definitely not," Marissa agreed as she poked her head into the office. "Me? I wish you would get run over by a bus."

"Thank you." I almost wanted to hug her. "That's what I want."

"You want everybody to pray for you to be hit by a bus?" Graham challenged. "Why would you possibly want that?"

"I don't want everyone hoping for that," I replied. "I just want people to be normal around me. At least Marissa isn't treating me as if I'm breakable."

"If only I could break you," Marissa mused. She seemed to consider it for several seconds, then turned to Rooster. "The parents are going to be arriving in ten minutes. We need to be in place to handle it."

"I'll be there in a second." Rooster gave her a "go away" look before focusing on me. "You said what you said because you're tired. I think it's time you get some rest. Your parents are handling your family. I'm going to handle this. Just ... go."

I narrowed my eyes. "You're not the boss of me."

"I sign your paychecks, so that literally makes me your boss."

I refused to acknowledge that he had a point. "I'm fine. See." I pointed at my face and smiled. It probably looked like something out of a Stephen King miniseries, but I was fine with that. "I just had a momentary lapse in judgment. I really am fine."

"I said you're going home."

I planted my hands on my hips and stared him down. Only one of us was going to win this battle.

. . .

"I CAN'T GO HOME AND CLIMB INTO BED and do nothing for the rest of the afternoon," I complained to Gunner as we got into his truck. It was still parked downtown from this morning so we'd had to hitch a ride from the school.

"You said you wanted to spend a day in bed," Gunner pointed out.

"Yes, but I want to spend a day in bed when we don't have Arachnids hanging over us."

"You should've been more specific."

I glared out the front window, debating what to do. Ultimately, I could only think of one thing. "Go to the cabin."

"That's what I'm doing. I'm going to get chicken on the way and then I'm going to get you naked." He looked truly happy, which made me feel bad because I was about to cause him to deflate like a balloon.

"Not our cabin. I want you to go out to the other cabin. I need to talk to Rick and Andrea."

"Why?"

"Because I don't want them blaming themselves for something that isn't their fault. This ... *thing* ... is my fault. I should've kept my mouth shut. I never do, though, so here we are."

Gunner narrowed his eyes. "Are you telling me you want to check on Rick and Andrea because you're worried about them?"

"I'm worried they're going to blame themselves, and it will be more weirdness."

"So, you are worried about them." Gunner broke out into a wide grin. "I'm so proud."

"I'm not worried about them in a whiny way," I warned him. "If that's what you're thinking, stop it right now, because that's not what I'm doing."

"Of course not. My Scout would never get whiny."

"If I got whiny and you got whiny at the same time, the world would stop spinning on its axis."

"Yeah, I'm just happy that we can both be whiny together. It's hard to wear the crown without any support. Now you can share the burden with me."

I shook my head. "It's weird to me now that I fell in love with you."

"Because you think I'm just too good looking?"

"Because you're just too whiny."

"You like that I'm whiny." Gunner winked at me.

In truth, I liked him just as he was. In general—Arachnid fear notwithstanding—he was perfect for me. He wasn't too alpha to be annoying. He wasn't too beta to be needy. He believed I could do whatever I set my mind to, making him my biggest cheerleader. He was willing to go the extra mile to help me. Most importantly, he didn't care if he looked like an idiot when making me laugh.

So, yeah, the whining thing wasn't a deal-breaker.

"Let's just go out to the cabin, huh?" I prodded in a low voice. "I need to talk to Rick and Andrea. After that ... we'll see where things stand. If we can squeeze an afternoon in bed onto the calendar, then we'll do that."

"Don't tease me, Randall," Gunner growled wolfishly.

I laughed despite the turn the day had taken. "We need to talk to Rick and Andrea before we make any other plans."

"Yeah, yeah, yeah. I'm already in bed with the chicken in my head."

Somehow, that didn't surprise me.

I WASN'T PAYING ATTENTION AS WE CRESTED the final hill that led to the cabin. I was screwing around on my phone and looking up Arachnid behaviors right up until Gunner sucked in a breath and took his foot off the gas pedal.

Immediately, I raised my eyes, and almost came out of my skin when I realized the same magical wall that had fallen when I'd let myself into Bonnie's lair was back up. This time, though, we were on the other side of it.

"Son of a witch!" I slammed the door with gusto upon exiting and stormed up to the wall, which was undulating like a snakeskin to the point where it seemed to be laughing at me.

"Do you think the same wall came back?" Gunner asked as he joined me. He was no longer messing around trying to make me laugh and was instead deadly serious.

"How would that work?"

"I don't know. I just ... I had plans. There's no way we're getting chicken in bed now."

He wasn't wrong. Tentatively, I reached out to touch the wall. The magic zapped me back quickly, leaving my fingers feeling a bit singed. "Ow." I shook my hand to cool my fingers.

"That's what happens when you touch a wall you're clearly not supposed to touch," Gunner fired back.

"Shh." I lifted my finger to my lips.

Gunner's eyes went wide. "Do you hear something?" he whispered.

"No, I'm just trying to get you to stop talking." Then, because I was frustrated, I kicked out with my foot and instantly regretted it when the wall threw me back. I hit the ground with enough force that I skidded against the gravel. I was feeling raw when I rolled to my knees and glared at the wall with murderous intent. Before I could throw magic at it, however, a figure appeared to my right.

"I wouldn't," Baron said as he surveyed the pulsating wall. He looked much calmer than I felt.

"You wouldn't what?" I demanded.

"I wouldn't try to burn that wall down."

"Not that I said I was going to do that, but why wouldn't you use magic to bring it down?"

"Because it's designed to absorb your magic," Baron replied. "It will just make the wall stronger."

"Freaking Bonnie," I grumbled under my breath.

"It seems she took your threat at the trailer park seriously," Baron agreed.

"So much for the Arachnids doing the smart thing," I muttered. I rubbed the back of my neck. "We have to get it down."

"We do," Baron agreed. "If only because we don't want her thinking that she's somehow won a battle."

Gunner moved closer to me, his phone in his hand.

"What are you doing?" I asked.

"I'm seeing if I can text through this thing," he replied, not looking up. "Your parents are over there. I'm just trying to see if they're okay."

"Oh, good idea." I watched him, hopefully. After a few seconds, he shook his head.

"They're not responding. It's possible they're not looking at their phones. They could be focused on the wall."

"If they knew the wall was out here, they would've texted us," I argued.

"Good point." Gunner nodded before sliding his phone into his back pocket. "So, what do we do?"

I didn't know what to do. I stared at the wall, bopping my head back and forth as I hummed to myself. "Well, actually, I'll just do what I did before and make a door." I moved to stand but Baron's hand landed on my shoulder before I could start forward.

"You can't do that," he said in a low voice.

"And why not?" I was about to say that it had worked the first time but that felt like a fluke.

"Because Bonnie knows that will be your answer going forward, and she's built in a little surprise. Any door you try to open will take you to a plane that can be entered but not exited."

It wasn't that I didn't believe him. I had my doubts, though. "How do you know that?"

"Because I can see through doors, and she's built a number of traps into this wall." Baron didn't crack a smile as he regarded me.

"You can't risk it. I could always try to force a door to rescue you, but I can't guarantee that will work."

"So, what are our options? We can't just sit here and do nothing."

"Did I say we were going to sit here and do nothing?" Baron challenged.

"No, but you're not exactly hopping to it to get anything done either."

"Shh."

I glared at him when he used my own tactic against me. Before I could tell him my opinion of his thievery, he strode three paces to the left, waved his hand and opened a door in the opposite direction, and stepped through it.

I watched with open-mouthed disbelief as he escaped. "What the hell!" I was about to chase him ... and maybe smack him around ... when he returned. He wasn't alone either. He had Poet tucked under his arm.

"What are you doing, you big moron?" Poet demanded. She looked furious. "You just can't manhandle me when you want something. In fact, I have a mind to..." She trailed off when she saw me and stopped fighting Baron. "Hello." She broke out into a wide grin.

I didn't know I was going to do it—it really went against everything I believed—but it had been a crap day and Rooster was right. I was overwhelmed. The second I saw her, I burst into tears, forcing me to bury my face in my knees.

"Oh, no." Poet slapped back Baron, who was busy arguing with Kade and two other men who had followed him through the opening. I knew who they were because I'd seen them on video chat before. Luke and Cole, the other members of her famed reverse harem.

"You can't just take my wife," Kade roared. "What were you thinking?"

"Screw that," Luke complained. "She's my best friend. That's way more important than her being your wife."

Poet ignored all of them and dropped to the ground next to me. "What's wrong?"

I gestured toward the magical wall.

"That can't be all that's wrong," she said. "I've never known a little magic to make you cry."

"This day sucks," I replied, going back to hiding my face.

"That's okay." She sat on the ground next to me and slid her arm behind my back. "We'll fix it."

"How can you be sure?"

"Because there's nothing we can't do when we're together."

And because I believed that, I started to cry harder. What in the hell was wrong with me?

22

TWENTY-TWO

"Go away," Poet ordered when Gunner tried to slip in and ... what? I had no idea what he was going to try to do. I wasn't a crier, though, and he looked as if he was close to melting down because of the tears.

"I can't just go away." Gunner looked scandalized. "She's my chicken partner."

"I have no idea what that's supposed to mean," Poet replied. "It sounds weird, though."

"Really? You think the chicken sounds weird?" Luke was blasé. "Have you seen the huge wall of magic that strangely resembles a snakeskin?"

Kade balked. "I don't like snakes. Why are we here? There shouldn't be snakes in snow."

"Oh, that's really a true statement." Gunner moved closer to the others. "I guess I should introduce myself."

I didn't watch the male meet and greet. I knew they would get along fine. Instead, I kept my face down. "I think I'm having a nervous breakdown."

Poet was the picture of serenity as she sat next to me. "And why do you think that?"

I told her about my mini meltdown regarding the Arachnids, and how it had backfired on me.

"Wait ... there are spider people too?" Kade hissed from somewhere behind Poet.

"Yeah, and they're gross," Gunner said.

"And I thought snake people were bad."

"Nothing is worse than the spider people."

I shook my head and blew out a heavy sigh. The crying had stopped when I was telling the story, but I didn't feel like myself. Everything was off.

"So, you didn't massacre the spider people, and it came back to bite you," Poet surmised. "That's not the worst thing in the world."

It felt like the worst thing in the world. "If I'd killed them, this probably wouldn't be happening." I gestured toward the magical wall.

"Something tells me that Bonnie was going to do this regardless," Poet replied. "Obviously, she's trying to get under your skin."

"She's good at it."

"Showing her she's good at it is just going to keep her doing this stuff over and over again," Poet replied. "She's trying to get a reaction out of you, make sure you believe that she's the big dog in the area, not you. It's probably not smart to let her have this amount of power over you."

"Thanks for the pep talk," I replied dryly. "I wouldn't have figured that out myself."

Poet sent me an apologetic look. "Sorry. I didn't think about that before I said it. I just meant that you can't let her believe she's winning. That will make her more difficult to deal with."

"I get it." I did. "I'm just...tired."

"You're dealing with more than any one person should have to deal with," Poet agreed. "It's not fair. Everyone expects you to have all the answers. You don't, though. You can't have all the answers."

"My entire family is on the other side of that wall," I said in a low voice.

Poet stilled, her eyes moving between the wall and me. "And you just got them back and now you're separated from them again," she surmised after a few seconds.

I made a face. "That sounds whiny. That's not it. I just ... we were going to have chicken in bed. Rooster thinks I'm weak. Now this? I'm just tired."

Poet narrowed her eyes. "Well, you need to suck it up." She didn't mince words. "Don't keep looking at the overall picture. Just look at one problem at a time. You can't focus on the family ... the Bonnie ... the Arachnids ... and the loas of it all at the same time."

Baron's shoulders squared. "What do I have to do with this?"

"We'll get to that," Poet replied. She didn't even look at him. She was too fixated on me. "Just focus on the wall. How did you get the last one down?"

"I didn't technically take it down," I replied. "I opened a door, invaded Bonnie's lair, and dropped a ceiling on both of us."

"And when Bonnie was knocked out, the wall dropped?"

I nodded.

"Hmm." Poet went back to looking at the wall.

One of her companions, a dark-haired man I didn't know as well as Luke and Kade, went to her side. "What are you thinking?" he asked. I knew his name was Cole even though I'd only gotten fleeting glimpses of him over video calls since Poet and I had reconnected.

"I'm not sure yet." Poet cocked her head as she extended her hands.

"Don't," I warned her. "It hurts."

Her fingers were singed just like mine before I finished saying it. When she waved her hands and frowned, all I could do was shrug.

"It's not like I didn't warn you," I said.

"You could've been a little more zealous with the warning." She stuck her index finger in her mouth and sucked on it as she glared at the wall. When she turned her ire on Baron, I wasn't surprised. "Why can't you get this thing down?"

"Because it's not my job." Baron met her glare for glare. "You can't rely on me to swoop in and solve every problem for you."

"Oh, yes, because that sounds just like us." Poet shook her head as she moved closer to the wall. "You can't do another door around it?" she asked me.

"Not unless I want to walk into a plane that doesn't have an exit," I replied. "Or, well, at least that's what Baron says."

"Huh." Poet made a popping sound with her lips. "I wonder if I can teleport to the other side."

"Wouldn't you be in the same danger as Scout?" Kade asked her.

Poet shook her head. "No. She opens plane doors. I just pop from location to location. In theory, I should be able to pop to the other side without an issue." To prove it, she winked out of existence.

"Poet!" Kade's irritation was obvious. "She's trying to kill me," he complained to nobody in particular. "That's the only explanation I can come up with."

Before I could respond, Poet appeared in the same spot she'd been standing in. "So, they're okay over there," she said quickly when everybody started exclaiming. "They're relieved to know we're on the case—apparently they've been trying to call but haven't had any luck—and I told them to sit tight until we figure this out."

"Can't you just bring them back over here?" Gunner asked.

"Sure." Poet bobbed her head. "It would take a lot of trips, but I could do that. It doesn't solve our overall problem, though."

"We need to send a message to Bonnie," I supplied.

"We do," Poet agreed. "We need to send this wall tumbling, and we need to do it sooner rather than later."

I forced myself to stand and look at the wall with fresh eyes. "This wall was designed to stop me. We need to figure out a way to use your powers to drop it."

"No, we need to figure out a way to work together to use your powers to do it," Poet countered. "That will send the right message to her."

"Okay." I blew out a breath as I considered it. "I can't teleport. I'm guessing pixie magic is out because she has Emma's powers." Something occurred to me. "What about straight-up witch magic?"

"Now you're thinking." Poet beamed at me. "She can't combat your witch magic."

I scuffed my foot against the ground as I studied the bottom of the wall. Then something occurred to me. "What if I used earth elemental magic to shake up the base of the wall? If I give it a good effort, it should topple the higher parts of the wall."

"And cause the whole thing to come crashing down," Poet agreed.

"We can use my fire magic to hurry the process along," Cole offered.

I was going to argue that I should probably do it myself when I realized I would have access to the powerful fire magic he had at his disposal even after he left. I always had Stormy...even if I didn't want to drag her into danger.

"I think we can knock it down," I said. "My issue is what happens when Bonnie realizes it's down. What if she comes here? We don't have a lamia present to take her powers."

Poet darted a look toward Baron. "I'm working on that. Let's just move forward under the assumption that Bonnie is not going to show up. Instead, she's going to sit in her lair and lick her wounds."

"That seems like wishful thinking," I countered.

"Yes, well, we can only do one thing at a time. Let's handle the wall first. Bonnie's retribution is a secondary worry."

"Okay." I glanced at Cole. "What can you do?"

His wink was charismatic. "Oh, honey, you wouldn't believe the things I can do."

"See, I feel I should be angry about the flirting," Gunner complained.

"Don't worry," Baron assured him. "He's only interested in the loud one. Now me, on the other hand, I would totally ruin her for you and all other men."

I shot him a dirty look. "You can't say things like that in this day and age. It's wrong ... and gross ... and wrong.

Baron rolled his eyes. "The problem with today's society is that everybody has gone soft."

"Yes, *that's* our biggest problem," Poet agreed sarcastically. "We're all soft and you're just misunderstood. It has nothing to do with you being a weird pervert."

"I am not a pervert."

"Blah, blah, blah. That's all I hear when you talk." Poet pointed toward the ground. "Aim there, Cole. Scout, wait until he has the fire going and then do what you're going to do."

I rubbed my sweaty palms on my jeans and nodded. This felt like a lot of pressure. The sort I didn't want to deal with. I had no choice, though. The wall had to come down ... and I had to get it together. I was completely off my game. Why, though? Why was I so off? I didn't have time to think about it because Cole had started throwing fire magic at the ground.

I watched it build, chewing my bottom lip, then I added witch magic to the mix. I made sure to avoid using my pixie magic. That appeared to be the right choice, because before I knew it, the wall had started moving upwards. The taller it got, the more unstable it grew, and within a few seconds, it started toppling inward and dissipating.

From start to finish, we worked for thirty seconds. When we were finished, smoke surrounded us, but we could see the cabin ... and my curious family watching from the other side.

"Well, that wasn't so bad, was it?" Baron dusted his hands off, as if he'd put actual work into the process. "See," he said to me. "When you think outside the box, great things happen."

I wanted to smack him. Hard. Instead, I merely shook my head and caught my mother's gaze.

"What did you do?" Andrea asked as she took a step forward.

"It's a long story. It's been a long day." I rolled my neck. "I don't suppose you guys are cooking up one of your fancy dinners, are you?"

"We're making fried chicken," Andrea replied.

That caused me to smirk. "Well, that's good, because we have guests." I gestured toward Poet's crew. "They helped."

"Not really," Poet replied. "You did all the heavy lifting."

"Hey." Cole shot her a dubious look. "I'm more than just window dressing, sweetheart."

Poet snorted. "Fine. Scout and Cole did all the work."

"And we have some things to discuss," I added. "We can do it over chicken."

"Now we're talking." Gunner beamed at me. "I'm sure they'll make leftovers for us to take home and eat in bed, too."

"Life is looking up for you, isn't it?" I teased. "Now you have two families cooking for you."

"Life started looking up for me the second you entered my life."

His words were schmaltzy and yet endearing. "I feel the same way about you."

EVEN THOUGH THEY'D BEEN CUT OFF FROM the rest of the world by a megalomaniacal lamia apex, my family seemed to be in good spirits. They gave us the table in the middle of the room and the ambiance was happy around us as we dug into the chicken, potato salad, and homemade fries.

"This is amazing," Gunner said around a mouthful of food. "I think I might orgasm."

Rick, who was sitting across from him, made a face. He didn't comment, though.

"So, tell me about yourselves," Poet said as she took a swig of her beer. Her gaze was on Rick and Andrea. "What were your lives like when you were separated from Scout?"

Rick paused with a piece of chicken halfway to his mouth. "You're the first one to ask us that."

Poet, who was on my left, sent me a dark look. "Really? Well, I'm interested."

"At first we spent months mourning our loss," Andrea replied. "Rick didn't get out of bed for weeks. Then, when he did, he went through the motions of trying to build a new community. We were on a different plane, but it wasn't all that different from this one."

My stomach constricted. I'd tried to force myself to think of what their lives had been like in the aftermath of giving me up, but all I could picture were the big parties they kept throwing now that they were all together again. Of course it hadn't been like that. They'd been struggling. Just like I had been struggling.

"We basically homesteaded and kept to ourselves," Rick explained. "We were trying to keep off whatever radar we could stay off of. When we left the farm, we left our stability. We tried to focus on that."

"There wasn't a lot of fun being had," Emma offered. If she was put off by the appearance of new magical beings, she didn't show it. "Everybody was sad. Then everybody became stoic."

"We made it for a long time, but the worry and curiosity got the better of us," Andrea said. "We knew a year before we left that we were going. We had to come back to this plane. Leaving wasn't easy, but we needed to do it."

"We had the prophecy to go by, but that didn't give us a time frame," Rick said. "Basically, we knew you would end up in Hawthorne Hollow. That's *all* we knew."

"We did go to Detroit for a bit," Andrea offered. "We got separated, though. It was bad enough being here not knowing where you were."

"You have to understand, we had no intention of interrupting your life," Rick added. "We just wanted to watch you from afar. Being alone, though..." He trailed off, his gaze significant when it landed on me. "You were alone, and it crushed us. I was too weak to be alone, though, so I went north and so did your mother. We decided, since we knew where you would end up, that we would make our lives here and wait for you."

"We got to know the town and the people here," Andrea said. "We were constantly on the lookout for dangers. We knew about Rooster's group, and we figured you would end up with them. I wish we would've known about Bonnie before you arrived. We could've handled that situation before it even became an issue."

"You couldn't have known about Bonnie," I countered. My mouth was dry, so I took a long swig of my beer. "I didn't know and she was with me. A lot. I was on the lookout for dangers, too, and she slipped right past me."

"Don't blame yourself, Scout," Rick chided. "Bonnie's entire reason for being was to slip under your radar."

"Well, she did a good job of it." I offered up a rueful smile. "I thought Marissa was going to be the one who turned out evil."

"Marissa is evil," Gunner said. "She just owns her evil."

"In hindsight, I realize that it didn't make sense for Marissa to be evil," I said. "She would've tried to ingratiate herself with me rather than constantly tick me off. Bonnie made the most sense as a mole, and yet I didn't see it."

"Nobody saw it," Gunner said. "She was part of the group before you came, and I never sensed anything off about her. Right up until we realized it was her...I just didn't see it."

"Yeah." I sighed.

"Tell me about your time in Hawthorne Hollow before Scout showed up," Poet prodded. "That must have been difficult for you, realizing that she was coming but not knowing when."

Rick and Andrea exchanged heavy glances.

"That was really hard for the first year," Andrea confirmed. "We were happy to have found each other again but not knowing when Scout would arrive ... it was painful."

"We busied ourselves working on the house," Rick supplied. "We also tried to watch everybody in town whenever we could ... without drawing attention to ourselves, of course. We were convinced Graham, Gunner, Rooster, and Whistler were clean fairly quickly."

"Gunner was too goofy to be evil," Andrea said on a grin. "For a while there, I was convinced you were a manwhore and thought maybe you were going to be a jerk, but you grew out of that phase, and I saw you become a great man. That's why, when Scout finally did arrive, we were happy you and she clicked."

"Some of us were happier than others," Rick said pointedly. "Still … your loyalty helped. We watched you from afar."

"How come you didn't approach her?" Poet asked. "Like … why didn't you introduce yourselves right away? You waited months, which doesn't exactly prove you were chomping at the bit to see her."

Poet was asking every question I didn't want to have answered and yet I could do nothing but sit there and watch her. Now that she'd asked, I needed to know the answers.

"It was fear," Andrea replied, her voice cracking. "Once she was there, she was real."

"At first, we wanted to see how she interacted with others, learn who she was," Rick said. "After that...we gave in to the fear. What if she didn't like us? What if she told us to get lost? What if she hated us?"

"We didn't want to be disappointed," Andrea offered. "How could we not be, though? So, we just watched her … and yearned."

Suddenly, I felt sick to my stomach and lowered my chicken. What was I supposed to say here?

Poet was the one who responded. She was better with people than me. "You're together now. You can't focus on the mistakes of the past. You need to let go of your guilt. Scout needs to let go of her anger because it's literally making her break down. It's time for all of you to move forward."

"That's what we want," Rick said. "We can't push her, though. She has a right to her anger."

I did, but when was enough, enough?

23
TWENTY-THREE

Baron spent the entire meal charming every woman in sight. The men didn't seem as thrilled with his presence as the women but Baron being Baron, he didn't care. Once dinner was over, we headed outside.

"We need to get back," Poet said. "If you need us, we'll be here, though."

Luke shook his head. "I won't."

Despite myself, I burst out laughing. "You were nowhere near as obnoxious as I thought you would be," I admitted. "You were almost fun."

"I can't kick you when you're down," Luke replied. "I'll kick you when you're feeling up again."

"Well, I'm looking forward to that."

Poet put her hand on my wrist and drew me away, her eyes serious. "You need to make an effort with your parents." There was no give to her tone.

"I've been better," I protested.

She arched an eyebrow.

"I have," I insisted. "I've been ten times better."

"Well, you need to get even better than that. Let go of the anger. They suffered, too. Nothing about what happened is okay, but we have to play the cards we've been dealt."

I nodded. "I think I'm just having a bit of a thing." I pointed toward my head.

"Like a breakdown?" Luke asked, proving he'd been listening. "I can see you having a breakdown."

I burned him to a crisp with a single glare. "How does anybody put up with you?"

"You get used to it," Cole replied as he joined us. "He's not so bad when his hackles aren't up. He's convinced you're going to try to steal Poet from him."

"Nobody can steal Poet from me," Luke declared. "We're bonded for life."

"Yes, and I'm bonded with Scout, too." Poet slapped her hand against Luke's forehead and pushed him back. "Now, give me a minute."

Luke didn't look happy with the order, but he didn't fight either. Instead, he slid away to talk to Cole and Kade in hushed tones. At one point, Kade and Cole both slapped him on the back of the head in tandem. That told me Luke was being Luke ... and I was okay with it.

"You're wound so tight right now that the excess energy you're feeling is leaking from your eyes," Poet said. "You need to let it go. All of it." She was firm. "The past can't be changed. These aren't bad people. Even though they let you go, they love you. Let them love you."

I wrinkled my nose. "You're kind of bossy."

"I am bossy," she agreed. "I'm also right."

Because I didn't disagree, all I could do was sigh. "I'm working on it."

"Well, get some sleep, and work harder tomorrow." She threw her arms around me for a hug and whispered the next part. "Everything you've ever wanted is here. Embrace it. Running from it is going to make you sick."

"I know." I returned the hug. "Thank you for coming."

"I'll always come." She was solemn when she pulled back. "When you need me, I'll be here."

"The same goes for me."

"Oh, I know." Poet's smile lit up her entire face. "You're a giver despite that mouth of yours. That's what's dragging you down now. Just let it go. Let others fill your well. You need it no matter what you think."

We embraced again, then she moved toward the others. "We're heading back," she said to Baron. "I assume you're staying here."

Baron's smile was easy. "I am. For now. I'll drop in to visit you when I can."

"I can't wait." Poet shook her head. "As for you ... call. I want to make sure you're okay."

I hated feeling infantilized. "I'm fine. I'm right as rain."

Poet narrowed her eyes. "You're a lot of things, but you're not fine."

That was disturbing to hear, but it was true. "I'll see you soon."

"Count on it."

I MADE SURE TO SAY GOODNIGHT TO Andrea, Rick, Ezekiel, and Emma. It felt necessary after what I'd heard. I waved to the others, but they didn't try to get too close. They merely waved in response, which told me that Andrea and Rick had laid down the law about pressuring me.

Gunner was quiet for the ride home. He didn't say anything obnoxious or try to be funny. Andrea had packed a box of chicken and container of potato salad for us, and he was seemingly happy with that.

I fed Merlin once inside. The cat shot me a disdainful look because we were late and then focused on his food. Once in the bedroom, I changed into flannel pajama pants and an oversized T-shirt before climbing into bed. That's where Gunner found me after putting the chicken away. I'd heard him talking to Merlin too, assuring him we hadn't forgotten about him. When he came into the bedroom, he gave me a long look before stripping out of his shirt and pants. He wore his boxer shorts to bed and crawled in next to me.

"Do you want to talk?" he asked in a low voice.

I shrugged. "We probably should. A lot has happened today."

"It has." He propped himself on the pillows next to me and took my hand. "Tell me what you're thinking."

"I fell apart. I'm embarrassed."

"You didn't fall apart, and there's nothing to be embarrassed about. Why are you always so hard on yourself?"

"I don't happen to think I am."

"But you are." He was firm. "You feel as if you have to be large and in charge under every circumstance, and it's not necessary, Scout. You're allowed to need help. You're allowed to want a break. You're allowed to take some time for yourself."

"I know. I just..." I blew out a sigh. "I had to do everything for myself when I was younger. That's how I survived. Poet was the first person I let in, and I lost her."

"I get that was hard."

"It wasn't hard, though. It just ... was. I had no choice in the matter. She was gone. I was the one who became harder. After that, I didn't let anybody in until Evan."

"And you lost him, too."

I swallowed the lump that had appeared in my throat. "It took me forever to trust Evan in the first place," I admitted. "He didn't give up, though. He just kept showing up. I was the grumpy to his sunshine, but he refused to let me wallow. Eventually, I let him in."

"And you love him still."

"Losing him was too much. I didn't think I would recover. And I didn't ... until I came here."

"And let me in." His smile was impish, but there was compassion in his eyes. "I've been careful not to push you too hard because I thought it would make things worse, but Poet is right. You can't hold what happened against Andrea and Rick any longer.

"It's okay that things are still awkward between you—that's to be expected—but holding a grudge over things that were out of their control is unfair," he continued. "They're trying really hard. They're not pushing even though you can tell they want to. They're playing the game by your rules. It's time to give a little."

"I didn't realize I wasn't giving it my all until Poet started asking them questions." It was hard for me to give voice to the guilt I was feeling, but I pushed forward. "I just didn't bother asking them the things I should've asked them. Why do you think that is?"

"I think you were afraid to hear the answers. You didn't want to know if it was easy for them to leave you. It wasn't, though, and you need to accept that they did what they thought was right. Now you need to do the same. No more hiding."

"Yeah." I rolled and rested my head on his shoulder, his arms automatically coming around me. "I'm not easy."

"I remember you being very easy."

I ignored his teasing tone. "No, I mean ... there are people out there who are easy to love. I'm not one of those people."

"You're wrong, Scout." Gunner was firm. "You're the easiest person in the world to love. I think your problem is that you told yourself a long time ago that you didn't deserve love ... and ever since then you've been trying to live up to that decision.

"I knew I was going to love you from the first moment I met you," he continued, shaking his head when I opened my mouth to argue with him. "Don't. I knew it. Being loved by you is like having the sun with you twenty-four hours a day."

"Oh, geez," I muttered, burying my face. "What is it with you and the schmaltz?"

"It's the truth," he replied simply. "Loving you is easy. Letting yourself be loved is hard. You're getting there, though."

"I have to try harder with Rick and Andrea."

"You do. Maybe you should start calling them Mom and Dad."

That seemed like a big step. "I'll think about it."

"That's enough for tonight." He kissed my forehead. "You need sleep. Tomorrow is going to be a big day."

"Yeah. I have to find the queen and kill her."

"You don't have to if you don't want to. We can figure things out."

"No, I *have* to." I'd already come to that conclusion. "I shouldn't have let her go in the first place. I was just trying for a different outcome. It wasn't realistic."

"I'm sorry."

"You don't have to be sorry. Some things just have to happen, and this is one of them."

"You need your rest first. We'll tackle the spider queen tomorrow."

"We?" I cocked an eyebrow. "I thought you didn't want to be part of any spider shenanigans."

"I don't, but I want to be with you more than anything, so I have to make compromises too."

"Sucks, huh?"

"I don't know. It seems worth it to me."

"And there's a fine bit of schmaltz to end our night on."

"I thought so too."

PERHAPS IT WAS THE EMOTIONAL UPHEAVAL. Perhaps it was seeing Poet and being able to spend time with her. Perhaps I was just completely exhausted. Whatever it was, when I slipped into sleep, it was like being plunged into a world where sight, sound, and smell weren't possible. I was in a void.

That's why, when my internal danger alarm started dinging, I was confused. It took me longer than it should have to climb out of the hole. When I finally did, I was in the same position I'd been in when I fell asleep. The familiar beat of Gunner's heart served as an anchor as I struggled to understand what had woken me.

Then I heard it again. My inner voice—which sounded a lot like Agnes this time as I was trying to get my bearings—barked a warning.

Get up!

I rocketed to a sitting position, all my senses firing on all cylinders. There was nobody in the cabin. Merlin's soft snores on the other side of Gunner told me that. If somebody was in the cabin, the cat would be investigating.

There was someone outside the cabin, though.

I left Gunner to sleep and went to the window. It was foggy outside, a brief warmup colliding with the snow to make it difficult to see. After a few seconds of staring, I found what I was looking for. There were three figures on the lawn, just outside the ward line. They appeared to have something that looked like a body next to their feet.

With grim detachment, I felt around the floor for my shoes. My initial instinct was to leave Gunner sleeping. He wouldn't like it, though, and it wasn't the smart move.

"Gunner." I gently shoved his shoulder to wake him up. "Graham Jr.," I said when he didn't initially stir. There was one thing that was guaranteed to get Gunner going.

"Don't make me hurt you, *Allegra*," he said in a sleepy voice.

I ignored the dig about my birth name. "Get up. There are people on the other side of the ward line. I think they have a body." I left him to sleep or get up—I didn't really care at this point—and headed into the living room. I assumed I was heading outside alone as I shrugged into my coat. Gunner appeared in the hallway, sweatpants and boots hastily thrown on. He didn't bother with a shirt. He ran hot so it wasn't necessary.

"Should I call for backup?" he asked. He was no longer sleepy. He looked angry more than anything else.

"No," I replied. "They wanted me to wake up. This isn't a fight. It's a message."

"Then let's send a message right back."

"Let's see what we're dealing with first." I made sure to shut the door behind us when we exited the cabin. I didn't want Merlin getting out, not that he showed a lot of interest in being outside. He was spoiled rotten and knew he was better off living with us than braving it outdoors.

The fog made it difficult to see who we were dealing with until we were practically on top of them. As I grew closer, it was impossible not to identify the squat bodies and broad shoulders of the three dwarves standing over the body.

I made certain to blank my face. No matter who they'd killed—and I could think of a hundred different people they might want to off to make an impression—I vowed I wouldn't react. Even being twenty feet away, at first I didn't recognize who was dead. Then one of the dwarves kicked the body and caused it to flip over.

I expected it to be someone from my family ... or one of the townspeople ... or maybe even Marissa. Instead, I found the Arachnid queen's open and frozen eyes—all eight of them—staring back at me. There was no doubt she was dead. How she'd gotten into that state was a mystery.

"Is this a present for me?" I asked finally. Really, what else was I supposed to say?

"Our mistress asked us to send a message," the dwarf in the center of the trio replied. He had a dark beard that was shot through with gray, and malice in his eyes. "There's only room for one queen in this town."

I pursed my lips as I looked down at the body again. "Okay, well, thanks for the tip. Is that all?"

The dwarf narrowed his eyes. "You're next."

"Yeah, yeah, yeah." I hunkered down to get a better look at the queen. If she was dead, that meant all the bitten minions we'd picked up at the school would be free of whatever curse she put them under. Bonnie had done me a favor, which I was struggling to accept. "Can you thank your mistress for me?"

"You want to thank the Dark Queen?" the dwarf demanded on a laugh. "Why would you possibly want that?"

"Because I thought I was going to have to spend my morning tracking her down and killing her," I replied. "Bonnie just made it so I can sleep in and have a huge breakfast."

"You thought she was on your side," the dwarf insisted.

"Actually, I didn't." I shook my head. "I thought I might be able to find a way not to kill her. I wasn't in the mood. Bonnie took care of that for me though." I held out my hands as I stood and grinned. "So, thanks. It's like Christmas in February."

The dwarf didn't look happy. "This was not supposed to be a gift."

"Well, I'm taking it as one." Now that I knew I was annoying him, I couldn't stop. "Thank you so much for being Team Scout." I launched a chef's kiss at him. "I can get a jersey made up if you're so inclined. Are you a large? I'm thinking extra-large will leave you swimming in it. You know, more like a dress. Maybe you would prefer that. I have a friend who knows a dwarf who loves dresses. Maybe there's a reason."

"This was not a gift," the dwarf spat. "There can only be one queen."

"Yeah, yeah, yeah. I heard you the first time." I flashed a flat smile at him. "Just out of curiosity, when Bonnie ordered you to bring her here, did she think I would kill you?"

The dwarf looked to be bracing himself. "I am willing to sacrifice myself for my queen."

"Okay, but that's not what I asked. Did she really think this would upset me? Because, if so, she's even loonier than I realized."

"Your ally is dead."

"She wasn't my ally. Bonnie brought her here to build her army. Then, when I upended things, Bonnie killed her in a fit of rage. On the off chance it would annoy me, she decided you three were worth sacrificing to bring her here."

They started breathing a bit heavier, but none of them ran. That was a testament to their constitution I guess.

"I'm not going to kill you, though," I assured him. "I'm just going to send you off with a wave and a smile. If I had balloons, I would give you those too. I don't, though, so you'll have to settle for this." I wiggled my butt and did a little dance.

"This is not a win for you," the dwarf seethed.

"On the contrary, it's very much a win." I linked my arm through Gunner's. "Thank you for my present. Next time, try to get me candy or something so it lasts longer. This is a good first offering, though."

With that, I turned Gunner and marched him back toward the cabin.

"What are we doing?" he asked in a low voice. "Shouldn't we deal with this?"

"Maybe, but we're not going to," I replied. "I think it's more fun to let them stew and deal with it in the morning. She's not going anywhere."

"True. What do you think happened?"

"I don't know. I'm dying to find out, though."

"Yeah." He dragged a hand through his long hair. "I'm going to have trouble going back to sleep. Do you want to wear me out first?"

The request would've seemed weird hours before. I was feeling better now. "Sure. Why not?"

"Oh, see, you do love me."

"I do. I might need to wind down too."

"I have just the thing."

"Somehow I knew you were going to say that."

24
TWENTY-FOUR

I woke up feeling strangely exhilarated the next morning. Gunner was still sleeping, so I left him to it, showered, and then headed outside to deal with the Arachnid queen's body. To my surprise, Graham was already standing next to it, a box of food in his arms. He looked perplexed.

"Did you do this?" he asked me.

I shook my head. "No, but I knew she was out here."

"And you just left her?" Graham's confusion was obvious.

"She wasn't alone. Some dwarves dropped her off. I figured it was better to wait until morning to deal with her. It's not as if she was still alive and I could've saved her."

"Plus, she was on your list to kill today."

"There's that, too," I agreed. "The dwarves seemed mad when I thanked them. They brought her as a warning from Bonnie."

"Why would you be upset about her death?"

"That I can't figure out." I shrugged. "They seemed upset that I wasn't crying in my Cheerios, though. I left them stewing about it and went back to bed."

"That was probably a smart move. It was foggy last night."

"Yeah." I cocked my head. The smell of the breakfast had my stomach growling. "I'm going to wrap up this body and drag it on this side of the wards so nobody else can grab her and then I'll meet you inside."

"I can help." He made to put down the box of food.

"No." I flashed a flat smile. "I actually want to do this myself. It feels somehow right. It won't take long."

"She'll be heavy. Dead weight."

"I can use my magic."

He hesitated. "Is this a woman thing?"

"It's a Scout thing. I'm trying to be more responsible, more open to affection, and less prone to histrionics."

He pressed his lips together, and it was obvious he was trying not to laugh.

"I'm a work in progress," I said. "Some other stuff happened last night. Gunner will fill you in." Then I remembered Gunner was still in bed. "If you really want to have some fun, you can wake him up. He was still down for the count when I left him."

"Don't tease me," Graham deadpanned. "Are you giving me permission to go into your bedroom?"

"Don't sniff my underwear or anything while you're in there, but sure. Wake Gunner up however you want. That might be fun."

He gave me a dirty look. "You always take it to a weird place. Why is that?"

I shrugged. "Just part of my charm I guess."

"You should try being charming a different way."

"I'll get right on that."

IT WASN'T HARD TO WRAP THE QUEEN'S BODY in a tarp and drag her close to the fire pit. We weren't going to bury her. She wasn't one of ours. We couldn't risk anybody in town seeing her anyway. Those eight eyes would get the conspiracy theorists going like mad. Later, after breakfast, I would search her clothing before burning the body in the pit. It was a long shot that she had anything of interest on her, but I would be remiss not to check.

By the time I got inside, I found Graham and Gunner sitting across from one another at the table. Gunner was still in his boxer shorts, and he didn't look happy.

"You don't put a pillow over someone's face to wake them up," he said in his surliest voice. "That's just ... wrong."

"It worked, didn't it?" Graham didn't look bothered by his son's attitude. "You should be ashamed of yourself anyway. You deserved what you got for making your girlfriend take care of a body all by herself."

"She didn't have to do it all by herself." Gunner shot me a death glare. "That wasn't the plan. She should've woken me up."

"Be thankful I woke you up last night when I decided I was heading out there," I countered. "I could've left you sleeping and dealt with the fallout this morning."

"Don't push it." He wagged a finger before turning back to his father. "She's tough. Obviously, she was okay."

"I just moved her to the fire pit," I replied. "I want to search her clothes later just to be sure. Then we'll burn her."

"Ah, how many men can say their girlfriends like to burn bodies?" He mock clutched at his heart. "What a lucky man I am."

I rolled my eyes and focused on Graham. "So, a few things happened since the last time we saw you." I took the container he offered me and opened it, grinning when I saw the eggs, corned beef hash, and toast. When he handed me a smaller container full of bacon, I fell head-over-heels for him. "If I wasn't already shacking up with your son, I would be all over you."

Graham's smile was fond. "If you hadn't shown the poor taste to fall in love with my son, I would be all over you. Unfortunately, that poor taste suggests you're soft in the head."

I laughed at Gunner's disgruntled look, and then launched into the tale of the night before. Graham listened with rapt attention as I explained about the wall of magic, Baron's admonishment on what might happen if I used my magic, Poet's arrival, and the downing of the wall. He didn't look happy when I was finished.

"So, let me get this straight." He sipped his coffee before continuing. "The loa is here—ostensibly to help—but whenever asked to help he says he can't. What's up with that?"

"I don't know." I mashed my eggs into the corned beef hash. "It doesn't make a lot of sense to me either. He pretends he came here because he wanted to flirt with me, but it's clearly more than that."

"What about the god?" Graham asked. "Wouldn't he be able to answer your questions?"

"I haven't seen him since the first incident." I thought back to what I knew about Cernunnos. "My understanding is that he's been focusing on business in Detroit."

"How do you know that?"

"I still have contacts in the Detroit office. We text occasionally, and about a week ago one of them informed me that Cernunnos was hanging around with reapers and there was some sort of zombie problem." I took a big bite and then had to hurry to chew and swallow. "Oh, they also told me that there's a traveler in Detroit."

Gunner and Graham both had blank expressions on their faces at the news.

"A time traveler," I pressed. "They were thought to be extinct. Nobody I know has ever seen one ... and yet Detroit has one."

"And Cernunnos is involved in that?" Graham prodded. "Doesn't that strike you as odd?"

"I think everything he does is odd. The same with the loas. They're clearly moving magical beings around a chessboard only they can see."

"What do you think it all means?"

"I don't know." I held out my hands. "I just ... don't know. It feels like their game, and we're pawns in it. Despite that, they're weirdly hands-off when it comes to certain things."

"Maybe there are rules," Gunner suggested, his mouth full of food. "Maybe they're working against another set of loas and gods—

this group evil—and they agreed to rules before they started working against one another."

Initially, I wanted to laugh. I couldn't pull it off, though, because it made a weird sort of sense. "Huh."

"Now you're wondering if there's another plane that plays host to a meeting room for evil loas, aren't you?" Graham asked.

"I kind of am. Are there evil loas?"

"Didn't Poet absorb an evil loa?" Gunner asked.

"Marinette," I confirmed. "I read up on her after. It said she was 'most dreaded,' and she was actually a cannibal back in the day."

"Well, that is a lovely picture you're painting," Graham complained. "Thank you so much for putting that image in my head."

I couldn't do anything but shrug. "Sorry. That's just what I read."

"Charlie Rhodes absorbed another loa, right?" Gunner asked. "That's the story that I remember hearing."

"Yes. Linto. He was supposedly a child spirit."

Graham continued eating ... and thinking. "Okay, well, what if you're right? What if there's a group of other loas and this group maneuvered their people into positions to take out the other loas they didn't like? How do we know that we're working with the right loas?"

That was an interesting question. "Because they've stepped in and saved people. They saved Poet. From what I understand of this Charlie Rhodes, the loa Erzulie actually put herself in a two-decade sleep to protect her from an evil witch. Why would they go out of their way to save others if they weren't good?"

"Maybe 'good' isn't the right word," Graham argued. "Perhaps they're just fighting for a specific outcome."

"Perhaps." I pulled out my phone and searched for a list of loas. "Wow. It says here that voodoo practitioners believe there are more than a thousand loas and only two-hundred or so are named. To me, that suggests there could be a lot of evil loas out there."

"Only the most dangerous loas ever make it to lists, though,"

Graham pointed out. "I'm guessing the lowest of the low aren't big worries. Maybe it's just a group of three or four that have the other loas fretting. Maybe that's why they've joined with Cernunnos, to make sure they don't come into power."

"Yeah." I tapped my fingers on the table and turned off my phone. "My other concern is Bonnie."

"Why wouldn't she be a concern? She's a concern for all of us."

"Yes, but what possessed her to believe that I would be upset about the Arachnid queen's demise?"

"I believe the queen went to Bonnie after your conversation and maybe tried to suss out the location of her lair. Because of that, Bonnie assumed she was now working for us and killed her."

That was an interesting theory. "But why wouldn't the Arachnid not just tell her about the conversation? She clearly didn't pull all her minions. Although ... I would think all the minions have to be free now."

"I can check in at the jail when I'm finished here," Graham offered. "It won't be hard to tell if the spell holding them has been broken."

"We should definitely do that," I agreed. "I have to make sure to burn the queen's body before we leave here. We don't want it bringing in creepy-crawlies."

"Definitely not," Gunner agreed.

"Have you considered that Bonnie sent the Arachnid queen's body as a warning after you so easily broke the spell out at the cabin?" Graham asked. "I mean ... she probably wasn't expecting you to manage it. She built in a lot of traps. You managed to drop it fairly easily, though."

"Not without help," I groused.

"Yes, this fire elemental you mentioned was a great deal of help. You have Stormy if you need more fire, though."

"I do have Stormy. I'm not sure I want to put her at risk, though."

"You need to get over that." Graham shook his head. "We're all in this together. We're one big powerful and messed-up family. You are not allowed to be a martyr."

"That's how you got into trouble yesterday in the first place," Gunner added. "You took too much on, and it almost broke you. That can't happen again."

"For once, I agree with my son," Graham said, causing me to glare at them both. "You have to start accepting help. This isn't going to be a short battle. It's going to be a long one. You have no choice but to let us help you."

I wanted to argue—oh, so very much—but they were right. I'd almost lost it the day before because things started feeling too big. I couldn't let that happen again. "Let's focus on the problem at hand right now," I countered, forcing myself to be calm as I dealt with the new stack of issues we had facing us. "The Arachnid queen is dead. That's actually good for us. At some point, though, Bonnie is going to realize she made a mistake killing her."

"I'm willing to bet Bonnie has already figured that out," Graham said. "Once the dwarves returned and told Bonnie you were laughing in their faces, she would've started thinking … and realized that perhaps things weren't exactly what she thought they were."

"Maybe she's not mentally stable," Gunner added. "I mean, just because absorbing Emma's magic made her magic stable, that doesn't mean her head is in the right place. You yourself said she was talking to Zeno."

"That's what Tiffany said." I rolled my neck back and forth. "Where are Tiffany and Brandy? I lost track of them after what happened."

"They're still at The Overlook," Graham replied. "At least they were there this morning."

"You spent the night again?" Gunner was perplexed. "You're an animal, aren't you? Just admit it."

"You spend the night with your girlfriend every single night," Graham pointed out.

"Yes, but we live together. We're serious." When Graham didn't respond, Gunner groaned. "I am not calling her 'Mom' and you can't make me."

Under different circumstances, I might've needled him. We had a problem, though. "If Bonnie is crazy, she's not going to get better. Like ... she's not going to suddenly be not crazy."

"Definitely not," Graham agreed. "Once the cycle starts, it only gets worse. Trust me. I know."

Yolanda. She'd tried to kill Gunner. Her time in a mental hospital hadn't helped her find clarity. While I was certain other people might've been helped at the hospital, Yolanda was a lost cause. Bonnie felt like one too.

"You know what? We're not burning the queen's body."

"We're not going to keep it as a decoration, are we?" Gunner involuntarily shuddered. "I don't think I can live with her in the yard, Scout. I'll have nightmares."

"We're not keeping her either. We're going to return her to her people."

"To what end?" Graham challenged.

"They were working for Bonnie. Bonnie killed their queen. What if we can convince them to work for us so they can avenge her?"

"What makes you think they would be loyal to us?" Gunner prodded. "I mean ... I'm loyal to you because you're adorable. They wouldn't be anywhere near as loyal as me, though."

"I don't need them to be loyal. I don't expect them to fight for us over the long haul. I do expect them to want to make Bonnie pay for turning on them, though."

"Basically, you want to use them as fodder," Graham surmised.

I hesitated, then lifted one shoulder. "I don't want them all to die. If they pick up stakes and leave as soon as this is done, more power to them. If Bonnie realizes that her former soldiers are working for us, though, it might cause her to change her tactics."

"Plus, they might be willing to share the information they have on Bonnie," Gunner said. "They weren't before, but things have changed now. They could tell us everything they know and leave.

Maybe we don't need them to fight. Especially if they have something good on Bonnie."

"I think that's a very good possibility." I smiled at the thought. "Maybe letting the queen live wasn't a mistake after all."

"That would be convenient, wouldn't it?" Gunner teased.

"It would make me feel better."

"Then we'll take the body." Gunner was resigned. "That means I'm going to have to lift it, doesn't it?"

"I'm afraid so."

"Ugh." He squeezed his eyes shut. "Why spider people? I would've been much more comfortable with ant people." He seemed to think about what he said after the fact. "Wait ... I'm not comfortable with that either. That's just all kinds of gross."

"It's definitely gross," I agreed. "Spider people are better than ant people."

"Just be glad it wasn't human praying mantises," Graham said. "You tend to lose your mind around women, and they rip off heads when they're done mating. That would not have worked out well for you."

Gunner turned positively apoplectic. "Oh, did you have to make me think about that? What is wrong with you?"

"I was just pointing out the bright side of things."

I cleared my throat to get them to stop bantering. "We have a plan. I don't know if it will work, but we know what we're doing next. That's more than we woke up with."

"What if they attack you?" Graham asked. "What are you going to do then?"

"Kill them." It wasn't even a question now. "I can't risk them going after us. I don't think they're going to do that, though."

"Because we're not their main enemy now," Graham said. "Now they have a bigger enemy."

"Exactly." I bobbed my head. "We might not be their friends, but there are worse things out there. And Bonnie is that worse thing."

"Good luck." Graham managed a smile. "Don't let the spiders get my boy. He'll cry if you do."

"I don't even know why I spend time with you," Gunner complained to his father. "You're the worst."

"It's okay." Graham patted his hand. "Daddy is here."

"Unbelievable," Gunner muttered.

I let them continue their squabbling. It was simply the way they communicated with each other. Me? I turned my attention to the Arachnids. They weren't going to like the news we were bringing them this morning. How would they react, though?

25
TWENTY-FIVE

Evan showed up not long after we were finished with breakfast. Gunner had texted him without me realizing, and I had to roll my eyes when Gunner suggested his back hurt from the previous evening and maybe—*just maybe*—it would be better if Evan lifted the queen's body into the back of his truck.

Evan rolled his eyes but picked up the body as if it was nothing and tossed it in the truck, which allowed me to search her pockets. All I found was a small journal—one of those pocketbook types most people use for shopping lists—and it was filled with a language I didn't recognize. I shoved the notebook in my pocket, thinking I would look at it closer later, and then glanced at Graham, who had been largely quiet through the process.

"Your son is kind of a baby about the spider people," I noted.

Graham nodded. "Do you blame him? She has eyes in her chin."

"Ah, like father, like son." I gave him an awkward side hug, which he returned. "Thanks for breakfast. You don't have to make a point of coming every day, though. Gunner needs to get used to the fact that you have a life too."

Graham seemed hesitant to speak. Finally, he sighed. "For years, we didn't have much of a relationship because I didn't know how to engage with him."

"You know how to engage with him," I countered. "You just let your guilt regarding Yolanda rule you. It's nice that you're not doing that any longer."

"I still feel it."

"You probably always will. It's better not to let it control you, though."

"Yeah. You should do the same."

"What do I have to feel guilty about?"

"About the way you've been trying to shut down your parents. It's okay if you're ready to move forward. They're going to take whatever you give them because they feel guilty, too. Maybe we should all let go of the guilt."

"Wouldn't that be nice?"

"You're getting there." He ruffled my hair. "You're a good girl. You try to pretend you're not, but at your core, you're soft and sweet."

"Are you trying to piss me off?"

He laughed, which was my intention. "I can remember what life was like without you, but I'm so glad you're in our lives. You make things better."

"Of course I do. I'm sunshine and light."

"You're ... something." Graham gave me one more side squeeze and then moved toward Gunner, who was eyeing the tarp-covered body with great dislike. "You know when spiders look like they're dead, when they curl up and you think they're gone, but really they're just waiting until they think you're not looking? Then they get up and keep crawling around again. I hope that's not happening here." He slapped Gunner's shoulder a little harder than was necessary and then started toward his truck, whistling.

"Why?" I complained to his back as Gunner stared at the body with fresh eyes.

Graham didn't turn around. He just shrugged. "Why not?"

When I turned back, I found Gunner had retrieved a metal rod from somewhere—it had to be the back of his truck—and he was poking the body.

"She's dead," I snapped.

"You don't know," he shot back. "Spiders do play dead."

I shook my head and flicked my eyes to Evan. "I'm sorry he texted you. We could've done this ourselves. I mean... I could've lifted the body in the back of the truck if it came to that."

Evan's shoulders hopped. "It's fine. I want to go with you."

"How come?"

"Because I feel we're getting close to some answers here—at least a plan—and I want to be there for that. You know I get FOMO."

My lips curved. "I still appreciate it. Gunner isn't going to be a lot of help when we talk to the spider people."

"I heard that," Gunner groused. He was still poking the body.

"Oh, I don't know," Evan said. "I think having your boyfriend and his bad back wait in the truck while you do all the heavy lifting is kind of cute."

"I wasn't going to stay in the truck," Gunner sniffed. "Also, I do have a bad back. Scout woke me up during my restorative sleep and now I'm in pain."

"Okay, buddy." Evan grinned at him. "I believe you."

"It's true," Gunner insisted, his imploring eyes coming to me. "Tell him."

"If you're in such pain, maybe you should stay here," I suggested. "Evan and I can handle this. You should get your rest."

Evan baby talked him. "Yes, the big, strong shifter should go back to bed. He needs his sleep."

"I don't appreciate the attitude," Gunner muttered. "I said I was going. I'm going."

"If we didn't have attitude, our conversations would be so much more boring," I noted.

"Yeah, yeah, yeah."

. . .

GUNNER DROVE. IT GAVE HIM SOMETHING TO do rather than obsess if it was the wind whipping the tarp we'd covered the body with, or if she really was rising from the great beyond now that she'd lulled us. I let Evan sit up front while I sat in the back and thought about how I was going to approach things. Subterfuge seemed like a bad idea. The spider people weren't smart enough to actually be manipulated. The straightforward approach seemed like the way to go.

This time Gunner pulled into the park. We weren't going to carry the body in because people on the road might be able to see what we were doing ... and that would be a whole other mess. There was no activity in the park, but I could feel hundreds of eyes—some likely in chins—watching us from the windows of the trailers.

I didn't waste time once the truck stopped moving and jumped out. I moved to the front of the truck—I could feel Evan behind me—and stared in various directions before I focused on one trailer.

"We need to talk," I called out.

Nobody answered. Nobody stirred.

"I'm not here to kill you," I offered. "Not yet at least. We have something that belongs to you, though." I nodded at Evan, who retreated to the back of the truck to retrieve the body. He was careful when he dropped her on the ground in front of me and removed the tarp.

I couldn't see the spiders. Nor could I hear them. I felt them, though, and there was a great amount of panic rolling through them inside the trailers.

"I need a representative of your group out here now." I let my frustration show. I didn't have time to deal with these guys. "Just send somebody out. We need to have a discussion."

Evan cast me a sidelong look as we waited for them to do ... whatever it was they were doing. "Do you think they're drawing straws?"

"I think they believe I killed the queen and whoever comes out here is going to die," I replied.

"You could tell them you didn't kill the queen."

"That's the plan. I don't really want to yell it, though."

"I can see that." Evan glanced back at the driver's seat, to where Gunner was making a big show of checking something on his phone. "What's with him and the spiders?"

I shrugged. "We all have phobias. I'm terrified of sharks."

"Yes, and you've been in the ocean a grand total of one time."

"Twice," I countered.

"Do you know the odds of being eaten by a shark?" Evan raised an eyebrow. "They're minuscule."

"I didn't say it was a rational fear. The thing with fear is that you can't control it or rationalize it. If we're attacked, you know darned well that he's going to jump into the fray because he won't let us fight without him."

"The one thing that frightens him more than spiders is losing you."

"You have fears, too," I reminded him, narrowing my eyes when I saw movement through the trailer window directly in front of us. They were sending someone. Good.

"I used to have fears," Evan replied. "I don't have them any longer."

I didn't believe him. "You're not still afraid of vaginas?"

"Oh, stop telling people that," Evan complained as the trailer door opened and a female Arachnid appeared. She looked pale, and terrified, so I opted to keep my gaze on Evan so she wouldn't flee back into the trailer. "I'm not afraid of them. I just don't understand them."

"What's to understand?"

"They're weird," Evan complained. "It's like a little doughnut or something."

I choked on a laugh. "A doughnut?"

"How would you describe them?"

"I think we need to buy you a female anatomy book."

"I'll pass." He moved his eyes to the approaching Arachnid. She was alone. "So ... they sent you out to your doom alone, huh?"

The Arachnid straightened and stared him straight in the eye. "If I die, then I'll know I died for a purpose greater than myself." Her voice was low and thin.

"We're not going to kill you," I said to her.

She darted her eyes to me—even the ones in her chin—and I didn't miss the brief glimpse of hope that registered in her eyes. Then she got control of herself. "You killed our queen."

I glanced down at the body, then shook my head. "Actually, I didn't. The lamia apex did. She had her minions drop the body on my property last night, though."

Confusion knit the Arachnid's eyebrows. "I don't understand."

"I don't either, but that's why I'm here. We're going to talk. Your people aren't going to do anything weird, and we're not going to kill you all for being lying liars who lie."

She made a protesting sound. "We don't lie."

My glare was withering. "Let's not play *that* game, huh?" I let loose the exhale I didn't know I was holding. "I laid down the law with your queen yesterday. She lied and didn't mention the Arachnids hanging out at the school. She then tried to lure my boss in to kill him—I'm guessing to use as leverage against me—but it didn't work. I was going to kill her today for that alone. Bonnie just beat me to the punch."

"I have no knowledge of that." The Arachnid crossed her arms over her chest.

"No?" I was amused despite myself. "How about we start with names?" I suggested. "I'm Scout."

"You may call me Charlotte."

I stood there a moment, convinced I'd misheard her. "Charlotte?"

"Like the spider with the web in the book?" Gunner yelled from the truck. He'd rolled down the window so he could hear but was still inside.

"Shouldn't your name be something weird like Elvira? Or even Shelob? That's more terrifying than Charlotte."

"You'll have to take it up with my parents," she replied stiffly.

"Okay, well, Charlotte, when was the last time you saw your queen?"

It was clearly not the question she was expecting because she did a double take. "I don't understand."

"I'm trying to put together a timeline. I mean ... I'm guessing that your queen went to Bonnie to tell her about the threats I'd lobbed. Bonnie being Bonnie decided she was a traitor and killed her. The story is simple, but it fits the facts. Since we were dealing with a trap last night before heading home—this was hours before the minions brought us the body—I'm just trying to wrap my head around things."

"I ... don't know." Charlotte looked frustrated now. "When you took over the school, she was enraged. She left in a huff."

"Was her name Shelob by any chance?" I asked. "I'm just curious."

"Amara."

"Well, that's disappointing, too."

Evan patted my shoulder. "There, there. Just be glad we haven't crossed paths with Aragog yet."

"Who told you about Aragog?" Charlotte demanded.

I pressed my lips together, rolled my eyes to the sky, and ordered myself to count to ten. When I was finished, I flashed a flat smile. "So, yesterday afternoon," I prodded. "That's the last you saw her, correct?"

"We thought you had taken her prisoner," Charlotte confirmed. "You moved a great number of us to your prison."

"Jail," I corrected. "The town is way too small for a prison."

Bafflement ran roughshod over Charlotte's face.

"Forget I said that." I waved my hand. "It doesn't matter." I focused on Evan. "She went to Bonnie after we took over the school. I'm betting Bonnie didn't kill her until we took down the wall, though. Rick and Andrea made it to the cabin okay. There was no barrier. They left the Cauldron before Rooster came to the school."

"The timeline fits," Evan agreed.

"Bonnie promised you guys a place next to her," I said to Charlotte. "Instead of following through—even though your queen didn't do the smart thing and leave like I told her—she killed your queen because she's not trustworthy."

Charlotte let loose an indelicate snort. "And you think we're going to trust you?"

"No, I do not. I don't want you to trust me. I don't want you to stick around in my town. I want you to take your queen and go."

Charlotte was obviously suspicious because she cocked her head. "You're just going to let us leave even though Amara lied to you?"

"Yup." I bobbed my head. When Charlotte started toward the body to collect it, I shook my head. "There's just one thing," I said. "I need to know what you guys know about Bonnie before you go."

Charlotte opened her mouth, then shut it. She seemed to be considering the offer, but she was still reticent. "How do I know we can trust you?" she asked finally.

"Because I'm the one who let you go yesterday, and you're the ones who double-crossed me," I reminded her. "Bonnie is the one who killed your queen. Not me. She thought your queen was working for me."

"We would never." Charlotte shuddered with revulsion. "Pixies are our enemies."

"Okay." That was news to me, but I filed it away to research later. "You should know that Bonnie is part pixie now. She stole my sister's power. That's neither here nor there, though."

"She did not tell us that." Charlotte looked appalled.

"I'm not surprised. I need to know Bonnie's plan. I'll let you take your queen and leave with all your Arachnids—the people in the jail who were bitten and taken over are staying though—if you tell me what you know about Bonnie and what she's going to do."

Charlotte's gaze turned calculating. "What makes you think we know anything?" she asked finally.

"Because Bonnie is as loony as they come, and she spends half her time talking to herself. You would've at least heard something. Tell me what it is, and you can go ... as long as you know that if you ever come back, I will kill you."

Charlotte looked resigned. "We don't want to be here. This place is cold ... and barren ... and your fight is not our fight."

"Then tell me what you know, and we'll call it a day."

"Can you guarantee the lamia apex won't come after us?" Charlotte looked hopeful.

"No, I cannot. Bonnie is unpredictable. I can promise that I believe her attention will be on me going forward. She won't even be looking at you guys because she thought she washed her hands of you when she killed your queen."

That seemed to make sense to Charlotte because she nodded. "All I know is that the lamia apex seems to believe the answer to beating you is in the past."

That was not the response I was expecting. "Now I'm the one who doesn't understand."

"She says the future is written in stone. There's a prophecy ... and you almost always win no matter the changes she tries to wreak on the timeline. That means she has to go to the past to kill you."

"But..." I licked my lips and turned to Evan. He looked as baffled as I felt.

"How is she going to travel through time?" Evan asked finally. "I mean ... that's not something people can just do unless they're predisposed to it. She's not, for the record."

"I don't know the specifics," Charlotte replied. "I just know she believes she's procured a device that will help her with her plan."

That's when it clicked into place in my head. "Whatever she stole from the harpies," I said to Evan. "It wasn't a device to suck them dry. I was right about that being a stupid thing to keep out in the open. They lied about what it was."

"Then I guess we need to question them again," he said, his expression dark. "They're still out at The Overlook."

"Then that's where we're going. We need to get the others out there, too." I started to move back toward the truck but stopped myself. "Take your queen and leave this town," I ordered Charlotte. "I appreciate the tip. I want you gone, though."

"We're leaving," she assured me. "We don't want to stay here."

"Not that I don't believe you, but we need to be clear," I stressed. "If I see any of you again—that's a single one of you—I'll kill you all. I'm done being magnanimous."

"This is not our fight," Charlotte said. "We didn't want to be part of it in the first place. The lamia apex offered payment, though, and we thought we could use the money to find a permanent home in the west."

"Well, the lamia apex was always lying to you."

"I know. Amara couldn't see that until it was too late, though."

"Then good luck on your travels." I turned my back to her. She wasn't a threat. "Try not to eat people."

"We won't eat anyone here before we go. That's all I can promise."

"I guess that will have to be enough."

26
TWENTY-SIX

Whatever was happening at The Overlook was loud when Gunner, Evan, and I let ourselves in through the front door. We could hear it from several rooms away.

"Sounds like it's coming from the dining room," Evan said.

I nodded.

"Oh, maybe that means they're having a late breakfast." Gunner rubbed his stomach.

"You already ate," I reminded him.

"Yes, but it's been a few hours, and I burned off a lot of calories thanks to that thing with the Arachnids."

"You mean 'that thing' where you sat in the truck and pretended to be reading something on your phone while Scout and I did all the work?" Evan challenged.

"What work did you do?" Gunner protested. "Also, I was giving Scout her space. I knew she wanted to do it on her own."

"Thank you, honey." I offered him a fake pretty smile. "You always put my needs first."

"I do," Gunner readily agreed. "I'm good like that."

"Yeah, yeah, yeah." I moved away from him and toward the

sound of the noise. If I wasn't very much mistaken, Winnie and Tillie were getting into it. That was hardly surprising given Tillie's constant shenanigans. It wasn't what I wanted to deal with right now, though.

I was careful when poking my head through the open doorway. To my surprise, it wasn't just Tillie and Winnie going a round. Bay, Twila, Marnie, Terry, and Landon were there too.

"I don't understand what the big deal is," Tillie complained. "It was one little dancing bear."

"You made the bear talk," Winnie snapped.

"Technically that wasn't me." Tillie was solemn. "I just added the tutu."

"And who put the sign around the bear's neck proclaiming that Margaret Little was trying to bring down Hemlock Cove with a case of genital warts?" Winnie hissed.

I ducked my head to get control of my emotions. Clearly Tillie had been on a tear.

"It wasn't me," Tillie replied. "I don't actually like the word 'genital.' I would've gone with something more dangerous ... like Syphilis."

"Oh, well, at least we have that going for us." Winnie threw her hands in the air and turned her back on her aunt. She was clearly in a mood.

"Syphilis can make you crazy if it goes untreated," Tillie said knowledgeably. "That's what I was trying to get at. Baron said that genital warts are grosser ... and they hurt more. We decided to compromise."

"Where did you get the bear?" Landon asked. His expression was hard to read. He was serious enough, and yet the way his lips kept twitching told me he was amused.

"It's Michigan," Tillie replied. "There are bears everywhere."

"Aren't they hibernating now?"

Tillie waved off the suggestion. "I have no problem waking up a bear. It's almost spring. It was going to get up anyway."

"And who picked the song?" Marnie asked. "I mean...*Baby Got Back* is a catchy tune. Did you have to make the bear show everybody his bottom while dancing, though?"

"He did that on his own," Tillie replied. "We just kind of lured him into town. And, before you give me grief about it, was anybody hurt?"

"Margaret had an incident," Winnie replied.

"What sort of incident?" Bay asked. She seemed to be nursing her coffee and picking at a cake doughnut. The conversation clearly didn't have her full attention.

"She was surprised by the bear for obvious reasons." Winnie could always keep a straight face, and yet she seemed to be struggling now. "Apparently ... um ... you tell them, Terry." She wrung her hands together.

For his part, Terry was a stoic mass of annoyance. "She crapped her pants," he replied.

Behind me, Gunner and Evan burst out laughing, drawing attention to us.

"It's not funny," Winnie insisted.

"Sorry." Gunner held up his hands. "Sometimes I have the sense of humor of a thirteen-year-old boy."

"And I only laughed because he did," Evan assured them.

"We laughed at the same time," Gunner argued.

"Yes, but I knew you were going to laugh, and it just sort of happened."

"Whatever." Gunner pushed his way into the room. "Where did that doughnut come from?"

Rather than answer, Winnie disappeared into the kitchen. When she returned, she had a platter of freshly decorated doughnuts with her. She wordlessly placed it on the table, where Gunner could sit directly in front of it, and he went to town as everybody else returned to the conversation at hand.

"People are saying you took photos of the defecation incident,"

Winnie said to Tillie. "You are not to put those photos on fliers and tape them up downtown. You've been warned."

"Technically it was an accident and not an incident," Bay noted. "We should stop calling it an incident."

Winnie ignored her.

As for Tillie, her mouth was hanging open. "First of all, do I look like someone who would put up fliers? That's way too much work."

Winnie rolled her eyes.

"Secondly, I did not take photos."

"Well, that's something," Marnie said.

"I took video. I'm going to put it to music and upload it to the Hemlock Cove website."

"No, you are not," Winnie snapped.

"How would you even know how to upload it?" Bay challenged. "It's not as if you're technologically gifted."

"I'm not," Tillie agreed. "Evan is, though. He'll do it for me."

All eyes turned to Evan, who was suddenly fascinated by the doughnuts. "Give me one of those." He snagged a bear claw—which seemed like an odd choice given the conversation—and bit in. "Wow. Who cooked these? I'm going to love you forever." He didn't need to eat to sustain himself. It was a nice diversion, though.

Winnie had no intention of falling for it. "Don't you load that video for her." She extended a threatening index finger. "Just don't even think about it."

"Okay," Evan replied easily enough. If I had to guess—and I would ask him about it later—he was already anticipating Easton being the one to put the video up. That was tomorrow's problem, though.

"Listen, I don't want to interrupt," I started.

"Then don't," Winnie fired back. She was clearly at the end of her rope.

"I don't have a choice. I need to talk to Tiffany and Brandy."

"They're upstairs." Winnie looked disinterested in the reason for my visit. "They're leaving today. They say they're going to rent a place in Hawthorne Hollow until their house is fixed."

"Okay." I turned to leave, but Bay stopped me.

"Has something happened?" she asked.

There was no reason to lie. "The Arachnids say that Bonnie's plan is to go back in time to kill me. Supposedly, she stole something from the harpies that would allow her to do that. I need to talk to them."

Everybody at the table forgot about Tillie and the defecation video—she would owe me for that later—and started talking at once.

"Are you kidding me?" Bay said when the din had died down. "Why didn't you lead with that?"

"I was enjoying the conversation," was my response. "Who doesn't love a good 'Margaret pooped her pants' story?"

"There." Tillie jabbed a finger at me. "She gets it."

"Yes, and now I need to get something else. Like information." I didn't hesitate this time before heading for the stairs. This was a conversation for sooner rather than later.

There was scrambling behind me, and when I looked, Bay had joined Evan and Gunner for the chase up the stairs. Tiffany's room was open when we arrived. She wasn't alone either. Her sister was with her, and they looked to be packing up.

I stood in the doorway and waited. It only took a split second for them to register my presence.

"Scout," Tiffany said. Her expression was pinched.

"You're Scout?" Brandy offered me a warm smile. "I'm glad you stopped by. I wanted to thank you for saving us. I wasn't awake when you were here, and I thought I was going to have to track you down in Hawthorne Hollow."

"You don't have to thank me," I assured her. "I was just doing my job." I moved my gaze back to Tiffany. She seemed to be able to read the room better.

"You know," Tiffany said. It wasn't a question.

"I know," I confirmed.

Tiffany abandoned the dresser and moved to the bed to sit down. She looked much better than she had when I'd removed her from the cairn days before, but there were still shadows under her eyes. She seemed tired.

"I was hoping it was just a coincidence," Tiffany offered. "The channeling stone looks like a sapphire. I thought maybe she stole it because she thought she could get some money for it."

"That doesn't appear to be the case," I replied. "Apparently, she wants to use it to go back in time and kill me."

Brandy's forehead creased. "Do you have any idea how much magic that would entail?"

"Well, since she's got apex lamia powers, Emma's pixie powers, and her own witch magic, I'm guessing she believes that she has enough power to carry out what she wants to do."

"Add to that the magic she stole from us," Tiffany said on a sigh. "That's the key, you realize. She's going to use our magic to power the stone."

"I didn't realize that harpies could travel through time," Bay interjected. She was clearly invested in the conversation.

"It's not a normal gift, but there are some lines that have that power," Brandy replied. "We're one of them."

"Do you travel through time often?" Evan asked.

"We've never traveled through time," Tiffany replied. "It's dangerous. Changing one little thing—turning right instead of left and causing an accident, even a fender bender—could change every-thing. We never wanted to risk it."

"Obviously, Bonnie believes that she needs to risk it," Brandy said. "Can you tell us why she believes that?"

I had a choice. I could keep them at arm's length and tell them to mind their own business. Or I could take a leap of faith. My heart told me I could trust them. So I did.

"There's a prophecy about a big battle here," I replied. "It's going to involve my people, friends from other places, shifters, gnomes ... you name it. That prophecy is the reason Gunner's mother tried to kill him when he was a child. She recognized him in it."

The sisters looked horrified.

"That prophecy has little changes all the time," I continued. "The big outcome is not shifting, though. Not with Bonnie killing Zeno and taking over. Not with Yolanda dying. Not with my parents coming back into the picture. The big ending remains the same."

"You winning," Tiffany surmised.

I nodded. "Bonnie wants to make sure that doesn't happen, for obvious reasons."

"You winning means she will die," Brandy said.

"Yes."

"So, she wants the channeling stone to go back in time," Tiffany deduced. "She's going to kill you. When do you think she's going to try and get you?"

That was an interesting question. "I don't know. My guess is she won't go back to the time when I was with my family. There are too many pixie witches there to risk a fight with. She would probably be better off going after me once I'm in the system. I was alone a lot."

"How would she know that, though?"

"Because I told her. We talked about my upbringing some when I joined the group up here. I ... we ... well, I thought we were friends. She was easy to talk to."

"And she probably led you to the information she wanted and you didn't even realize it," Tiffany said. "It makes sense that she would go after you when you were still a child. Your magic would've been weaker then."

"I didn't even really come into my magic—at least enough to realize what I was dealing with—until I was older," I confirmed. "If she goes after me as a child, I won't be able to fight her off."

"Then we need to stop that from happening," Gunner said. "I'm not losing you."

"If Bonnie kills Scout as a child, everything that has happened will be rewritten," Brandy countered. "It could be catastrophic. It won't just be that Scout never existed. Although it will be like that for you. She'll have existed for her parents but have been lost. You just won't remember her. Or, more likely, there will be some local legend about a pixie apex who was supposed to save the world, but the prophecy died."

Gunner briefly closed his eyes. "We can't let this happen." He rested his hand on the doorframe. "We just ... cannot let that happen." His voice sounded ragged.

"We can't," Evan agreed. He was the one who comforted Gunner by putting his hand on his shoulder. "Listen, that's not how it's going to go down. That's why we're here. We're going to make sure she can't go back in time." His gaze was imploring when he turned it on the sisters. "How do we do that?"

"Guys, take a breath," I instructed. "I'm right here. There's no reason to get upset."

Gunner burned me with a look. "Really? Because Bonnie dropped a body to distract us last night. She knows she doesn't have a lot of time to do this. That means she's going to be doing it today. Maybe even right now."

"I know, but we're going to stop her." It was lame to say, but it was all I had.

"We're also going to ensure that we can fix it if something goes wrong," Bay said, catching me off guard.

"How are we going to do that?" Evan asked.

"I'm going to have Aunt Tillie cast a spell," Bay replied. I noticed she wasn't asking my permission. She was deadly serious. "It will make it so we can see both timelines if this one changes. We'll remember Scout."

Gunner let out the breath he'd been holding. "Will we be able to get her back, though?"

Bay's expression twisted. "Gunner, when I said 'we' would be able to get her back, I meant us. Aunt Tillie and me. We can't cast the spell for you. It has to be a witch."

Gunner briefly closed his eyes. When he opened them again, he was calmer. "You won't let us lose her."

"Of course not," Bay assured him. "It's just a precaution. We're going to make sure this doesn't happen."

I turned back to the sisters. "How do we stop this ... what is it called?"

"It's called the Loden. At least that's what our people call it." Tiffany absently scratched her cheek. "The only surefire way I know to stop it is to destroy it. If Bonnie already has it activated, that's what you need to do."

"But only if she hasn't walked through the door to the past," Brandy stressed. "If she manages to get through that door, you have to follow her to stop her."

"Which means I'm going to have to go to the past and kill her," I surmised. "How would I get back?"

"The Loden should bring you back," Tiffany replied. "There are no guarantees, though. It's better if you destroy it before she manages to engage it."

"To do that, we need to know where her lair is." I shook my head. "We don't know that right now."

"We don't," Bay agreed. "I'm willing to bet a certain loa does, though."

"He didn't intimate as much last night when he was helping us drop the magical wall Bonnie erected around the family cabin."

"Well, there's no way he doesn't know." Bay was firm. "He's walking a very narrow tightrope right now. I'm guessing he didn't want you to know what Bonnie was planning in case you panicked. He was hoping you would find another way to stop her and it wouldn't be an issue."

"Well, that doesn't seem to be the case," I said darkly.

"Aunt Tillie can find him," Bay said. "We'll cast the spell, so we won't forget. Then you, me, and Aunt Tillie will go to find him."

Gunner balked. "I'm not leaving Scout."

"It's not a *Sophie's Choice* situation," I assured him. "I need you and Evan to go to the Rusty Cauldron. Get everybody together ... including Rick and Andrea. If I'm about to be erased from the present timeline, they should know."

"That's my girl," Evan whispered. He looked proud. He also looked terrified. I didn't know which one of those things freaked me out more.

"Make sure the team is prepared," I ordered. "We'll be heading out as soon as we have a location."

"What about Bonnie, though?" Evan challenged. "We still don't know what we're going to do with her powers. If we kill her and don't have anybody on hand to step in and take the lamia powers..." He trailed off. He didn't need to finish it out. I already knew what was bothering him.

"We don't have a choice," I replied. "We'll have to try not to kill her. If we can destroy the Loden and get her to run, that will have to be enough."

"We can also try to put her in stasis," Bay added. "Aunt Tillie has been working on a spell. I'm not sure if it's going to work yet, but it's worth a shot."

"What does stasis mean?" Gunner asked.

"It's not a forever fix," Bay warned. "We can freeze her, though. We can make it so she's floating and can't get out. It will buy us time until we find a new lamia apex."

Gunner perked up. "I'm all for that."

"It's our best shot," I agreed. "We have to worry about the Loden first, though. If Bonnie can travel through time, it's going to mean bad things for all of us."

"She can only do it once," Tiffany said. "She doesn't have enough power to do it multiple times because we didn't have enough power to do it more than that. She's got one shot."

I blew out a breath. "Okay, we have a plan. Let's get it together."

"Scout..." Gunner reached for me. He looked torn.

"It's okay," I assured him. "We're going to fix this. Just ... have a little faith."

"I have endless faith in you. I'm still afraid."

He wasn't the only one.

27
TWENTY-SEVEN

"Are you sure this will work?" Bay was dubious as she regarded Tillie.

"Of course it will work." Tillie eyed the cauldron she'd been slaving over for the past hour, the potion inside swirling and making for an unfortunate puke color. "I'm not new."

"You might not be new, but I don't remember you ever doing a spell like this," Bay argued.

"That's because I've never had to do a spell like this. There's a first time for everything, though, right?" Tillie's smile was bright. "I have done memory spells before. This one is just a little bit different."

"Explain it to me," I prodded.

"Why?" Tillie cast me a dubious look. "Are you going to demand a new potion if this one doesn't work? It's not as if we have time for that."

She was right. Still ... I wanted to know. "If I disappear, I won't know any better. I'll just be gone. Right now—just for right now—I would like to know what you're going to do to fix it if it happens."

Under normal circumstances, Tillie would give me a hard time and call me weak. This time, however, she just sighed. "Bay and I will take the potion," she said. "We could give it to everybody, but as long as it's the two of us, that's all that matters. The others will believe us regardless."

I nodded but didn't say anything.

"We'll remember this happening," Tillie continued. "We'll remember this timeline, so even if it changes, we'll know to go look for you."

"How do you know you can fix it, though?" That was the part that bugged me. "If time travel was easy, everybody would be doing it."

"I don't think it's going to matter," Bay assured me. "We just want to make sure that we remember you so we can find you again."

Just because they wanted to find me, that didn't mean they would. "I guess at least you guys will remember." I thought of Evan and Gunner. "Maybe it's better if they don't."

"No." Bay was firm when shaking her head. "That is not even remotely true."

"If I'm going to be gone anyway, it's better for them," I argued. "If you don't think you can get me back, don't tell them, okay? Just ... let them go on with their lives."

"Why are you assuming that we're going to get to the point where we lose you?" Bay demanded. She looked annoyed.

I shrugged. "I don't know. I just have a weird feeling. Like ... it's been building to this for days. It's as if something inside of me knew it was going to be over."

"Yes, well, you have been off your game," Bay conceded. "I get it. This is all too much. It's not going to get to that point, though."

"How can you be so certain?" I wanted a little bit of her faith.

"Because this is the answer to the riddle."

"And what riddle is that?"

"Why Baron is hanging around."

Realization dawned on me. "Oh, crap."

She nodded as my eyes went wide. "This is why he's here."

"We wondered, but obviously he was assigned to make sure there was no time travel," Bay said. "It's the only thing that makes sense. He's been hanging close all week, but not too close. He's been taking off to do his own thing, too. He's here to make sure there is no time travel."

"Why Baron, though?"

"Well, actually, I've been doing some research on him." Bay glanced around as if she expected him to pop out of the woodwork. "He has dominion over the dead. He can grant and take life. I think he wants to make sure that, if Bonnie makes it to the past, she can't take your life. He can literally stop death."

That was an interesting tidbit. "Poet never mentioned that."

"It might not have come into play with her."

"Maybe," I agreed.

Bay pulled up her phone. "See this here. This is an online group dedicated to studying and dissecting the loas. They've had a lot of good insights."

"You've been hanging around in a chatroom?" I was amused despite myself. Then something caught my eye on her phone screen, and all traces of mirth were gone. "Wait ... what's that?"

I pointed toward the squiggle drawings on the screen. It jogged something in my memory. What, though?

"What's what?" Bay followed my finger. "Oh." She nodded. "That's called a veve. I think they're neat. You know how there are certain pictures to depict the saints? Well, the loas are the counterparts. Each one has its own veve. This one is Baron's."

It took a few seconds for me to remember where I'd seen the drawing before. "The Beechwood sisters had runes in their house. Unlike the drawings for the four corners, their runes had these on them." I indicated the veve again. "Why do you think that is?"

"I think that they worship differently than we do," Bay replied. "It's possible they knew what was coming, though."

"We were just up there," I argued. The Beechwood sisters had left since our discussion. "Why wouldn't they say anything?"

"Maybe it's none of our business. Maybe they have different business with the loas. Just because Baron is here, that doesn't mean we're the only ones he's working with."

I hated that she had a point. "I'm annoyed."

"I don't blame you." Bay was matter of fact. "The truth is, he could've told us what was going on and saved us a lot of grief."

"Maybe he can't," Tillie argued. She'd been quiet for several minutes. "Maybe he can only involve himself to a point."

"Did he say something to you?" I demanded.

"No." She gave me a dirty look before wagging a finger. "And don't take that tone with me. I'm just saying ... he might not be able to involve himself to the extent you want him to involve himself. That's not him being a jerk. It's him having to follow rules ... and they're the sort of rules he might not be able to tell us about."

"Just because he's a loa, that doesn't mean he doesn't answer to anybody," Bay hedged.

"I guess." I rolled my neck and shook my head. "I guess it doesn't matter. It doesn't matter about the harpies either. They're going to do what they're going to do ... and now we have to do what we're going to do."

"We do," Bay agreed. Her gaze was seeking when it roamed my face. "We've got this. The potion is just a backup."

"Yeah." I scratched my cheek. "I guess I should suck it up and cast a locator spell."

"We still need to know where Bonnie is," Bay agreed. "We should get ready. We'll have the others head out when we're on the road. Then we'll all meet at the rendezvous."

"Oh, you do listen to me," Tillie crooned. "You've been picking up on my military speak. I'm so proud."

Bay made a face. "Actually, Landon and I have been watching this reality show so we can make fun of it where they make people go through boot camp. Landon eats an entire bag of chips himself when he's watching. That's where I heard it."

"You can't pretend you listen to what I say just for once?"

Bay shook her head. "Apparently, I can't."

"You are the worst."

Bay smirked before sobering. "No, I think the worst is yet to come."

WE HAD TO WORK TOGETHER TO CAST the locator spell. Bonnie had done something to baffle my magic when I tried it for the first time. I wasn't all that surprised—now that she had Emma's magic, she could thwart a lot of my pixie magic—but it was annoying all the same. When Bay and Tillie cast a locator spell with only their magic, however, it worked ... and it led us right back to Hawthorne Hollow.

I called Gunner and the others, and they were ready when we passed by. They filed right into line behind us. We didn't have to delay things. Time seemed important now.

Very, very important.

We were at the front, which seemed like a detriment because I wasn't familiar with the area where the locator spell was leading us. Surprisingly, when we came around a final corner, I recognized our location.

"Wait." I leaned forward. "This is the ghoul house."

"What ghoul house?" Bay's eyes crinkled at the corners. She was the one behind the wheel ... but mostly because nobody trusted Tillie to drive when there were real stakes on the line. She was a menace behind the wheel. We had taken her plow truck, though.

"A few days ago—right when this all started—we got sent out to deal with ghouls," I explained. "We climbed the hill that way. We didn't come in from this direction. This is where we were, though."

Bay studied the house. She'd stopped driving, so we could only catch a small glimpse through the trees. "Maybe she came out here because she knew it was empty. Once you took her cave, she was struggling to find a new headquarters. It probably made sense to go to a place where you'd already been."

"Maybe," I agreed. "Or maybe she just doesn't care. She thinks this is her big shot to take me out."

"It kind of is." Bay cocked her head and sent me a rueful smile. "I mean ... it's ingenious when you think about it."

"Yeah. It's a smart move." I tried to smile ... and failed. "At least she can only make one jump. That's what the Beechwood sisters said. She only has enough power to make that one jump ... so if she fails, then it's done."

"Then let's make sure she fails." Bay made an attempt at a smile, but it was more of a grimace than anything else. "Are you ready?"

"Not even remotely."

"Are you prepared to do it anyway?"

"Yup." I pushed open the door and hopped out, absently helping Tillie down—despite her slapping my hands and telling me she could do it herself—before raising my chin to greet the others. Nobody looked happy about the turn of events. Well, other than Marissa. She looked positively gleeful at the possibility of me being wiped from the timeline. We were all determined to make sure that it didn't happen, though.

"I see they tapped the big dog," I said to Mama Moon when I realized she'd tagged along for the ride.

"They did," she confirmed. It was rare for her not to look smug. Today, however, she seemed stressed. "We're going to make sure this doesn't happen."

"Okay." I flashed a smile I didn't feel. "Thanks for coming."

"We created a potion," Bay explained to Mama Moon. "If something happens, then we'll at least remember her."

"And try to figure out a way to erase Bonnie's attempt at messing with the timeline," Mama Moon surmised. "It's smart. Potentially fruitless, but smart."

"Hey!" Gunner snapped. "I don't want to hear about anything being fruitless. You got me?"

I sent him a sympathetic look. "Gunner, it's okay." I reached over and squeezed his hand. "We're going to make sure nothing bad happens."

He didn't look convinced. "Let's just do this. I'll absorb Bonnie's powers if I have to. Let's just kill her today."

"You won't survive that," I argued.

He glared at me. "Maybe I'm willing to sacrifice myself so you don't have to."

"No." I was firm when shaking my head. "Nobody is going to sacrifice him or herself." I meant it. "That includes me. We're going to figure out a way to get all of us out of this. That means we can't kill Bonnie yet."

"But we can put her in stasis if the opportunity arises," Bay said. "We've got every angle covered. We need to get in there, though. If Bonnie realizes we're here, she could try to use the Loden and then we're really screwed. We need to move."

Gunner was annoyed but game. "Fine. I'm sticking close to you, though," he said to me.

"There's nowhere else I would want you to be," I assured him. "We've got this."

When he smiled, I hoped I'd done my best to convince him. My biggest issue was convincing myself. There was no time for that, though. We had to move right now. We were out of options.

I took the lead for the walk up to the house. I could feel people watching—dwarves?—but didn't bother knocking. I reached out with my senses, determined the wards were low, and burned through them with my pixie magic before throwing open the front door.

"Honey, I'm home!" I declared.

The dwarves, who were armed, threw knives at me. Three of them had taken up positions in what had once been a living room. The house was probably beautiful at one time—how Gunner and I wanted to update our cabin someday—but it looked as if it was one bad winter from toppling.

By the time I was finished, it would be gone. I would make sure of it.

I managed to dodge one knife and deflect the other two with my magic. When I was in Detroit, knives being thrown was commonplace. I had gotten out of the habit of dealing with them during my time in Hawthorne Hollow. It was like riding a bike, though. It was one of those things that you didn't forget.

"I don't think so," Evan growled as he grabbed the nearest dwarf, who looked to be reaching for another weapon. He shook the creature until it stopped moving and then threw him against the wall like he weighed nothing. It was brutal, but nothing compared to what we would unleash if Bonnie didn't relinquish the Loden.

The other two dwarves tried to retreat, but Gunner grabbed one and killed it without wasting a single breath, his shifter claws coming out to play. I kept my face impassive even though there were chills running up my spine.

That left the dwarf in the middle, and I cocked my head to slow his pace. "Now would be the time to run," I warned him. "You don't want to be here for this."

The dwarf seemed to consider it. His eyes glittered, his chest heaved. There was no smoke coming out of his ears, but he was clearly thinking hard. Then he bowed his head and acted as if he were going to leave. It was too good to be true. I braced myself. When he was even with me, he lunged to the side, brandishing another knife. Evan caught him before he could move more than a foot, and he died with his friends.

I moved to the next room, which had likely been a dining room at one time. That's where I found Bonnie. She looked frantic, and it gave me a small thrill to see her obvious panic. In the middle of the floor, the huge sapphire stone rested on a stand. It was glowing, but not swirling enough to suggest that a door had already been opened.

"I think you're done," I said to her.

"Not even close," she hissed. She threw more magic than I was expecting at the stone. It was a bright green color, so when it mixed with the blue, the stone turned turquoise as it immediately kicked to life and started swirling magic all around it.

It was almost as if I'd jinxed myself. "Stop!" I fired as much magic at her as possible, but it did nothing to dissuade her. Now she was the one feeling full of herself as the door took shape.

"Your time is done," she announced as she straightened. The gleam in her snakelike eyes had my insides shriveling. "Now I will end you."

She leapt toward the swirling light. I tried to stop her with my magic, but it was already too late. There was only one thing I could do.

I didn't say goodbye to my friends. I didn't tell Gunner I loved him. I just took a leap of faith and followed her through the light.

I didn't know where I was going. I just knew I only had one chance to stop her.

One.

28
TWENTY-EIGHT

I chased Bonnie through swirling mist in a world that seemed to have no definition. No ceiling. No floor. No sound. Well, the last part wasn't entirely true. There was some sound. I could hear Bonnie laughing like the Joker on crack. She was ahead of me, and seemed to know where she was going. All I could do was follow.

When I finally emerged in what appeared to be the real world, I had to look left and right for Bonnie. I didn't immediately see her. I was on a busy street. The skyline told me I was in Detroit, and I had to suck back a sigh when a case of nostalgia caught me in the feels. Then I remembered I was on a mission.

I had to find the when because that would inform the where. If I knew what year it was, I could find myself and stop Bonnie from doing ... whatever it was she was going to do. It would be ugly, of course. If I stopped her, though, that would be enough.

Although, getting home was a whole other issue.

Rather than try to find Bonnie—that would be a lot of wasted effort—I pointed myself toward discovering what year it was. That led me to a newspaper box. That alone told me that I was in the past. You didn't see newspaper boxes most places these days. I had quarters on me, and the box didn't seem to have a problem with them even though they were from another time. When I pulled out the newspaper, I was struck by several things at once.

The first was that it was thicker than any newspaper I'd seen in a long time. I'd forgotten that newspapers used to be robust and important. Nowadays people didn't want to pay for their news. They wanted it for free on the internet...whether it was true or not.

The front page's biggest story was the Sandy Hook shooting. There was also another story mentioning an issue in Libya. There were a lot of conspiracy theories tied to a bombing over there. The date in the corner said it was December. More than a decade before. I would've been an adult, not a child.

So why had Bonnie opted to take on an adult Scout and not the child?

Slowly I turned, and almost came out of my skin when I found Cernunnos leaning against a building watching me, arms crossed. "Seriously?" I gave him a dirty look. "What are you doing here?"

"You know me?" He looked momentarily confused. Then he caught himself. "Of course you know me. You're from the future. I'm sure my future self would've wanted to know you, so it makes sense that you know me, but I don't know you."

Was that supposed to make sense to me? "Um..."

"I'm Cernunnos," he offered amiably, extending his hand.

I eyed it before snagging gazes with him. "Hello, Bob," I said dryly, mimicking Zoe Lake-Winters, the mage who messed with Cernunnos every chance she got.

He paused, his expression going hard before he cracked a smile and dropped his hand. "Of course, you know Zoe. From everything I've heard, you and she are two peas in a pod."

"I don't understand this," I admitted. "What are you doing here?"

"I received an urgent message from the future. I'm to help you stop whatever you're here to stop."

"But you're not the Cernunnos I know," I prodded.

"I am what he was. I will grow into what he will become. I simply have not crossed paths with you yet."

I grew frustrated and made a growling sound.

"Try not to think on it too hard," he said. "You'll give yourself a headache, and maybe an ulcer."

I wanted to shake him. I didn't. He was my only backup, and I didn't have much time. "I need to find myself," I replied. "I need to find the other me."

"Sure." Cernunnos was agreeable enough as he bobbed his head. "Let's find the other you."

We fell into step together, and I cast him an odd look. "Just out of curiosity, how did you know to come here?"

"I told you. I received a message from the future."

"From whom?"

He shrugged. "It's hard to say. Let's focus on why you're here." He was calm, but there was a hint of nerves fueling him. "Where would you be at this time?"

"I was living in a rat trap apartment over on Woodward," I replied.

"Okay. Was that public knowledge?"

"I ... don't understand." I slowed my pace. "Why does that matter?"

"Because the warning I got to help you suggested that we need to cut corners to save time. You're going to look at the place you *know* you are. Where does your enemy *think* you are?"

It was a preposterous question on the face of it, and I opened my mouth to tell him just that. Then I realized he was right. "The halfway house after I left the group home," I replied. "I didn't want to stay there. It was for transitional cases. I found out a few years ago that the people running it listed me as one of the residents—and got paid for it—but I was never there."

Cernunnos nodded. "Then that is where she will go."

I didn't argue with him. He seemed to know what he was talking about.

"Do you know where it is?" he asked after a beat when I hadn't started walking.

"Oh, right." I put my head down and started in that direction. It was an uncomfortable walk. Eventually, I slowed my pace and regarded him. "Can't you just poof us to where we need to go?"

"Of course. I thought you might want to talk, though."

He wasn't wrong. There were a few things I wanted to discuss. "It's at least ten miles from here."

"Ah, then we'll poof there—as you call it—and have a discussion once we arrive at our destination."

"Fine." I eyed his hand when he extended it. "What?"

"You have to tell me where we need to go."

"Oh." I was really off my game here. Everything felt far too surreal. I took his hand. "The intersection of Sherman and Griffin Avenues. I don't remember the exact address. I just know it's over there. I'll be able to find it."

"Good enough." He squeezed my hand tightly. "Let's go." With that, the world around us blinked out, and before I could register it, we were in a different neighborhood.

I immediately released his hand as I looked around. "There." I pointed at a familiar house. It was two stories—plus a basement if I remembered correctly—with yellow siding that was sagging in multiple places and what had once been white shutters. Most of the shutters had fallen, along with the trim.

"That's where they keep children?" Cernunnos looked appalled.

"No." I shook my head. "That's where they keep eighteen-year-olds who don't have anywhere else to go. I was a ward of the state. I didn't have a lot of options."

"And yet you didn't come here," Cernunnos said.

"Actually, I came long enough to check it out. I knew it wasn't for me right away. I didn't have a bad deal at the last group home I was staying at. I still wanted to get out on my own. I just didn't know what I was going to do when I got there."

"And what did you do?"

"I was aimless for a few months. I lived in a rathole. Then I was in the park one day and saw a group of monster hunters wipe out a ghoul nest. I knew that's what I needed to be doing. It called to me."

Cernunnos nodded. "And now, here you are trying to stop your own assassination. It seems to have worked out well."

I cast him a dark look. "I don't need the judgment."

"I wasn't judging you. I just find it all interesting."

"Whatever." I rolled my eyes back to the house. "What do we do here? Do we stand out in the open and wait for Bonnie to come to us?"

"That doesn't sound smart."

"Yeah." I rolled my neck. "Let's find a place across the road, behind that house over there." I pointed toward a structure that was clearly abandoned. "When we see her show up, we'll..." That's where I lost the through line. "Crap. What are we supposed to do?" I shifted my wide eyes to him. "We can't kill her. I'll die in the process." I tried to picture Gunner's face if I never came back and died in the past. "Why were you sent here?" I demanded.

He managed a smile. "Your instincts are good. I can see why you went into your chosen field. I am here for a purpose."

"And what's that purpose?" I had to know. If he was an additional enemy, I didn't know what to do about it. I had to know, though.

"You're supposed to be here, Scout." His voice was soft. "I was warned that you would be difficult, and prone to sacrificing yourself for others. I'm not to allow that. I'm also not to allow you to interact with your younger self."

"That shouldn't be an issue," I fired back. "I'm not here."

"That's good." He was calm, the same god I knew, just not quite as familiar with the players. "You can't kill her, Scout," he said in a serious voice. It was as if he was reading my mind. "You're not meant to end things here. There's still too much for you to do."

I shook my head and paced the small area behind the house. It was overgrown, with weeds sticking out in various places. Some of those weeds were big enough to trip a person. "Someone knew I was coming to the past. Who?" I demanded.

He blinked. Then he sighed. "I was warned that you wouldn't quiet yourself without answers."

"Well, it's good that you were warned about that," I replied. "Being quiet is not in my wheelhouse." My eyes practically dared him to mess with me.

"We don't have a lot of time," he said. "Bonnie will be here soon. When she arrives, you're going to let me handle her."

That was not the response I was expecting. "You're going to kill her?"

"No, I most certainly am not going to kill her." He let loose a low chuckle. "I am, however, going to move her to a different place."

"Move her to a different place?" I repeated the words back to him, my brow furrowing. "I don't understand. I..." Then it hit me. "You're moving her to a plane where there's an entrance but not an exit." I wasn't certain how I knew that, but it made sense ... to the point where I'd been considering handling her that way myself to buy us time.

"She'll find a way off that plane even though there's no exit," he said. "The thing is ... she won't find it right away."

I touched my tongue to my top lip and nodded. "It's just a stopgap."

"It's a way to allow yourself the room you need to breathe," he clarified. "You need it."

"How can you know that?"

"Because the person who warned me ... was me."

An image popped into my head—two horned gods—and I had to force myself to exhale. "I knew you guys were up to something," I muttered under my breath.

"Of course we're up to something," he agreed. "What you need to understand is that we are trying to do what's right for you."

"I didn't actually doubt that."

"Good." Cernunnos was deadly serious now. "You need to listen. We don't have a lot of time."

I crossed my arms over my chest so my hands wouldn't start fluttering. Then I braced myself.

"I cannot kill this woman," he explained. "I cannot safely absorb her powers any more than you can. That's why she has to be moved. She's here to kill you in a time before you were strong enough to fight back. Why do you think she didn't come when you were a child?"

"I ... don't ... know. I was wondering about that, though."

"I'm sure you were. The short answer is, you were hidden as a child. The protection that was placed on you disappeared when you became an adult."

"And this is the place where I would've become an adult and still been at my weakest," I surmised.

He nodded.

"Who hid me?"

"Your parents to some extent. They did what they could. It wasn't enough, though, so we lent a helping hand." He leaned closer. "You're important for what's to come. We cannot fight the fight for you, but we can help our gladiators ... and you're one of ours."

"Good grief," I complained. "You're just as obnoxious now as you are in my time."

"Yes." He nodded. "I'm not done. Time grows short, however. You shouldn't be here. It's dangerous. You could change too many things. So could she. There is a traveler coming to this area in the future. Time will ... shift ... then. We cannot shift it now."

I waited for him to finish it out.

"That means, when we see her, you are going to let me handle it." He was firm now. "We can't risk you getting hurt. We can't risk you dying. We can't risk her dying either. She simply needs to be removed from the equation for the time being."

"Okay." I nodded. "You're going to shift her to another plane."

"Yes. I want you to distract her. I'll shift her. Then it will be done." He put both of his hands on my shoulders and talked to me as if I were a child now. "Do not do anything else. Promise me."

He seemed desperate about the possibility, which was unlike him. Of course, I'd never traveled through time before. I had no idea what sort of terrible things could happen. The fact that he was so serious had me agreeing even though I wasn't certain it was the right decision. "I won't do anything. It's just … how am I going to get home?"

He smirked. "We've got that handled too. A door will open when it's time. A door fashioned from the other side. Just focus on the apex for now. You will distract her. I will make her leave."

It sounded far too easy. "What are you guys afraid of?"

He started to shake his head, then stopped himself. "If something were to happen here that stopped you from going north, it would be the end of us all. We need things to stay as they are."

Something occurred to me. "Will the prophecy still be true after this?"

"I don't know anything about the prophecy," he replied. "You'll have to take that up with the other me."

"Okay." I nodded. He was too earnest to ignore. I'd theorized that the loas and Cernunnos were working together to ensure a specific outcome. What I hadn't realized is that they weren't looking beyond, at the prophecy. No, they were worried about the right now. That's why all of this had come together the way it had.

"Here she is." Cernunnos inclined his head toward the front of the house, to where a car had screeched to a stop.

Bonnie stumbled out of the car, her eyes gleaming as she took in the house. Her snake exterior stood out here even more than it did at home.

"Now is your time to shine," he said. "I'll approach her from the other side."

"Where did she get the car?" I asked absently. "She didn't kill someone to get that car, did she?"

"Kill? No. That's why nothing too terrible has happened yet. We have to make sure it stays that way."

I was resigned. "Fine. I'll distract her. Just ... end her quickly."

"I will do what needs to be done," he promised.

My feet felt heavy for the walk back up to the front of the house. Bonnie was focused on the group home and didn't look over her shoulder to check for enemies. That made it easy to get close.

"I'm not in there," I offered when I was about twenty feet away.

She whipped her head around, her eyes going wild. "How did you...?" She trailed off.

"It wasn't hard to figure out what your plan was," I said. "You have a problem, though."

"And what's that?" Bonnie sneered. She clearly wasn't happy with my presence. She hadn't yet realized just how much trouble she was in, though.

"I'm not in that house. The other me I mean. I never was. They collected money from the state for me, but I never lived here. Right now, I'm downtown somewhere. That's where I spent all my time at this age."

Bonnie vehemently shook her head. "You're lying. I had Doc look up your official records one day. He had access to the records. Of course, he didn't know why I had him looking you up. That doesn't matter, though."

"It doesn't," I agreed. "Just because the state has a record of me being here, though, that doesn't mean it's true. I wanted to be on my own. I didn't trust this place."

Bonnie cast another look at the house, then squared her shoulders. "Then I guess I'll just kill you."

"You could," I readily agreed. I'd realized something in the past few minutes that nobody else had brought up. "If you kill me, though, the same thing that will happen to me will happen to you."

"And what's that?" she hissed.

"You'll absorb my magic ... and it will be too much for you. You'll die."

For a moment, I thought Bonnie was going to laugh at me. She was deranged to the point of no return after all. She didn't, though. There was still part of her that could see reason. "But..." Her mouth opened and shut, then opened and shut again.

Before I could taunt her—because I really wanted to—a door began swirling behind her and I knew it was too late. Cernunnos was holding up his end of the bargain.

"I'm sure I'll see you soon," I offered lamely.

"You're seeing me right now," she snapped, crashing back to reality. "Are you blind?"

"No, but you're not staying." I gestured toward the door that was now so big there was no escaping it. "Don't worry. I'll still be around when you get back."

"No!" Bonnie tried to scramble away from the door, but the new plane's gravitational pull was too great. She disappeared through it and the door closed almost immediately in her wake. It all happened so fast it was almost as if she'd never been there.

When I looked up, I found Cernunnos watching me from afar. "I don't understand what you did here, but I'm going to figure it out," I promised.

He nodded. "That's also the other me's problem." He pointed to a spot over my shoulder, and when I looked, I found another door swirling. "Don't delay. Go through it. We got lucky here today. Keep it that way."

Because I knew my friends—Gunner, Evan, Bay—were on the other side, I moved toward the door. "Will the other you remember this?" I asked him before walking through it.

The horned god's smile was enigmatic. "He always has."

With that, I walked through the door and back to my people. The past had to remain in the past.

29
TWENTY-NINE

When I emerged back in my time, I found quite the sight. Gunner was on the ground in front of the cabin Bonnie had been using for a lair, his face buried in his arms, which rested on his knees. The shaking of his shoulders told me he was crying.

Evan stood a few feet away, his back to Gunner. He wasn't crying, but the way he was holding himself told me all I needed to know. He was bereft too.

Baron sat on the porch drinking from a flask. He looked none the worse for wear. Next to him sat Cernunnos, who also didn't look worried. They were the first two I focused on.

"We should talk," I said to them.

Cernunnos smirked even as excitement exploded around me and Gunner practically tackled me with an effusive hug. "Of course we'll talk," he said as I was dragged to the ground and effectively smothered.

"Where did you go?" Gunner demanded. His eyes were red rimmed and puffy. "Where the hell did you go?"

"Exactly where you think I went." I hugged him tight—he

seemed to need it—and met Evan's gaze over his shoulder. My best friend's eyes were bloodshot, suggesting he had shed a few tears as well. "How long have I been gone?"

"About two hours," Rooster replied as he stepped forward. His eyes weren't puffy, but I swear it looked as if he'd aged ten years. "What happened? Where's Bonnie? Did you...?" He trailed off.

"Kill her?" I managed a smile. "No, I did not. She's out of our hair for a little bit. I'm not sure how long." I patted Gunner's arm to get him to release me but that only made him hug me tighter.

"I'm okay," I assured him, struggling for the right words to make things better. "Absolutely nothing happened to me."

"I wouldn't say nothing," Cernunnos countered. He remained in his chair. "You did exactly what you were supposed to do, though."

I wrinkled my nose as I regarded him. "How long have you been here? This version of you I mean."

"Are there other versions of him?" Andrea asked. She stood next to Rick, their hands clasped, and looked as if they'd been through an ordeal. Of course, they *had* been through an ordeal. All the sacrifices they'd made to get us to the finish line must have flashed before their eyes when I disappeared.

"Well, I got to meet the Cernunnos from more than a decade ago," I replied. "He's just as much of a tool."

Cernunnos's smirk remained firmly in place, but he didn't respond.

"How come you didn't act as if you knew me when we first met?" I demanded. "You'd obviously met me before."

"Time is not a straight line," Cernunnos replied. "And, if you recall, I never said you were a stranger. Also, I didn't pretend that I was unaware of your reputation."

"So, you were playing games."

"I was playing to win," he replied, letting loose a sigh as he stood. "Let's take a walk." He looked as if that was the last thing he wanted to do, but there was determination in the grim set of his jaw.

"You're not taking her anywhere," Gunner snapped. "No. It's not happening. I'm taking her home."

I patted his arm again. "It has to happen," I said in a low voice. "Trust me."

Gunner looked torn.

"We'll walk with you," Evan offered. "It can't hurt to have a couple more sets of ears present for this conversation." He said it in such a way that Cernunnos dared not argue with him. The god merely nodded.

"Why don't you guys finish with cleanup?" I suggested to Rooster. "Burn the cabin down. I don't want anybody else using it as a lair."

"As soon as Tiffany and Brandy are done inside, we'll do that," Rooster promised.

I stilled. "I didn't realize they were here."

"They arrived with him." Rooster jerked his thumb at Cernunnos. "They're the ones who opened the door so you could come back. At least that's what they said they were going to do. It took a lot longer than we were expecting, though."

"Right." I scratched my cheek. "You planned all of this," I barked at Cernunnos before I could gain control of my emotions. "You knew all of this was going to happen."

"We didn't *know* all of it was going to happen," Cernunnos replied. "We simply knew that it *could* happen and made adjustments."

"Like telling your other self where to go to intercept me?"

"That would be one of the adjustments that we made," he confirmed. He showed no signs of walking away now. Apparently, this discussion was going to happen in front of everybody.

"Bonnie couldn't touch me when I was under the age of eighteen —although I'm not sure what importance that number means when it comes to magic, but whatever—so she had no choice but to arrive right after I turned eighteen. She had access to my records thanks to Doc."

Doc wasn't there—something I was grateful for because he would've turned whiny—but I didn't suspect him of working with Bonnie. She'd merely manipulated him because that's what she did.

"The problem Bonnie had was that my records from that time were a lie," I explained. "The loas and the gods banded together to enhance the pixie magic that was used to hide me. They made sure I couldn't be found when I was too young to defend myself. The state records in Michigan show I was at a halfway house then. I wasn't, though. I left on my own and they still collected the money."

Rooster's eyebrows hopped halfway up his forehead. "How lucky was that?"

"I don't think there was a lot of luck involved in any of this," I replied. "We were positioned like chess pieces and played our parts. Cernunnos sent his older self to act as a guide to make sure I didn't interrupt the timeline. Apparently, if something happened that caused me to never come up here, we'd be in a world of trouble."

"And where is Bonnie now?" Rick asked.

"Cernunnos—the other one—shoved her through a plane door. She's locked away on a plane without an exit."

"So ... she's gone for good?" Gunner looked hopeful.

I shook my head. "They said she would find a way back. It's a stopgap. My question is—and the other you said I had to ask you—is the prophecy even still correct?"

"You shouldn't have been living your life by the prophecy in the first place," Cernunnos replied. "You should've been going on your instincts and nothing more."

"That's not what I asked," I gritted out.

"I don't have an answer." Cernunnos extended his hands. "I don't know if the prophecy stands. What I do know is that you have to handle the minions Bonnie already called to this town and prepare for her return."

He leaned forward, reminding me of the other him. His eyes were clear when they locked with mine. "This isn't done. When Bonnie returns, the final fight will be here. You have to be ready for it. You have to know what to do with her magic.

"That thing you told her in the past, where if she kills you she will die too because she can't handle your magic?" he continued. "That's true. She will spend her time plotting as she figures out her escape. You must do the same."

I made a growling noise deep in my throat. "I really can't stand you right now."

"I know." His smile was back with a vengeance. "I happen to like you a great deal, though."

"So, what are we supposed to be doing here?" Evan demanded. "If you guys have set all of this in motion, how do we finish it?"

"You're not puppets," Baron replied. He looked bored more than anything else as he stood. "We help where we can. We guide where we can."

"Like you and the harpies," I surmised. "They worship you. They had your runes. You made sure they were here to bring me back."

"We did what needed to be done," Baron replied. "You have free will, Scout. If you don't want to fight this war, you can leave at any time. Something tells me you're not going to do that, though."

He was right. I couldn't leave this war for others to wage. "So, basically you're saying we have to prepare ourselves for the big battle, even though we don't know when it's coming."

"The war has already started," Baron countered. "Bonnie had more forces here than you realize. You just have to fight it. One step at a time."

I exhaled heavily and shut my eyes. When I opened them again, I was resigned. "So, basically you're saying we just have to keep on keeping on."

"That's exactly what I'm saying," he confirmed.

"Great." I threw up my hands and looked around. It was Andrea and Rick who drew my attention. "I don't suppose they're whipping up something good to eat for dinner at the cabin, are they?"

Andrea nodded. "Yes. Ham and scalloped potatoes."

"Sold." I gave her a thumbs-up. "Let's hang out with the family. We're going to start including them in this. It's not just my war. If we're going to fight this, we're all going to do it together."

Andrea's grin was so wide it threatened to swallow her entire face. "That sounds like a great plan to me."

"Yeah, it's going to be awesome, a real day at Disney World." I glanced at Gunner. "You hungry?"

"Aren't I always?" He brushed his fingers through my hair. "I could eat. After that, though, we're taking tomorrow and not getting out of bed. Just like we both want."

Actually, it was something we both needed. I didn't make that clarification, though.

"Then, the day after tomorrow, the war begins," he said.

I leaned into his hand when he cupped my cheek. "That sounds like the perfect plan to me."

"I was hoping you would like it."

Bonnie was gone, but she wouldn't stay gone. It was the ties of family that would push us over the finish line. I could no longer be a baby and worry about what the past meant for my future. No, the future was upon us.

And I had to be ready for it.

Made in the USA
Middletown, DE
05 September 2024

60437295R00177